By Nicholas Christopher

FICTION

Tiger Rag (2013)

The Bestiary (2007)

Franklin Flyer (2002)

A Trip to the Stars (2000)

Veronica (1996)

The Soloist (1986)

POETRY

*Crossing the Equator:
New and Selected Poems 1972–2004* (2004)

Atomic Field: Two Poems (2000)

The Creation of the Night Sky (1998)

5° and Other Poems (1995)

In the Year of the Comet (1992)

Desperate Characters: A Novella in Verse (1988)

A Short History of the Island of Butterflies (1986)

On Tour with Rita (1982)

NONFICTION

*Somewhere in the Night:
Film Noir and the American City* (1997)

EDITOR

*Walk on the Wild Side: Urban American Poetry
Since 1975* (1994)

*Under 35: The New Generation of
American Poets* (1989)

TIGER RAG

TIGER RAG

✳ ✳ ✳

A NOVEL

Nicholas Christopher

THE DIAL PRESS

NEW YORK

Copyright © 2013 by Nicholas Christopher

Published in the United States by The Dial Press, an imprint of The Random House Publishing Group, a division of Random House, Inc., New York.

DIAL PRESS is a registered trademark of Random House, Inc., and the colophon is a trademark of Random House, Inc.

LIBRARY OF CONGRESS CATALOGING-IN-PUBLICATION DATA
Christopher, Nicholas.
Tiger rag: a novel/Nicholas Christopher.
p. cm.
ISBN 978-1-4000-6921-7
eBook ISBN 978-0-679-64534-4
1. New Orleans (La.)—Fiction. 2. Louisiana—Social life and customs—20th century—Fiction. I. Title.
PS3553.H754T54 2013
813'.54—dc23   2012013491

Printed in the United States of America on acid-free paper

www.dialpress.com

2 4 6 8 9 7 5 3 1

FIRST EDITION

Book design by Dana Leigh Blanchette
Title-page photo: © iStockphoto
Photo of Edison cylinder on page ix by the author

In memory of my father
who introduced me to early jazz early in my life,
and shared his passion

TIGER RAG

AT THE TURN OF THE TWENTIETH CENTURY, THE PREMIER JAZZMEN — KID ORY, MANUEL PEREZ, JOHNNY ST. CYR — WERE CUTTING CYLINDER RECORDINGS. BUT NO RECORDINGS SURVIVE OF THE MAN THESE MUSICIANS SAY INVENTED JAZZ. RUMORS OF A RECORDING HAVE CIRCULATED EVER SINCE, YET HIS REPUTATION IS ENTIRELY BASED ON WORD OF MOUTH, FROM THOSE WHO HEARD HIM IN THE BARS, DANCE HALLS, AND PARADES OF NEW ORLEANS. IT IS GENERALLY BELIEVED THAT WHEN THE LAST OF THOSE WITNESSES DIED, THE SOUND OF HIS MUSIC WENT WITH THEM.

NEW ORLEANS—JULY 5, 1904

Suite 315 at the Hotel Balfour on Oleander Street, the honeymoon suite. The heat was stifling. In the large sitting room the windows were shut tight. A long mahogany table and two chairs were pushed up against the wall. A carpet had been nailed over the door, to block out sound. Myriad scents— lavender hair oil, talcum powder, cinnamon—were interlaced. Also the lingering smell of lunch: fried catfish and roasted corn. On the table there was a bucket of beer, a pitcher of ice water, glasses. The musicians were accustomed to performing at night, so at four o'clock, with the city bathed in sunlight, they had drawn the curtains.

The Bolden Band. Seven musicians in a semicircle tuning their instruments: drums, guitar, stand-up bass, valve trombone, two clarinets, and a cornet, played by Charles Bolden himself. All of them tuning to the cornet, including the drummer, Cornelius Tillman. Bolden would not be accompanied by

*untuned drums. And he would only play a Conn Wonder, man-
ufactured in Elkhart, Indiana, a triple-silver-plated cornet, the
inside of the bell gold-plated, the finger pieces inlaid pearl. In
the right hands, Bolden's hands, the Conn could project a powerful sustained sound on a single breath.*

*The musicians were in shirtsleeves, sweating, all except the
trombonist, Willie Cornish, who never took off his chalk-striped
jacket, even when his shirt was wet through. He kept his hat
on, too, for luck. He was studying the sheet music, running his
finger along it, pointing out something to Bolden, who nodded
and looked away. Bolden didn't want to think about notes on
paper when he could already hear himself playing them, could
see them dancing in the air. He and Cornish were the only band
members who read music. Bolden had learned in church as a
boy, Cornish taught himself while working as a pressman at
Montgomery Brothers, musical publishers. Bolden was wearing a red shirt, red tie, and yellow silk vest. His handkerchief,
too, was red, and after he mopped his neck, the dye ran so that
the drops of sweat on the floor looked like blood. Which he
was aware of. Also that this was the honeymoon suite, which
amused him.*

*Oscar Zahn, the recording engineer, was a stocky young
man with sharp eyes and a heavy brow. He spoke with a
slight German accent. He too was perspiring heavily in a
high-collared shirt and a bow tie. He had a pencil behind his
ear. A Turkish cigarette between his lips. He was sitting on a
stool in the corner screwing the wax cylinder onto the mandrel
of the Edison recorder. It was one of the new Edison Gold
Moulded cylinders, hard black wax, playable hundreds of
times. Its four-minute capacity was double that of the old car-
nauba wax cylinders. Zahn had learned sound engineering at*

*the W. T. Bellmon Studios in St. Louis, recording opera singers
and barbershop quartets. He came to New Orleans with his
wife and daughter, hoping to save enough money to open his
own studio. In the meantime, he was learning how to capture
sound cleanly in spaces like this, or—when the money wasn't
there—far more cramped spaces in basements and back rooms.
But Buddy Bolden had the money. He was in demand, every
night of the week. In addition to performing with his band, he
sometimes made the rounds of a half dozen dance halls, social
clubs, and fairgrounds, all for a handsome fee. If you doubled
that fee, he would play your private party, sitting in with the
hired band and laying down a couple of solos, the flashier the
better. But he had never cut a cylinder. He had resisted, not,
like some musicians, because he feared his techniques could be
stolen—he knew no one could truly imitate him—but because
he was certain the recording companies would make good
money off his recordings while he got clipped. Oscar Zahn had
sworn he wouldn't let that happen, and Bolden, knowing how
many musicians were starting to record steadily, making a
name for themselves outside New Orleans, finally decided to
take a chance.*

*Zahn's assistant, Myron Guideau, was stuffing a towel be-
neath the door. He was slope-shouldered, wearing a cheap
checkered suit. His eyebrows met over his nose and his mustache was untrimmed, tobacco-stained. He glanced sidelong at
the slender girl in a yellow dress reclining on the sofa, ankles
crossed and her shoes kicked off. Yellow was Bolden's favorite
color and he had bought her the dress that morning. Her skin
was oak-colored and her long black hair was speckled gold,
catching the light. Her eyes, too, were golden. They were fixed
on Bolden, who was standing very still, the cornet at his lips.*

The girl smiled at him, and stomping the floor one-two-three, *Bolden launched into the rag known to every band in the city as "Number 2." Except, as often happened, his opening solo was a variation the band had never heard before, an electrifying eight bars, after which Cornish entered, cornet and trombone playing off each other as the bass and drums rumbled in, setting the tempo for the guitar and clarinets, all of them working in sync now, flying apart and coming together again like shavings to a magnet. The piece was fast, high-pitched: veering, accelerating, peaking, before Bolden closed it off with an explosive solo.*

Take One: *three minutes and forty-nine seconds.*

Bolden shook his head. He wasn't happy. Zahn lit another cigarette. Tillman replaced a cracked drumstick. Willie Warner, the B-flat clarinetist, cursed under his breath: he had never played a better solo in his life—for nothing. Guideau handed Zahn a fresh cylinder. Zahn removed it from its gold tube with the photograph of Thomas Edison on the side and screwed it onto the mandrel. He tightened the worm gear, tested the spring, and adjusted the sapphire stylus. Sitting against the wall, Guideau waited for the stylus to dance on the turning cylinder. Four inches high, two inches in diameter, the cylinder revolved one hundred twenty times a minute as the stylus cut grooves thinner than capillaries into which the music flowed. The device still amazed Guideau, who had grown up on a pig farm in Hiram, Ohio, where there were tools, but no machines.

Bolden stomped the floor, one two three, and the band began to play.

Take Two: *three minutes and fifty-four seconds.*

Bolden immediately signaled Zahn that he wanted to do it again. He was even less happy this time around. The segues were rough, the solos disjointed. The opening was fiery, but his closing solo felt flat.

Bolden told the bassist, Jimmy Johnson, to tune up again, that his A string was off. Nineteen years old, Johnson had already performed with half a dozen bands. Bolden recruited him after hearing him play with Johnny St. Cyr at the Algiers Masonic Hall on Olivier Street. Johnson started as a saloon pianist, but the bands didn't use pianos, which were too cumbersome to transport. Johnson rode to performances on a Columbia bicycle with his bass strapped to his back.

Frank Lewis, the C clarinetist, took off his Panama hat, lit a cigarette, and blew a smoke ring that floated to the ceiling.

Willie Cornish was staring at the guitarist, Brock Mumford, who had missed his cue. Six three, two hundred thirty pounds, Cornish rarely smiled except with his children. At twenty-five, he had three daughters, the youngest, Charlene, named after Bolden. He had left the band in 1898 when he was drafted to fight in Cuba against the Spanish. As Cornish's troop ship embarked, the Bolden Band, sans trombone, was performing rousing numbers on the dock. Then Bolden played a plaintive solo of "Home Sweet Home" that inspired some of the soldiers to jump into the harbor and swim to shore, AWOL in less than an hour. Cornish had sailed on to Havana and received an honorable discharge eleven months later. He had a scar on either side of his shoulder, where a bullet had gone through. When the band was in a cutting contest with the Robichaux Orchestra or the Onward Brass Band, it was Cornish who blew most fiercely, and nearly as loudly as Bolden. He called his silver

Distin trombone "the tornado," and he could finger the three valves twice as fast as a slide trombonist, with the dexterity of a trumpeter.

Bolden was smiling again, buffing his cornet on his shirt-sleeve.

Where'd you find that opening? *Cornish said.*

Bolden laughed and pretended to snatch something out of the air.

Most bands used two cornetists. It was a matter of endurance, not sound: the cornet was the lead instrument, exhausting to play, and two men, alternating, could withstand the strain of a seven-hour engagement. But Bolden went it alone, playing deep into the night, only breaking for an occasional snort of rye and a smoke. Afterward he rubbed his cracked lips with camphor and palm oil.

He filled a tin cup with red whiskey and wandered into the bedroom sipping it, the fumes filling his head. When he met his wife Nora, she told him he moved like an alley cat. Slow then fast then slow. Always in rhythm. But lately he had been freezing at odd moments, startled by movements—darting shadows, flickers of light—that he caught out of the corner of his eye. He soon realized that no one else saw them. And that each time, it required more willpower to regain his bearings. Most nights he was afraid to be alone. He imagined he was like a ship spinning, unsteerable, as it neared a whirlpool.

Only Cornish called him Charles, never Buddy. Watching him pace the bedroom—not in a straight line, but a loop—Cornish opened his mouth to call out, but the word never left his throat. Charles. *This drifting in circles had been happening more frequently. When Bolden came out of it, as if out of a*

dream, the world became all sound, so acute it blinded him—
insects' wings, horses' hooves, workmen hammering, a boy
whistling by the river. The other musicians thought it was his
moods—the airs of King Bolden, who could be, and could
have, whoever he wanted whenever he wanted—but Cornish
and Nora knew better. They understood he was slipping in and
out of this world, each time returning a little less himself. Day
by day the clock inside him not so much running down as running faster. Still he boasted to Nora that for every calendar
year, he lived five years. She retorted that he was going to die
accordingly. As fast as you play.

Bolden lingered in the bedroom, staring out the window
at two boys sitting laughing atop a hill of coal in a horse-
drawn cart, their cheeks so black they gleamed like coal nug-
gets. Bolden himself was a coppery brown. He shaved close,
clipped his hair short. Many musicians were laborers by day,
with rough hands. His hands were smooth. He waved to the
boys, who didn't see him. When he closed his eyes, that coal
reddened into embers, inflaming the air and consuming the
cart.

He walked back into the living room, to the sofa, purpose-
ful again, and whispered in the girl's ear. She laughed. Her
beautiful teeth caught the lamplight. Her perfume, a cloud of
spices, filled his head. He could have inhaled it all day. Her
name was Ella Hayes. She was eighteen years old. Cornish
watched the two of them, then turned away, frowning. Bolden
ran his palm across Ella's cheek, his index finger along her lips.
He was cradling the cornet. During their entire three hours at
the hotel, setting up, rehearsing, recording, he never put it
down. He carried it with him everywhere. It was in his lap

when he sat for a haircut, by his plate when he ate, beside the cue rack when he shot pool, at the foot of the bed when he was in a sporting house. Ella blew him a kiss.

Zahn signaled that the third cylinder was ready.

Bolden looked into the face of each musician. He winked at Cornish. Then he stomped the floor and raised his cornet.

Fly, he shouted, putting the mouthpiece to his lips.

Take Three: *exactly four minutes. Feverish drumming from Tillman, taut solos from Cornish and Frank Lewis. Bolden closed it off with yet another extended improvisation, a sizzling, intricate variation on the new opening. It took even him by surprise, since he had not heard it in his head until that moment, and the band listened in amazement as he bent his knees, dropped his shoulders, and, turning his back to them, leaned forward and blew into the corner, the music flowing up the blue shadow that ran to the ceiling.*

After Bolden held, extended, and released a high B-flat, Cornish clapped softly and Frank Lewis danced in place. Goddamn, *Brock Mumford muttered. Ella opened her damp lashes and smiled broadly as the room continued to echo with Bolden's solo.*

King Bolden, *Oscar Zahn said,* nobody ever played "Number 2" like that.

I expect they haven't, *Bolden said, catching his breath. He shook his head.* "Number 2"—what kind of bullshit name is that?

Needs a new name now, *Lewis said.*

Bolden began pacing, working it over in his mind. He looked at Ella, who lifted her palm as if to blow him a kiss, but instead, in a throaty voice, sent him a word: Tiger.

Tiger, *Bolden repeated, his eyes locking on hers.*

Ti-ger Rag, *she whispered.*

He smiled. Tiger Rag. I like that.

So be it, *Zahn said.*

The crowds at Johnson Park had crowned him King Bolden in 1900, after he won all the cutting contests. At the end of each number they cried out, King Bolden, play it again! *He was twenty-three years old.* Play it again, and bring us home! *People started addressing him as* King Bolden. *Housepainters, dockworkers, the ladies on Basin Street, bartenders, commissioners, doctors, even the police.* King Bolden. *In July 1904 he and the band were at their peak. The previous day they were first among all the bands, leading the Fourth of July parade along the traditional route: Elks Place to Gravier to St. Charles to South Rampart, around and down to Esplanade, through the French Quarter, then to Chartres and Canal and back to Elks Place, where the city councilmen, dressed like undertakers in black coats and stovepipe hats, sat cross-armed in the reviewing stand, their wives in flouncy pinks and whites and yellow sunbonnets sitting behind them. King Bolden liked those bonnets.*

The biggest venues in the city were Johnson Park and Lincoln Park. They were three hundred yards apart, separated by Short Street, both parks fenced in. Some warm nights, the air heavy with vapor, Bolden would stick his cornet through a gap in the fence and blow as hard as he could, summoning the crowd from Lincoln Park. And no matter what band was playing there, the crowd would come running. He was that good, and that loud. Some musicians claimed you could hear his horn from a mile away, others that you could tap your foot to his music all the way down Melpomene Street and across the Mississippi (carrying fast across the water) to Algiers.

He played louder than anybody else, *according to Frank Lewis.*

Louder and clearer, *Willie Cornish would say shortly before his death in 1942.* Like a knife flashing light, a shark's fin cutting through water. And Charles always played in B-flat.

Always.

✳

At dusk they began to leave the Hotel Balfour. First Warner and Tillman. Then Mumford. Then Johnson, who disappeared down Fern Street on his bicycle.

The three Edison cylinders left that room separately:

Take One *went with Myron Guideau, who was supposed to deposit it at his boss Oscar Zahn's studio on Richelieu Avenue on his way home.*

Take Two *with Zahn himself, who dined with Frank Lewis at Ferdinand's Steakhouse, then rode the ferry to his house in Algiers.*

Take Three, *Bolden's copy, with Willie Cornish, to whom Bolden entrusted it for safekeeping. He knew Cornish was going directly home to dine with his wife while he himself was not going home at all but to the Hotel Marais on Perdido Street, a hotel for gentlemen where he rented a room by the month to take his girls. That night Ella, his favorite.*

Honeymoon's over, *Bolden laughed, putting on a white derby and heading for the door with Ella on one arm and his cornet cradled in the other. An hour later, still wearing the hat and enveloped in steam, he was being sponged down in the bathtub by Ella and her cousin Florida Jameson, who wore only yellow stockings and was telling him in a husky voice that, yes, Florida was her real name, which she shared with her mother, grandmother, and great-grandmother, none of whom had ever set foot in that state, though she herself planned to live there one day.* In a yellow house, King Bolden, with yellow sheets, *she whispered, and before the night was out Bolden had two favorites.*

The first cylinder disappeared sometime before dawn. En route to Richelieu Street, Guideau stopped at the Calabash Tavern for a drink. He found two friends there at a table with a bottle of Liberty rye. The three of them finished the bottle and had two more rounds. The friends were heading for Mrs. Vance's sporting house on Franklin Street, and Guideau decided to join them. Guideau was a white man who liked mulatto girls. He paid in advance for an hour with a girl named Tina. She had hazel eyes and small hands. They took a bottle of whiskey to her room. Guideau had another drink, fucked her, and fell asleep. When his hour was up and Tina couldn't wake him, Mrs. Vance's son Orson did. Orson, who was six feet four and formerly laid track for the Illinois Central Railroad, watched Guideau pull on his pants and button his rumpled shirt. He asked for and received a dollar for the whiskey Guideau had drunk (Tina as always had been drinking whiskey-colored tea in a short glass) and then followed him downstairs. The next morning at six, Guideau woke with a start in his one-room apartment off Cochran Park, his head splitting, and looked around the room for the cylinder. It dawned on him that at some point he had stopped carrying the cylinder around in one of Zahn's leather bags, but he couldn't remember where. He dressed hurriedly and retraced his steps, to Mrs. Vance's, where Orson, drinking a warm beer, was just locking up.

No, nothing was found in Tina's room, *Orson told him*, and anyway, there was three or four johns up there after you.

Guideau went on to the Calabash Tavern and waited for the day bartender to arrive at nine. The two of them searched without success the places where a lost item might be stored: the coat closet, the back room, behind the bar. The bartender promised to ask Ferguson, who came on at six, if he'd found anything the night before. With some difficulty that sunny morning, Guideau went on to track down Tina, fast asleep in her boardinghouse. All he got from her were the first names of the three johns that had succeeded him upstairs. She also told him that there was another john, who had been entertained by the girl that shared the room with her. The girl's name was Philippa, and Tina didn't know where she lived. Maybe in Algiers, *she shrugged. At ten-thirty Guideau reported to work and confessed to Oscar Zahn that he had lost the cylinder. He started telling him how it had happened, but Zahn didn't want to hear it. He gave Guideau forty-eight hours to recover the cylinder or he was out of a job. Zahn had not fully trusted Guideau ever since he learned that he had changed his name from "Guiteau"—a name still universally recognized and reviled twenty years after Guideau's deranged uncle, Charles Guiteau, had assassinated President Garfield.*

Zahn himself had placed the second cylinder in a locked walnut cabinet his grandfather brought to America from Prussia. Painted on its door was a likeness of Kaiser Wilhelm I, on a rearing white horse, framed by thunderbolts. There were a dozen other cylinders on the top shelf of the cabinet, each

marked neatly in white ink with a musician's name—THEOGENE
BAQUET, FREDDIE KEPPARD, ALPHONSE PICOU—*a song title,
and a date. And now* CHARLES BOLDEN—"TIGER RAG"—
5 JULY 04.

Willie Cornish likewise put Bolden's cylinder, the third cylinder, which had additionally been marked FINAL, in his wife's
linen chest, where their most precious finery was stored. Of
late Bolden had not been sleeping in the same bed two
nights running, and both men knew Cornish could better keep
the cylinder under wraps until it could be copyrighted and
reproduced by one of the two big outfits, Edison's National
Phonograph Company or the Indestructible Cylinder Company. Whoever paid more. Zahn had intended to keep the
other two cylinders, the ones Bolden found unsatisfactory, as
backups—one in his home and one at his studio—to be destroyed after the third cylinder was reproduced.

Bolden trusted Willie Cornish more than anyone, including
his own family. He made clear to Cornish that, unlike other
bandleaders in New Orleans, he actually expected to be well
paid for the rights to his recordings. He wanted a contract, put
in writing by a lawyer, and nothing left to chance.

After that, the band can make another recording, and another after that.

Zahn had told Bolden that the National Phonograph
Company would soon be able to reproduce the staggering
total of one hundred fifty cylinders a day and sell them for a
dollar apiece. Enormous profits were going to be made, and
Bolden wanted a piece of them. If not, I don't want no one to
hear the music at all, *he instructed Cornish.* Not if it's for nothing. So, if they won't pay, I'm going to keep this thing to my-

self. You do the same, if anything happens to me. My father died young, like his father before him, so I don't have a day to waste.

The Bolden Band never made another recording.

That same week, in a courthouse in Trenton, New Jersey, National Phonograph lost the right to mass-produce its Edison cylinders when a judge ruled in favor of Indestructible. Thomas Edison hired a team of crack patent attorneys to appeal the verdict, but until the case was settled two years later, neither company was allowed to mass-produce cylinders.

By then, the Bolden Band had dissolved, and the three cylinders they recorded on that summer afternoon were either missing or under wraps.

SAINT GEORGE, SOUTH CAROLINA— DECEMBER 20, 2010

There was a time when Ruby Cardillo did not obsess twenty-four/seven about what her husband and daughter were doing (or undoing) *at that moment,* and how their respective actions might impact her own, and what the repercussions might be *from that moment on.*

A time when melodrama repelled her, when she did not feel trapped in her own head, gasping for a pocket of air like the victim of a cave-in.

A time when even if she was at wit's end, running on fumes, she could maintain her composure and in a crisis appear coolly detached.

A time when she awoke without a stab of anxiety in her Key Biscayne villa, gazing out the picture window at the Atlantic, parrots squawking in the palms and the gardener hosing the bluestone around the pool.

A time when she was not furious that the world was slow-ing to a crawl while she was speeding up—*with no choice but to speed up.*

A time, above all, when she was not working two full-time jobs that had dangerously overlapped: the practice of anesthesiology, her occupation for two decades, and the job of losing her mind, which was new to her.

But that was before the following three events, which occurred in quick succession, but to Ruby had felt like a single lingering explosion:

First, Marvin Joseph Sheresky, cardiologist and self-proclaimed "doctor to governors"—having performed quadruple bypasses on two Florida chief executives—was declared her ex-husband in the Miami–Dade County Courthouse and immediately, publicly, went to work on Ruby's own heart, marrying his twenty-six-year-old nurse in a lavish ceremony on his refurbished yacht, the *Virginia,* renamed after his new bride.

Next, Ruby's twenty-five-year-old daughter, Devon, jazz pianist, convicted shoplifter, former bartender, and sometime journalist, had been arrested at Miami International for possession of twenty-eight peyote buttons with intent to distribute—a charge Devon tried to refute by insisting the peyote was for her personal use.

And then Ruby had been called on to arrange her mother's funeral and cremation at the Baptiste Brothers Funeral Home in Fort Lauderdale.

Though the latter had occurred just days before, Ruby was far more concerned with Devon, who had recently completed her community service, trash picking on Florida highways, and was sitting beside her *at that moment* on I-95 in a hailstorm that pockmarked the roof and hood of Ruby's silver Mercedes E550 coupe.

Ruby fretted about many things, but never, anymore, about her possessions. The objects of value in her life, both sentimental and material, that once included expressionist paintings, Mexican ceramics, Devon's baby clothes, and her grandmother's inexpensive jewelry now held no allure. Anything her husband had given her, except money, she had destroyed or discarded. But it wasn't just about possessions; the physical world, and the laws of science that ruled it, felt increasingly unreal to her. And that included the science of medicine, to which she had devoted her life.

Abandoned by both her parents, Ruby was eventually, belatedly, raised by her grandmother in a stable household. She was a loner by nature, very shy, but prodded by her grandmother, she evolved into the alert, studious girl who sought validation by acing exams, winning ribbons at science fairs, and attending medical school on a full scholarship. She married a wealthy fellow student, the son of a doctor, who seduced her on their second date. During their twenty-six years of marriage, she worked in operating rooms, cold and harshly lit, watching men like him—narcissistic, Napoleonic, oversexed—saw open chests, reroute arteries, and transplant hearts. She had been a working mother well before that was considered admirable. And now, in middle age, she had abruptly been thrust back into the treacherous world of her early youth, where deception and denial were the rule and people's worst qualities outpaced their best. She saw that what she had thought were the best years of her life were in fact the labyrinth of a sleepwalker. When she finally emerged, she was unprepared for the traps and trip wires that surrounded her. In the previous year, she had taken a crash course in betrayal and learned that, many rungs up the social ladder, she was no more immune to humiliation than when she had been a dirt-poor kid.

True to form, she had gone through her divorce alone, keeping her few friends at arm's length. She retained a divorce attorney as famous for her high-profile clients as Marvin Sheresky was for his celebrity patients. She was a woman her own age, coolly flamboyant as her name, Fortuna LeRoy. She spoke softly in a steely voice, never harsh or hurried, unruffled by the aggressive antics of Marvin's lawyer. The latter insisted that the recorded grounds for divorce be incompatibility, not adultery.

"Our clients are physicians," he said gravely, "and it would not be good for their reputations."

"Only your client is an adulterer, however," Ms. LeRoy replied. "Dr. Cardillo has an impeccable reputation. We're not here to whitewash Dr. Sheresky's marital transgressions. The grounds are adultery. The terms are nonnegotiable: fifty percent of their joint assets and she keeps the house in Key Biscayne and the deed to the adjacent lot."

LeRoy had urged Ruby to go after a portion of Marvin's trust fund as well, and to subpoena other financial documents. "He's concealing assets—I'm sure of it." But Ruby declined. She was getting enough. That adjacent lot, purchased two years earlier to extend their property, would be worth plenty if she sold it. She also had had enough of Marvin and his prick of a lawyer. Being around them made her feel sick. Not once during the hearing, the conferences in the judge's chambers, the chance encounter in an elevator, and the infuriating twenty minutes the state of Florida required them to spend alone in a room at the courthouse—to test the possibility of an eleventh-hour reconciliation—did Ruby speak to her husband. Ten days later, he remarried.

Now, having left Miami, what preoccupied Ruby above all else was *the moment at hand,* and the fact she could no longer fill it or be contained by it: this had become her definition of madness—superior, she thought, to those found in her old medical textbooks.

A *moment,* after all, is inhabited by billions of people whose actions ramify into trillions of situations, themselves ramifying by the trillions. And so on.

With that sort of explosive potential, with numbers appropriate to the realm of atomic fission, *a moment is not a safe place.*

But it is the only place.

They were driving through the worst hailstorm to hit South Carolina in fifty years. Hailstones the size of golf balls grew to be like tennis balls. "And what next," she said to Devon after one of their long silences, "basketballs, maybe?"

"What?"

"Are you hungry, dear? I'm hungry. Let's pull off, find a place, have lunch."

"We just ate breakfast."

"I know, but I'm hungry."

Devon didn't argue. Her mother's idea of breakfast had become half a tangerine and a Ry-Krisp. For dinner the previous night Ruby had eaten two scallops and a cup of rice sprinkled with rice vinegar. She was down to one hundred twelve pounds.

"I'm doing it for my heart" had become Ruby's standard line on the subject. "I've been overweight for fifteen years. In the OR I've seen blocked arteries. Ventricle valves gone floppy. Hearts encased in fatty tissue. Not pretty."

"Mom, you were not fat."

"Easy for you to say, you're like a rail. You have maybe ten percent body fat. Other issues, sure, but there's no fat around your heart."

"What issues?"

"Scarred lung tissue from cigarettes. Ditto your throat and mouth. Liver and spleen overtaxed by drugs. Irregular menstrual periods—am I right?—from going on and off the pill."

"Okay, okay."

Ruby cut across two lanes and braked smoothly onto a narrow exit ramp. "But I wasn't thinking physiologically," she said softly. "I was thinking emotionally."

"Spare me, Mom."

Ruby shrugged, then turned up the stereo. "I love the refrain." For the last forty miles she had been playing a CD she burned: Joan Jett and the Blackhearts singing "I Hate Myself for Loving You" over and over again.

"I can't bear to hear this song again," Devon cried, covering her ears.

"There are two songs," Ruby corrected her.

"Right. The other song." Ruby had looped Joan Jett ten times in a row, then there was one track of the Stones singing "It's All Over Now," then back to Joan Jett.

"I find it therapeutic."

"But it's driving me crazy. Can we just listen to the radio for a while?"

"Sure. Let's hear the weather. This hail is amazing." After searching the radio frequencies for a few moments, Ruby pointed out the window. "Here we go," she said, turning sharply into a strip mall parking lot. "A steakhouse. How many do you think there are between here and New York?"

"I'm a vegetarian and you don't eat steak."

"No? Watch me."

Ruby ordered the largest steak on the menu, a two-pound porterhouse, with a baked potato and buttered peas. Then she demanded the wine list.

"We don't have one," the waiter said.

"All right, then, I'd like a 1988 Chateau Latour."

The waiter was Devon's age, wearing a white jacket a little short in the wrists. His haircut was choppy, his hands chafed. He shook his head in bewilderment. "We only have merlot and chardonnay," he said.

"Then bring me a shot of Jack and a glass of ice water."

"Mom."

"And an iced tea for the young lady. Because you're going to drive, Devon."

"Coffee, black, please," Devon said.

Devon hadn't told Ruby that it was seventy-one days since she had picked up a drink or drug. Ruby knew that at Devon's sentencing, in addition to community service and a year's probation, she had been ordered by the judge to undergo spot drug tests and attend six AA meetings a week. Reluctantly, gratingly, Devon had gone to all twenty-four required meetings—open and beginners' meetings, step meetings, NA meetings. What Ruby didn't know was that Devon had surprised herself by going to a twenty-fifth meeting of her own volition. And another, and another.

Devon could have used a meeting right then, but the last person she wanted to discuss that with was her mother. When it came to her family, she was grateful for her anonymity. She only wished she could have come by it sooner.

As a teenager she had told her parents she wanted to be a musician, and it didn't sit well with Marvin. He saw it as a hobby, not a profession. He tried to discourage her, and when that didn't work, he turned to his typical means of persuasion, sly ridicule and innuendo. He gave her a new nickname, "Piccolo." As in, your talent is small and your interest ought to be commensurate. When Devon confronted him about it, he told her she was oversensitive. "Maybe because you have your own doubts . . ."

When Devon went to her mother, Ruby assured her that her father was only concerned about her future and intended no unkindness. As for nicknames, Ruby told Devon that her father only assigned them to people he cared about. "Out of affection." That's not how Devon figured it. She knew his penchant for them had more to do with his competitiveness and his need to control. She had heard him pin nicknames on friends and colleagues that were anything but affectionate. An overweight nurse was "Mama Cass," a poor golfing partner "Sandpit," a neighbor who had lost a fortune to junk bonds "Fast Buck." Ruby had always explained away his attitudes, attributing his arrogance to the fierce stresses of his profession. This was Ruby's blind spot. It had been confusing to Devon as a child, for in all other respects, her mother was steady and strong. Devon had to conclude that her mother's passivity toward her father was simply reflexive, a product of his overbearing character, her own zigzag history, or maybe just a part of her DNA. No matter the source, it had lasting repercussions for Devon. If she couldn't trust her mother on the subject of her father, the whole of her small familial map became enemy territory. Ruby tried to compensate for Devon's unhappiness by showering extra attention on her—music lessons, concerts, CDs—a strategy that boomeranged because Devon read it as a joyless program of self-improvement. Something her father might have instigated. The harder Ruby tried, the greater Devon's resentment, until finally, as a teenager, she pushed her mother away altogether. This was painful for Devon, but not as bad as the knowledge that it was unnecessary for her to push her father away since he had already beaten her to the punch.

The waiter delivered their food. Ruby didn't touch her steak. She pushed the peas around her plate and munched on a sesame stick. She ordered a second shot of Jack.

Devon crushed a Saltine into her tomato soup and ate it slowly. She had never seen her mother like this. The progression had been rapid. During her divorce proceedings, Ruby had first clammed up and then assumed her professional persona: focused, straight-ahead, clear-eyed. Afterward, all of that changed. There was still a protective skin in place of the old armor, but it was invisible, flexible. Too flexible.

First, she began dressing differently. Gone were the dark, well-tailored pantsuits from Bergdorf. The sensible doctor's pumps with rubber soles. The black hose. The button-up blouses in muted colors. Now it was a new look daily, everything up for grabs, the one constant an obsession with purple. Some item—shoes, belt, kerchief—had to be purple. Lately it had become more than one item, leading to the day, Devon imagined, when every garment and accessory would be purple, head to toe.

To begin their trip, Ruby had put on a purple silk T-shirt and tourmaline earrings, complemented by tight black jeans, bought at her new weight, and a red leather jacket with—Devon had counted them—fifteen zippered pockets. The zippers were purple. Her red boots matched the jacket, as did the skulls on the yellow bandanna she had borrowed from Devon that morning.

"I didn't always dress like a doctor, you know," Ruby had

said cheerfully as she backed out of their driveway, burning rubber when she threw the Mercedes into drive.

She often borrowed now from Devon's eclectic wardrobe: a purple jersey with a bull's-eye on the back, a vintage lizard belt with turquoise studs, oversized sunglasses with mirrored lenses, and a purple suede vest. Devon had told her to keep all of it, including the vest, which unbeknownst to Ruby, Devon had shoplifted in Key West.

At a time when Devon was doing coke, she had stolen to support her habit. She shoplifted the easy stuff, scarves and belts at boutiques, cosmetics from drugstores, and whatever she could drop into her handbag off the wall racks at Radio Shack. Predictably, the more strung out she got, the more recklessly she stole, until her luck ran out. She met a skinny, fast-talking guy named Al Hanson at a Mexican restaurant. While doing lines of coke in a back booth he mapped out for her how they could steal three cases of cigarettes from a delivery truck outside a bowling alley in Miramar. At twenty cartons to a case, the haul would be worth five thousand dollars, split down the middle. Hanson told her he once worked at the bowling alley and knew its delivery schedules inside out. More valuable than beer, light enough to carry, cigarettes were a cinch to steal. Except that a cop in an unmarked car saw them approach the back of the truck furtively, grab the cases, and duck into a parking lot. Devon pleaded nolo contendere and paid her fine by auctioning a mint set of Fats Waller 78s and a vintage clarinet on eBay. But she had a criminal record now, which made the judge at her subsequent drug trial that much harder on her.

More disturbing was the fact that the urge to steal didn't

disappear after she got clean. Twice she acted on it, lifting things she could easily afford to buy. She was afraid that stealing had become, not just a tool of her drug addiction, but an addiction itself, lessening the anxiety of her withdrawal. But petty theft was a dangerous sedative for someone on probation who could be tossed into prison for the slightest infraction. She talked about her stealing at two meetings and felt better for it. But she wasn't about to try to return the vest with an apology, as someone in the program suggested. Instead, she mailed $93.28 in cash, which included the 6 percent sales tax, to the owner of the Golden Starfish Boutique.

After the waiter took away her steak, untouched, Ruby ordered a piece of ice cream cake with mocha icing.

"This is the dessert you serve at an engagement party," she instructed Devon. "But with a better presentation: say, a halo of raspberries and a sprig of mint."

"Good to know," Devon said dryly, sipping her coffee.

"Do you think you'll ever get married, dear?"

"Excuse me?"

"I know you don't share these things with me."

"There's nothing to share, Mom."

"There was the guy in Chicago."

"Josef? I mentioned him to you once—I'm surprised you remember."

"I remember everything you tell me."

"Really? Well, we broke up in January. I haven't seen him since."

"That doesn't mean anything," Ruby said, signaling the waiter for another shot of Jack.

For the last week, Devon had wondered whether her mother

was playing with her or was genuinely spaced. She concluded that it was both. "You know, you haven't exactly been waxing ecstatic about marriage yourself."

"It's not a black-and-white question."

"No? What about 'I Hate Myself for Loving You'?"

"That's after the fact. Anyway, we're not talking about me." Devon tapped a Camel on her palm.

"You know that's loaded with asbestos," Ruby said, nodding at the cigarette.

"I didn't know."

"Makes them burn slowly. Unfortunately, it also destroys the capillaries in your lungs."

"Whiskey isn't good for you, either."

"This is sour mash. Fermented grains. No additives."

"You make it sound like health food."

Ruby picked up the cigarette pack and studied the palm trees and pyramids on the label. "Did you know the Chinese put formaldehyde into their beer as a preservative?"

"You're exhausting me, Mom."

"It's inevitable. We have so much ground to make up."

"What do you mean?"

"I feel like I've only known you one way, with blinders on."

"That's right. You're my mother."

"And I admit it: I haven't been all I should be as a mother."

"I didn't say that."

"I should have protected you more from Marvin. I was a coward. I have to deal with that."

Devon was stunned. Her mother had never said anything remotely like this to her.

"You think I don't know?" Ruby went on. "Anyway, I got what was coming to me."

"Betrayal? You didn't deserve that."

"No? I'm only sorry you had to pay a price, too."

"Mom—"

"You have to let me say I'm sorry. Otherwise, where do we go from here?" She finished her whiskey and put the glass down with an air of finality. "To be continued."

Devon nodded. "Okay."

And Ruby shifted gears again. "Did I ever tell you one of my great fears when I was a kid, maybe thirteen years old? Cardiac arrest in my sleep. I'd read about it in a magazine. Some girl in Oklahoma my age. I remember her photograph, slightly fuzzy, the way they make the dead. Her heart just stopped and they found her in bed. Of course I didn't know how rare it is in people that young."

Devon waited to see what she was getting at.

"People think it's better to die in your sleep. Quick, painless. Not true. You think the soul leaves the body without a fight?"

Devon had never heard her mother use the word "soul," either.

Ruby leaned in closer. "At best it's like a boat that snaps its mooring and is swept out to sea—in the dark."

"I get it." For the umpteenth time in their recent conversations, Devon was wary.

"I talked to my shrink about this fear."

"You're in therapy?"

"Was. A long time ago. But the talking cure didn't work for me. If it had, I would have ditched your father. Saved us all a lot of grief." She shrugged. "I wasn't suited to be deputized."

"What do you mean?"

"Well, that's what it is: the shrink's the detective and you're the deputy, uncovering clues. And if you're lucky, you solve the case. You save yourself, not just from other people, but from the worst in yourself. Like in the movies. Except it doesn't happen often enough." She paused to take in what she'd just said, losing her train of thought. "As for my mother, she had no idea how to save herself. I doubt it crossed her mind. At a certain point, I knew I wasn't going to try."

"You always kept me away from her."

"Why wouldn't I keep you away?" Ruby said. "She was toxic. Anyway, she only came to Miami again this year, when she was desperate. For twenty-five years I didn't have an address or phone number for her. Not in Kansas City, or Tulsa, or anywhere else. I doubt that Camille Broussard herself could remember all the places where she lived." She patted Devon's hand. "Thank you for coming when I called."

"Please don't thank me for that."

"I can't say sorry and I can't say thanks."

"Come on."

"Okay, want to hear something funny? My mother was terrified of toxins. Except alcohol, of course. She worried about milk containers, hairspray, pesticides. She never did anything about it, she just worried. It got worse when she finally stopped drinking. No one dies naturally, she used to say: you get killed, you kill yourself, or it's slow poisoning."

"Are you going to eat that cake?" Devon sighed, signaling for the check.

"Of course."

Ruby skimmed a forkful of icing, tasted it, and pushed the plate away. Ten minutes later they were back on the interstate and Devon was driving fast, thankful that Ruby had dozed off within minutes of buckling up. She could throw back shots without blinking, Devon thought, but after years of abstemiousness, her tolerance was low.

At forty-eight, Ruby was still a beautiful woman, her features supple and symmetrical, her skin clear. Devon had inherited her dark blue eyes and the curve of her lips. Her mother's hands, too, the long fingers that had helped her as a pianist. That's where the resemblance ended. And at five eight, she was three inches taller than her mother. Devon was a blonde, much fairer than Ruby. Her father's mother and sisters were blondes, and Marvin Sheresky himself was sandy-haired, tall, lean and fit. Devon also had her father's very straight teeth, with the same singular imperfection: extra molars crowding her lower jaw. Like her father, when Devon had her wisdom teeth extracted, the periodontist took out six teeth, not four.

The previous week, two days after Devon completed her community service, Ruby had phoned her in the predawn to say her mother had died. The news didn't move her—her grandmother had long been a ghost to her—but Devon was shocked when Ruby asked her for help. They had been estranged for some time, and virtually incommunicado for four months, since Devon's drug conviction. Ruby had emailed Devon when she filed divorce papers, and then again when the divorce was finalized. Devon hadn't known what to say; twice she had dialed Ruby's number and hung up before the phone could ring. Finally she emailed back: I'M SORRY. And that's where things had stood until Ruby called about her mother.

"Come over as soon as you can," Ruby had said hoarsely. "I'm alone."

The two of them had been riding a roller coaster ever since. Driving her old Thunderbird across Miami from her cramped apartment in Little Cuba, Devon arrived at her mother's door weary and bedraggled. Her hair was unwashed, her eyes bloodshot. She had a toothache and an onset of the flu. During her final week of trash picking, in ninety-degree heat, she had nearly succumbed to sunstroke. It was about the worst she had looked since getting sober.

Devon always thought of her mother as having a steel spine and antifreeze in her veins. She had expected to find her sitting in the living room in prim physician mode, staring straight ahead, containing her feelings, heeding the Hippocratic oath and working overtime to heal herself. Instead, the curtains were drawn, scented candles were burning, and, wineglass in hand, Ruby was bobbing her head to Joan Jett, her long black hair loose and wild for once. She was wearing a scarlet robe and matching heels.

"What happened?" Devon said.

"A stroke," Ruby replied, misunderstanding that the question was about her. "Massive. Quick. Blow out one of these candles—it was like that."

"I'm really sorry, Mom."

"My mother and I were on the outs for most of my life—and for all of yours. Only after I put her in the hospice last month did we have a connection again, even if it was just a thread." Ruby turned down the music and took Devon's hand. "I don't want what happened to my mother and me to happen to us. It's not too late."

Devon was uncomfortable. The music, her mother's mood shift since their phone conversation, the robe and heels—she was trying to take it all in.

Ruby didn't wait for her to respond. "The funeral's tomorrow," she said. "Will you come?"

"Yes."

"And will you stay here with me? I mean, for the week?"

This was the biggest surprise of all for Devon. "You're sure that's what you want?"

"I wouldn't ask you otherwise." Ruby finished her wine and refilled the glass. "First the divorce. Then your father's marriage. Now this. My mother wanted to be cremated. No church, no ceremony. So it's not going to take long." She turned the music up again and stepped back, as if she were seeing Devon for the first time. "Devon, what's happened to you?"

For the rest of the day, Ruby remained solicitous, concerned. She didn't mention her mother again. She took Devon to her dentist. Sat with her in the steam room at her health club. Had her hairdresser make a house call. She started Devon on antibiotics and injected her with vitamin B_{12}.

But Ruby couldn't keep up that level of interest—she could barely focus on her own affairs, much less someone else's—and soon enough Devon would find that to be a blessing.

NEW ORLEANS—JULY 7, 1904

In a steady rain Myron Guideau climbed the rickety outdoor stairway to the attic apartment at 429 Cherokee Street. Water was pouring off the slanted roof. The door rattled on its hinges when he knocked. It was opened a crack by a girl with jet hair and eyes to match. She couldn't have been more than seventeen. And she didn't like what she saw: a skinny white man with a two-day beard, his hat dripping, his eyes darting. And there was whiskey on his breath at seven A.M.

The previous night, after giving up on finding the three johns who had been with Tina after him, Guideau returned to Mrs. Vance's sporting house. He bribed Orson into telling him which of the girls might know where Philippa lived. Orson directed him to a girl named Faith. Guideau found her half naked in one of the rooms. She started to unbutton his shirt. Another time, *he said,* and after she had mulled it over, for a half dollar she gave him an address that supposedly was Philip-

pa's. It was the first of three addresses, each more run-down than the last, where she had lived in the previous four months. At the second one, above a butcher shop, the butcher who owned the building told him to try the address on Cherokee Street. Here she could barely make rent, *he said.* Down there's a lot cheaper.

Are you Philippa Benoit? *Guideau asked the girl who answered his knock.*

You police?

No.

You don't look like police.

I need to speak with her.

'Bout?

Are you Philippa?

No.

Can I come in?

She shook her head. You from the landlord?

No.

And you not police.

My name is Myron Guideau. I'm a recording engineer.

A what?

I'm not the police. I need to ask Philippa about a man she was with at Mrs. Vance's on Friday night. Late.

I don't know what you're talkin' 'bout.

I think you do.

She shrugged, but he could see in her eyes she was interested. This was her, all right. There's a reward, *he said.*

For what?

Guideau took a silver dollar from his pocket. Tell me about him and this is yours.

She thought about it for a moment, then opened the door.

The room felt like a closet. Walls that had once been painted green. An oilcloth over the window. Clothes hanging on nails. A mattress. Two chairs. The smell of sweat and kerosene.

The girl was wearing a torn shift. She was thin and flat-chested but had good legs. Guideau looked her up and down, which she was used to.

They sat in the two chairs. Guideau unbuttoned his wet coat and waited for her to speak.

Only man I was with Friday late was tall, good-looking. Wore a green suit. Young. Never seen him before.

How young?

Maybe nineteen.

What else?

She thought about it. He was smoking a cigar, *she said, putting her hand out for the coin.*

What was his name?

Never said.

You're sure?

Uh-huh.

Guideau made as if to pocket the coin.

All right, *she said.* When he left, I heard one of the other girls call him Buck.

Buck?

They were down the hall, but it sounded like Buck.

Do you know who that girl was?

Could've been any girl. There's a full shift on Fridays.

He put the silver dollar into her hand. Anything else you remember about him?

Like?

Anything unusual he said or did?

She cocked her head. S'what he didn't do.

Oh?

He never done his business. Paid up front, but he never touched me, never lay down, nothin'. He hung up his jacket and sat down to take off his boots when he seen something under the bed. He went down on his knees and got it.

Guideau kept his voice level. A small bag?

She nodded. He asked me if it was mine, and I said no. He opened it and looked inside and put his hand in and looked some more. He asked me who left it and I said I didn't know nothin' about it, and that's the truth.

Then what did he do?

Just sat quiet, like I wasn't there anymore. Put on his jacket and give me another dollar and walked out.

With the bag?

Yeah, with the bag.

Damn.

Made two dollars off him. And now with your dollar, three. Anything else you want to know, Mister?

Guideau returned to Mrs. Vance's and found Orson in back eating bacon and eggs, drinking black coffee. He was annoyed that Guideau was interrupting his breakfast.

You got a burr up your ass? *Orson said.*

You know a man named Buck? He's the one was with Philippa Friday night.

I don't know no Buck. And I already told you, I don't know who she was with. There's twenty girls and more here. The johns come and go.

Young man, good-looking, wearing a green suit. Smokes cigars.

Orson hesitated, stabbing a slice of bacon with his fork. Don't know nobody like that. *He looked up.* What you want with him, anyway? He owe you money?

Something like that.

Well, I don't know him. And he don't owe me nothin'. *He put the bacon in his mouth.* And I'm ready for you to be on your way.

※

Guideau spent an entire week searching for the cylinder. After a while, it wasn't to pacify Zahn or get his job back, but out of pride. He was furious at the man who snatched the cylinder. And he was puzzled. Why would this man prefer an Edison cylinder with Bolden's name on it to the enjoyment of Philippa's charms? It made Guideau think he might be a musician, or someone who knew music, rather than an indiscriminate thief, who more likely would have gone to bed with the girl and then run off with the cylinder. But even if he happened to be a musician—a good many of whom patronized Mrs. Vance's— what could he possibly hope to do with the cylinder? It was no secret that Bolden had never been recorded, and such a recording might be worth some money, but how could that benefit anyone but Bolden himself? Zahn would sic a lawyer on any music dealer tempted to bypass Bolden.

Guideau had returned to the sporting house, and after greasing the palm of a more compliant Orson Vance and questioning some of the girls, he came up with three men, regulars, who might have been in Philippa's room that night. Two Bucks, a housepainter and a bargeman, and one Bunk. Two of the girls said this Bunk liked to light a cigar before he took his pleasure and then finish it afterward. Guideau grew excited.

He knew of only one Bunk around Storyville, and he was a musician.

Bunk Johnson was an ambitious young cornet player who had auditioned unsuccessfully for the Bolden Band before landing a spot in Lorenzo Tio's Triangle Band. None of the girls had actually seen Bunk Johnson enter or leave Philippa's room, but one of them swore he had been at Mrs. Vance's that night. Guideau thought it almost too ripe a coincidence that of all the johns, and more specifically all the musicians, who might have entered Mrs. Vance's and asked for Philippa, it would be Bunk Johnson, a man with a mighty grudge against Bolden. It was the sort of ill-fated coincidence that Bolden himself, quoting his childhood preacher with mock solemnity, would describe as one of Fate's dispensations.

Guideau tracked down Johnson's address, a rooming house on Vine Street. But the landlady said he was out. Try his brother's pawnshop on Lafayette, she said. Raoul Johnson's pawnshop specialized in musical instruments. Musicians congregated around the bench in front, drinking rye and trying out the wares. Freshly discharged after the war in Cuba, military band members had hocked dozens of trombones, cornets, and tubas with pawnbrokers like Raoul. The old man in a leather vest watching over the pawnshop said Raoul was gone for lunch and that Bunk could be found most afternoons at Moorhead's Saloon. It ain't no secret, he added, relighting his pipe.

Moorhead's was a low dark bar on Julia Street with a pair of stuffed herons in the window. The clientele were black and mulatto. Bunk Johnson was there all right, in a back booth, sharing a pitcher of beer with Frankie Dusen, the trombonist, and Lorenzo Staulz, a guitarist. Johnson was tall and well built. He had a wide forehead and square jaw and his eyes seemed fixed, as if he had to turn his head to shift his gaze even slightly. His shoulders bulged beneath his jacket, and even indoors, he didn't like to remove his wide-brimmed hat. With no greeting or introduction, Guideau slid in beside Dusen and said, I know you took that cylinder, Bunk. I want it back.

Johnson didn't blink. Who the fuck are you?

The man who left an Edison cylinder at Mrs. Vance's sporting house.

Johnson remained poker-faced. I don't know what you're talking about.

Hey, get the hell out of here, *Frankie Dusen said, and Guideau smelled something stronger than beer on his breath.*

My name is Myron Guideau. I work for Oscar Zahn. He recorded the Bolden cylinder.

Staulz and Dusen exchanged glances.

I know Zahn, *Dusen said casually, sitting back.*

Yeah? Then you know he'd be unhappy someone took one of his cylinders.

Bolden made a cylinder? *Staulz said, affecting the same nonchalance.*

Guideau knew Bolden had once fired Staulz from the band. He ignored him and turned to Johnson. I want it back. No questions asked.

I had enough of this shit, *Johnson said, jumping up and reaching into his jacket.*

Suddenly they were all on their feet.

You gonna pull a gun on me? *Guideau said, wondering where he was coming by the courage—or madness—to challenge a man a head taller than him and twice as strong.*

I don't like guns, *Johnson said, flashing a knife.*

Put that away, Bunk, *Staulz said, genuinely alarmed that the*

*three of them, black men, were threatening a white man with a
knife.*

Any man call me a thief, *Johnson said,* I'm gonna cut him.

I didn't say you were a thief, I said you took something.

Dusen leaned close to Guideau. You better leave, Mister.

Are you crazy? *Staulz said to Johnson.*

I'm gonna cut him.

You ain't gonna do nothin', *Dusen said.*

Let me know where you want to return it to me, *Guideau
said, backing away from the booth,* and I'll be there.

In hell, *Johnson shouted after him.* You'll be in hell.

*Walking back down Julia Street, his hands shaking, Guideau
knew he had found his man. He couldn't prove it yet, but he
knew. But what would Johnson do now? Why would he want
to keep the cylinder? And why has it become a point of honor
for me to win the respect of a man like Zahn, who doesn't respect me in the first place? Maybe I am mad, like my uncle who
failed at everything, but was convinced if he murdered the
president he could become president. When they hanged him,
he was sure the spectators loved him, that he was a hero. He
ruined my father's life, and my brothers', dirt farmers who lost
everything and had to leave Ohio. I ran away first, changed
that one letter in my name which maybe I should've changed
altogether, and here I am, tired of running. I'm no murderer,
but up to now I've been a failure, like my uncle. Up to now.
Because if that damn cylinder is so hot, I'll keep it for myself.*

*At Moorhead's, Johnson banged the table and shouted to
the bartender,* Rye. Send the bottle.

You know anything about this, Bunk? *Dusen said.*

What?

You do know, *Staulz said.*

Johnson drained his beer. It's my business.

You took it, *Dusen said.*

Johnson shrugged.

Why?

It was there for the taking.

Shit, *Staulz said.*

A waiter brought the rye and three tumblers. Johnson poured a shot and downed it.

You know what's on it? *Dusen said.*

Johnson poured himself another and glared at Dusen. I'm gettin' tired of your questions.

Take it easy.

You take it easy. *Johnson practically inhaled the second shot.* Yeah, I know what's on it, Frankie. I listened to it down at Bailey's music store on his Edison. Sounded like old "Number 2."

"Number 2"? *Staulz said.*

Yeah. But with a twist I ain't never heard before.

What kind of twist? *Dusen said.*

He just took it somewhere else. *He grimaced.* Anybody could do it.

Yeah? *Dusen said skeptically.*

Staulz shook his head. Man, I don't believe this.

So what you gonna do with it? *Dusen said.*

I'm gonna sell it, and put it out there.

As your own? *Staulz said.*

Why not?

You can't do that, *Dusen said.*

Who's gonna know?

Come on.

You gonna spill?

Jesus.

Are you gonna spill?

Keep it down.

Don't tell me that. Who's gonna know it's not me on cornet?

Who? *Dusen rolled his eyes.* How about anyone who's heard Bolden play?

Fuck you.

Come on, Bunk, *Staulz said.*

He ain't that much better than me.

He's better than everyone, *Dusen said,* and you know it.

You know how I feel about Bolden, *Staulz said,* but Frankie's right.

Fuck the both of you.

You gonna make a fool of yourself, *Dusen said,* and cross a lot of people, not just Bolden. It could be big trouble for you.

You calling me a fool?

I'm saying it will be big trouble.

From who?

The music stores, the krewe . . .

I don't give a shit about them.

Fuck it, *Dusen said.* Go ahead. Fuck yourself up.

Bunk sat back, thinking hard. Maybe there's something else, then.

Like what?

Like he give me jack to get it back.

Staulz's eyes widened. You want to squeeze Bolden?

He's got jack to spare.

What about Zahn?

Zahn is nothin'.

Listen to me, *Dusen said.* Bolden's got some rough boys owe him down on South Rampart. They could take you apart.

They're plenty rough, *Staulz added.* Louis Coe and the Ellis brothers.

Fuck 'em. I can be plenty rough. Why you keep runnin' me down? You fuckers not my friends.

Bunk, this don't work from any angle, *Dusen said.* Give it up.

He's right, *Staulz said.*

Johnson stood up angrily and threw down some coins. I'll give it up, all right. And that piece of shit Guideau with it. And the two of you can kiss my ass.

He stormed out into the street. Dusen and Staulz watched through the window as he disappeared. Then Dusen poured them each a shot.

He's crazy, *Dusen said.*

Staulz shook his head. I wouldn't want to be that white boy.

I wouldn't want to be Bunk. If you hear what he does next, don't tell me. I don't want to know.

✳

It was called Skeleton's Bend because dead bodies floating downriver never made it past the western bank. The water there was deep, and muddy right to the surface. The bodies, some newly drowned, others bloated, carried all the way from Cairo or Memphis, sank slowly as they turned the bend, and after they came to rest the fish picked them clean, leaving the skeletons suspended upright in the currents.

Bunk Johnson was standing on that bank in a torn shirt and muddy boots. He had a pint bottle in his back pocket. He once knew two boys who dove to see the skeletons. One came up breathless, screaming that they were there, all right, dozens of them, dancing. The other boy's body was never found.

*Far out on the river, the lanterns on the fishing boats flick-
ered. At night, it was the walleyes and the yellow catfish that
bit. Johnson used to go night fishing with his uncle, a roofer,
who one morning came home to find his wife in bed with another man, shot them both, and was hanged two months later
in the prison yard in Amesville.*

*Johnson was sweating. The mist off the water was more like
steam. Snakes slid in and out of the mangrove roots, bats
swooped through the trees. He could hear his own voice, somewhere outside himself in the darkness. He was cursing that
bitch Agnes he lived with, with her big ass and sweet lips, who
ran off with his money and had better be hoping he didn't find
her. And that son of a bitch Guideau who would never bother
him again. And, most of all, Bolden, with his mighty airs—King
Bolden—who was no better than him, no matter what anyone
said, and one day they would all know it.*

*He took a final swig from the bottle and threw it into the
river, then reached into his coat and took out the Edison cylinder and flung it as far as he could, so hard that he lost his balance and slid halfway down the riverbank. He heard a splash
in the darkness as he sprawled out in the mud, laughing and
cursing, telling himself that the only ones who would hear that
music now were dead men. Let them dance to it.*

FLORENCE, SOUTH CAROLINA—
DECEMBER 20, 1:30 P.M.

Driving north on the interstate, as the hail turned to freezing rain and the temperature plummeted, Devon had mixed feelings about leaving Miami. Though she was jobless, behind in rent, shitlisted by the local narcs, it seemed like a bad move to embark on a road trip with her mother. Ruby might have a concrete destination, where professional business awaited her, but it still felt as if she was fuguing. And Devon was along for the ride. After years of estrangement and uneasy truces, of brief obligatory phone calls, Devon was listening to Ruby's patter for hours on end. And this when, for the first time in memory, her mother frequently made little sense.

Her own mother's funeral had been just as Ruby promised: short and unceremonious. She and Devon sat alone in the first of six rows of folding chairs and viewed the body in its rosewood casket. Ruby had ordered three wreaths of white carnations, and their scent was overpowering. She insisted that she and Devon wear white, not black, and ordered dresses from Neiman Marcus, which a fitter brought to the house.

For her mother Ruby had picked out a pale blue dress, blue kerchief, and white gloves with pearl buttons. She saw Devon staring at the gloves and whispered, "Arthritis made her hands like claws. She would want them covered."

Devon had only met Camille Broussard once, when she was thirteen. Ruby had broken with her long before that. She had come to Miami for a single day and stayed in a motel. She found Ruby's office address in the phone book and sat in the waiting room until she arrived. It happened that Ruby had just picked up Devon at school, and Devon never forgot the expression on her mother's face when she saw the sallow, red-haired woman in a gingham dress sitting there pensively: in a matter of seconds, it went from astonishment to anger. She calmly ordered Devon to go into her office. Assuming the old woman was a patient, Devon didn't understand her reaction. Ten minutes later, Ruby joined her, looking pale and drawn herself, and sat down behind her desk.

"That was my mother," she said. "Your grandmother. I explained to you last year, when I thought you were old enough to understand, why I never saw her and never wanted you to see her."

"Because she abandoned you," Devon said meekly.

"She did worse than that. She all but encouraged me to abandon her. That was the kicker. She couldn't wait to be rid of me. I promised myself I would never allow her near me or my family. And I won't."

"She's gone?"

"She was never here."

Those words echoed in Devon's ears again as she looked

down on her grandmother's body. She didn't recognize her. The mortician had applied plenty of makeup, making her appear younger in death. Her wrinkles were gone, her white hair neatly coiffed.

By email Ruby had placed the same obituary in the *Miami Herald* and the New Orleans *Times-Picayune*. "That was her hometown," she explained, then read the obituary aloud from her laptop:

Camille Broussard, age 75, died December 11, 2010, at the Saint Francis of Assisi Hospice in Fort Lauderdale. She is survived by her daughter, Dr. Ruby Cardillo, and grand-daughter, Devon Sheresky. "When ye hear the sound of the trumpet, all the people shall shout."

"What's that quote?" Devon asked.

"Book of Joshua, 6:5. Her favorite. After her conversion, she spouted it all the time."

"Because your father was a trumpeter?"

"Who knows?"

Devon didn't know much about Ruby's father except that he was a trumpeter. That had intrigued her, especially since her mother had no apparent musical talent and did not even listen to music very often. Devon wondered if her own musical incli-nations had been passed down from her grandfather. His name was Valentine Owen, and according to Ruby, whose only source was her own mother, he claimed he was originally from New Jersey. That his father was a drummer. That his mother named him after Saint Valentine, patron saint of musicians. His father ran out on them. His mother took a job as cashier in the gift shop at the Dorset Hotel. They moved into a railroad flat in Hell's Kitchen. Owen took up the trumpet and became good enough to make money as a sideman. He dropped out of school, and for a long time, he lived out of a suitcase. It all sounded tough and romantic to Devon, but Ruby felt otherwise. "He was a guy who always watched out for Number One, and the hell with everyone else. The details don't matter."

Sitting before the casket, glancing sidelong at her mother, Devon couldn't read her thoughts, nor even venture that they had anything to do with the present circumstances. A high window allowed a thin shaft of sunlight to penetrate the room. Ruby seemed to be observing the motes of dust tumbling within it. The windowpane was stained red and blue and the dust was colored accordingly. Her face looked relaxed. Only her eyes, intensely bright and unblinking, betrayed the fact that she was getting very little sleep. That and the blurring of her lip gloss in the heat.

Befitting her profession, Ruby had always worn minimal makeup, but that, too, had changed of late: she took care each morning applying eyeliner and mascara, blow-drying her hair, and touching up her nails. "Devon, my grandmother used to say: worry about your brains first, your looks second. But you don't have to be a bimbo to get dolled up. Of course, some bimbos don't even bother. Take the new Mrs. Sheresky. No matter the occasion, she dresses as if she's going to a yoga class. I used to see her waiting outside the courthouse wearing a tank top and running shoes."

Devon had encountered her father's new wife only once, by chance, emerging from his office building, and didn't think she possessed anything like Ruby's natural beauty. Atop the drop-dead body, honed in hundreds of Pilates classes, and beneath the cascade of red hair, was an unformed face. There was nothing going on behind the eyes: not intelligence or mystery, not a modicum of her mother's allure. Her father's blindness infuriated Devon as much as his infidelity.

As the minutes ticked by, it struck Devon that Ruby was capable of sitting there in a daze for hours. Devon signaled the funeral director hovering in the doorway. On cue, four attendants in black suits entered, lifted the casket, and carried it off.

Later, in the director's office, Ruby was handed a bronze urn engraved with a pair of herons. Devon wondered at its symbolic significance until she discovered it was a stock item, one of a dozen in a nearby cabinet. The silver hair, the clawlike hands were a moot point now, Devon thought. That urn contained all that was left of her grandmother: roughly five pounds of powdered bone, not ashes, as Ruby informed her.

"At two thousand degrees Fahrenheit, the flesh is vaporized," her mother explained in her clinician's voice. "Afterward the bone fragments are removed from the furnace and pulverized in a remains processor—yes, that's what they call it. They sift out the jewelry and dental fillings, the knee and hip replacements that have survived the flames, so the processor won't be damaged."

Beneath Ruby's flat tone, her anger was palpable. Devon knew that Ruby was happy to talk about the years she lived with her grandmother—buckling down to her studies, working in her grandmother's dry cleaning business, preparing for college and medical school—but kept to a bare minimum the details of her childhood with her mother. That was off-limits.

Once outside the funeral home, Ruby walked to her Mercedes through the bright sunlight and placed the urn on the rear seat. She drove to North Beach on the expressway.

"I don't want to talk right now," she said calmly, before Devon could say a word.

After finding a space in the parking lot, Ruby headed directly for the beach, the urn tucked under her arm. Realizing with horror what she had in mind, Devon hurried after her.

"Mom, you can't do that here."

"Why not?"

"You can't. There are people swimming."

"There's room for one more in the water."

Sunbathers crowded the sand. In her long dress and stiletto heels, Ruby threaded them with surprising agility, leading Devon to the water's edge.

"Mom!"

Ruby kicked off her shoes and waded into the surf. Devon didn't follow her. She didn't want to raise any more fuss. It was too late, though. Children were laughing at the sight of a fully clothed woman in the water. Swimmers looked on in bewilderment, and a few who realized what she was carrying shouted angrily. An old man beckoned the lifeguard perched on an elevated chair down the beach. In knee-deep water, her white dress billowing, Ruby unscrewed the top of the urn and poured out her mother's ashes. Then she returned to shore, picked up her shoes, and made for the parking lot, sand sticking to the hem of her dress. "You're sick!" the old man called after her as the lifeguard trotted down the beach, but by then Ruby had dropped the urn into a trash can and started her car.

"Shhh," she said when Devon opened her mouth to speak. "You can say everything you need to say later."

By the time they got home, Devon was too stressed out to talk. She stretched out on the living room sofa and fell asleep. Ruby threw a blanket over her.

At two A.M. she was awakened by loud music. She walked down the hall to the study and found Ruby at her desk, writing on a legal pad with a fountain pen. Beside her was a half-empty bottle of Veuve Clicquot and a bowl of purple jelly beans. The home page of her computer was a photograph of a lightning storm at sea. Ruby looked up and said, "You know, Devon, I'm giving a speech in New York on the twenty-third."

"What?"

"To a group of anesthesiologists. My brothers and sisters. In September they invited me to give a speech. I have my topic, but I haven't had a chance to write it."

"And you're going to go through with it?"

"Why wouldn't I? I always meet my obligations."

"What's the topic?"

"POCD. Postoperative cognitive disorder. How anesthesia may cause memory loss. I believe it does, but many of my colleagues disagree. I'll tell you all about it, if you're interested."

"Sure."

"Will you come with me to New York? I'm going to drive. I haven't made that drive in years. It will give me time to think."

Devon felt queasy. "Can we discuss it in the morning?"

"It is morning."

"I mean, like when the sun comes up."

Ruby put down the pen and sipped champagne. "I know you have things to do, but it might be good for you to get away. It would mean a lot to me."

"All right. But let's talk it through in the morning."

Devon returned to the living room sofa and immediately fell into a deep sleep.

The following day, it already seemed like old news that she was going to accompany Ruby to New York.

For the next few nights, before their trip, the two of them dined by candlelight at one end of the cherrywood table that seated twelve. The glass doors of the dining room opened onto the garden. Lush scents of jacaranda and frangipani wafted in. The stereo, with Ruby's iPod in the dock, blared eclectic selections that amazed Devon: Jefferson Airplane, Blondie, Brazilian Forró, the Kinks, Senegalese drummers, and plenty of Joan Jett. No jazz, she thought ruefully. Ruby had recently hired a Vietnamese chef to prepare healthful organic meals, which she barely touched. Instead, she subsisted on midnight snacks at all hours—celery, onion dip, Spanish olives, Jell-O—washed down with tequila sours. At the dinner table she dawdled, applying fingernail polish, paying some bills and tearing up others, scribbling to-do lists (of things to avoid or buy, remember or forget), which devolved, or, from Ruby's point of view, crystallized, into a list of her lists. Devon, meanwhile, began to enjoy the chef's assortment of stir-fries, her vegetable spring rolls and garlic tempeh. Soon enough, Ruby would get restless, uncork a one-hundred-dollar Barolo, and begin pacing the Turkish carpet or wandering outside to clip calla lilies. Sometimes she remained on the lawn, tossing birdseed, long after the birds had retired. Or she disappeared into the small greenhouse at the edge of the property and tended to her herb garden. It had been built when Devon was a child and was off-limits to everyone, including the gardeners. Devon had only been allowed to enter with her mother. So of course when Ruby was out, Devon used to take the key from her mother's desk drawer and unlock the glass door. The interior had a spicy, earthen smell. There was a potting table, copper sink, humidifier, and dozens of herbs in clay flowerpots, carefully labeled. None of it seemed all that mysterious to Devon except the names of the herbs: bloodroot, balm of Gilead, boneset, coltsfoot, horsetail, calamus, and— Devon's favorite—life everlasting. So far as Devon could tell, only a handful, like turmeric and fennel, ever found their way to the kitchen for cooking. Apparently Ruby grew the rest for her own pleasure. She said she found it relaxing. What had always been odd to Devon, even as a child, was that, aside from picking flowers, her mother rarely spent time gardening and left most landscaping decisions to the gardeners.

After dinner, Ruby invariably suggested a swim. They would change into their suits, but true to form, Ruby would lose interest even before they reached the pool. Wineglass in hand, she reclined on a chaise longue and watched Devon glide through the turquoise water. Ruby wouldn't stir until Devon stopped swimming. Realizing this was one way to slow her mother down, with the added benefit of getting herself back in shape, Devon lapped the pool until her muscles ached.

Devon didn't need to consult the DSM-IV in her mother's study to figure out that Ruby was manic. Nearly every symptom listed in chapter 4 was applicable: grandiosity, lack of appetite, self-absorption, compulsiveness, indifference to danger. Devon realized that Ruby was running through the settlement money from her divorce at a frightening rate. Except that Ruby wasn't frightened. Or was so deeply spooked by other matters that what happened to her money was the least of her fears. In her spending sprees she was acquiring bizarre objects: a gold-studded saddle from Argentina, though Ruby had no horse; a deep-sea kayak, still under a tarp on the lawn; a Sung Dynasty credenza that remained boxed in the garage after express delivery from Macao. In recent days, she had moved on to seeking things that almost certainly didn't, or couldn't, exist: a red marble statuette of a five-footed fox and a silver barrel hooped in bronze and inscribed with the Sanskrit word for "secret," *guhya*.

"I thought maybe if I wanted these things enough," Ruby explained, "I would find them."

"You mean, you would wish them into existence?"

"Why not? How do we know that all things originate in the same way? If you project hard enough, maybe an object can move from the second dimension to the third. Or maybe the other way, from the fourth dimension to the third." She sighed. "But it hasn't happened. Doesn't mean it can't happen. But it hasn't."

Devon had hung out with plenty of strung-out people, but it was nothing compared to what she was experiencing with her mother. Ruby was doing the drinking, but Devon had the hangover. Ruby wasn't sleeping, but Devon was exhausted.

Even in less turbulent times, it would have been strange for Devon to revisit that house and bunk down in her former bedroom: the dresser filled with old clothes, a poster of Duke Ellington in tails over the bed, the clarinet she played in the school band on a shelf. As a kid, she had taken lessons on the Steinway grand in the living room, which she hadn't played in years. She moved out of the house at seventeen and rarely returned. She had taken her small collection of vintage instruments—two trumpets, a mandolin, a saxophone once played by Johnny Hodges, and the clarinet she sold—and two thousand CDs, nearly all jazz, that were stacked around her tiny living room overlooking Corona Boulevard. As a kid, she was always plugged into a Walkman. She had a good ear. She augmented her lessons by playing along to Earl Hines and Horace Silver, to McCoy Tyner's bop and Memphis Slim's boogie, mimicking their licks as best she could. She became as much a student of jazz as a musician. Her tastes were broadly eclectic: she was equally attracted to James Johnson's stride piano and Jason Moran's historical fusion, which took a famous piece like Johnson's "You've Got to Be Modernistic" and improvised a dozen sequences around the ragtime core. But she found her real model in Ahmad Jamal, the pianist she most admired. Classically trained, endlessly inventive, Jamal worked a broad canvas. He was ambitious, referring to his trio as an orchestra, exploring every jazz form that preceded him, and experimenting on the electric piano. His renditions of "Perfidia" and "But Not for Me" set the standard for Devon: the radical chord shifts, subtle colorations, and Afro-Cuban rhythms.

After dropping out of college for good, Devon had rented her apartment in Little Cuba. She liked it there, being an outsider. She played in a succession of jazz bands, appearing at second-tier clubs from Charleston to Key West. She never got the kind of break that would have landed her in New York or L.A. The demo she sent to various record labels barely elicited a response. She ended up working small clubs in Miami as part of a quintet. They made some good music, but their chemistry was terrible. They could never agree on their repertoire or their drummer (four in six months), haggled over money, and consumed vast amounts of booze and dope. After they broke up, Devon stopped playing. She was burned out. She tended bar in the same clubs where they had performed. And she started freelancing reviews for music magazines. A former classmate hooked her up with solid contacts at *JazzTimes* and *Jazz Review*. She wrote about jazz and rock. She landed a few interviews with musicians performing in Miami. She was getting good at it, almost earning enough to give up bartending, when she—literally—blew a big interview for *DownBeat* with a famous sax player in from L.A., sharing lines of coke in his hotel suite and then scratching up his face when he came on to her and got rough, ripping her blouse, slapping her around. The hotel called the cops, and when her criminal record came up on the squad car LCD screen and the sax player laid everything on her, they let him go and hauled her in for possession. The magazine promptly fired her. She beat the coke rap, but a couple of months later was busted with the peyote, coming within a hair of going to the women's prison outside Ocala.

And the fact is, she wasn't lying to the judge at her trial: the peyote buttons really had been for her personal use. A tai chi instructor turned shaman who called himself Ciguri had turned her on to the drug in Key Largo. He claimed his mother was a member of the Tarahumara tribe in Mexico whose religion was built around the peyote cactus. The Tarahumara believed hallucinations induced by the drug were scenes from the future, and therefore sacred. They said their distant ancestors fell from the sky and roamed the earth. And that every man has a dormant Double who awakens at the instant of enlightenment and joins him in his life's journey but will turn on him with a vengeance if he deviates from the true road.

The first time she ate peyote, Devon dreamed of a mountain range where rocks danced, plants spoke, and the terrain was a desert by day and a lake at night.

Ciguri nodded, smiling, when she told him. "You just visited the Sierra Tarahumara, home of the tribe. In order to integrate your warring selves and become an initiate, you ought to eat twenty-eight buttons in as many days. That is the next step toward enlightenment." He paused. "Which nevertheless you may not achieve."

It became a moot point when, arrested, convicted, and put on probation, Devon knew she'd have to find a different route to enlightenment—like sobriety.

❄

Devon had found an unlikely reason of her own for going to New York. It began the day before Camille Broussard's funeral, when Ruby told her about her last conversation with her mother. Camille Broussard had only been living in Miami for seven months when her health began to fail in late November. Ruby had checked her in to the Saint Francis of Assisi Hospice, a Catholic facility run by nuns, with a first-rate medical unit. Her mother shared a room with two other women, who played gin rummy incessantly at a Formica table. Ruby visited every few days. She would wheel her mother to the lounge. They didn't talk much. Her mother had no energy. Usually she dozed off after five minutes, at which point Ruby would get on her cellphone to her lawyer, who was overseeing the implementation of her divorce agreement—transfer of assets and deeds and so on. On that last visit, her mother had been too weak to get out of bed. She had just returned from the medical ward after suffering an angina attack. The doctors said she was stable, but Ruby thought otherwise the moment she saw her. Her blood pressure was high, her pulse irregular. Her surgeon wanted to install a pacemaker. He had telephoned Ruby that morning for her okay, and the operation was scheduled for the following week.

Propped up in her wheelchair, her mother interrupted Ruby's description of the procedure. "Let them do whatever they want, honey," she said in her Louisiana drawl. "No matter what, it's in the Lord's hands."

Ruby winced, as she always did when her mother waxed pious. "Sometimes he needs help," she said, trying to keep the contempt out of her voice.

"Never."

Sitting on a plastic chair beside the bed, Ruby hadn't taken off her raincoat.

"Don't go yet," her mother said.

"I wasn't leaving."

"You were." She started coughing. "I need to tell you something."

"That's a nasty cough."

"Listen to me. When you close up my apartment, Ruby, there's some effects I want you to have. You can throw away everything else. It's mostly junk, and seeing as you're rich, you wouldn't want any of it. But there's a cabinet in the living room that's got my keepsakes, including everything I ever had of your father's."

Ruby hadn't been expecting this. "What kind of things?"

"Have a look." She started coughing again, and this time she didn't stop. Ruby called for one of the nuns, who administered a sedative.

Camille Broussard suffered a stroke the next day, so those were her last words to Ruby: *Have a look.*

Ruby had taken Devon to her mother's apartment on Mosby Avenue to get a dress for the mortician. Devon was shocked by the shabbiness of the place: the chipped appliances, frayed carpets, cracks like spreading veins in the ceiling plaster.

"Feels like home," Ruby said, shaking her head. "Like every other place she ever lived in."

When Ruby opened the cabinet in the living room, she was greeted by a pocket of stale air. The dusty shelves were lined with odds and ends: empty perfume bottles, hotel ashtrays, AA pamphlets, yellowing road maps. There was an Annie Oakley doll. A replica of a steamboat named the *Camille*. A New Year's party hat emblazoned *1956*.

At the base of the cabinet, behind shoes and hatboxes, they found a battered leather suitcase labeled VAL in Magic Marker. It was also affixed with faded travel stickers, ROME (back-dropped by the Colosseum), PARIS (the Eiffel Tower), LONDON (Big Ben), and KANSAS CITY (a steer). Ruby pulled the suitcase out and snapped it open. She and Devon found an assortment of Valentine Owen's possessions, including a trumpet embouchure, a pair of pearl cuff links, and a coaster from the Oasis Lounge in New Orleans.

"That's where she met him," Ruby said, unrolling a pair of black gloves monogrammed V.O. "This must be the stuff he left behind when he took off. She's been lugging it around ever since. Pathetic . . ."

There was a small stack of LPs with worn covers. Devon grew excited, rifling through them: Louis Armstrong, Sidney Bechet, Bix Beiderbecke, and, at the bottom, an LP entitled *Undercurrents*, by Tex Mayeux's Hurricane Band. Wearing white tuxedo jackets with silken lapels, the band members had been photographed with their instruments before a neon-blue curtain, circa 1959. Tex Mayeux, a big man with a lopsided face, was front and center at his piano, showing a lot of teeth.

Ruby put her finger on the trumpeter, a tall unsmiling man

with a square jaw and slicked-back brown hair. He was the only one in the band looking directly at the camera. "That's my father," she said. "My mother played this record all the time. I did, too, when I was around twelve. Then one day I couldn't stand it anymore."

"How come you never mentioned that he cut a record?"

Ruby shrugged. "I never listened to it again. And I doubt you would've thought it was any good."

"I would've liked to have heard it."

"I've told you, your becoming a musician had nothing to do with him. You have more talent than he ever did."

"I never cut a record." Devon turned back to the LP. "Looks like he played a Selmer trumpet. You can tell because it's unusually long. Made in France."

"Evidently that trumpet was his prized possession," Ruby said, slipping on one of the gloves.

"The liner notes say the band toured South America as well as Europe. I've listened to a ton of music, but I never heard of these guys."

"I'm not surprised. This was their moment, and it didn't last. My father didn't last. According to my mother, he never played with a real band again. He went back to being a session man, a fill-in. He scraped along. It was his solo on 'This Can't Be Love' that she used to play over and over again."

"Did you ever hear him play?"

"Once." She took off the glove and folded it. "In Saint Louis."

"You never told me that, either."

"I'll tell you about it some other time."

"I don't know most of this playlist, except the standards. 'Body and Soul.' And there's one Monk."

Ruby had already moved on, sifting through the rest of the suitcase. "I never had a single thing of his," she muttered.

"Why didn't she give you any of this before?"

"Because it was hers," Ruby replied matter-of-factly. "This was what she got from him, and this is what I'm getting from her. No money, no property. This is their legacy."

"Did he have other family?"

"I wouldn't know. He may have married, had other children. Like my mother, he lived in a lot of places. He got his big break with Tex Mayeux right here in Miami. The rest is history," she added dryly.

"All you ever told me was that he and your mother met in New Orleans."

"Met, mated, and parted. March 1960."

"You lived in New Orleans yourself for a while, right?" Devon knew she was pushing her luck.

Even in her agitated state, Ruby didn't take the bait. "That's another story," she said brusquely. She looked around and shivered. "Let's get out of here."

When she realized Ruby was ready to leave the suitcase there, Devon quickly repacked it and carried it out with her.

When they got home, Ruby took a bath. Her stereo system included a turntable, and Devon took the opportunity to put on the Hurricane Band's album. Her mother was right: they weren't very good. Brassy but bland, they reminded Devon of the resident bands on late-night shows.

Ruby returned in her kimono and mixed herself a vodka martini and lit some scented candles. She was in her own world again. Devon was sitting on the floor in front of the open suitcase.

"If you want any of that stuff, it's yours," Ruby said off-handedly.

"I want that Selmer trumpet."

"Good luck finding it."

Devon unzipped an interior pocket in the suitcase and removed a packet of envelopes. "Look, there are some old letters." She flipped through them. "From your father to your mother, it looks like. Do you want to see them?"

Ruby sipped her drink. "Leave them on the table. Would you play the piano for me, dear? You play so beautifully."

"Now?" Devon hadn't played for her mother in years.

"Whatever you like: Schumann, Liszt—or some jazz."

"Mom, I don't play much anymore."

Ruby waved away her reply. "Please. Play me something. Can I fix you a drink?"

"No, I don't want a drink."

Devon sat down at the piano and, closing her eyes, launched tentatively into "Criss Cross." If Ruby was listening, she didn't show it. She had moved on again, arranging some flowers, watering a plant. Finally she circled around and picked up the packet of letters. She curled up on the sofa, scanning several letters, then examining the postmarks on the envelopes instead. Devon began improvising, losing herself in the music. She was surprised at how easily it was coming back to her.

"Devon," Ruby called out.

Devon did not want to stop playing. She looked over at her mother.

"Two of these are postmarked in Chicago, two in New York, one in Atlanta," Ruby said. "They were sent over just a few years, when I was small. I wouldn't have expected that."

Devon lifted her hands from the keyboard. "Love letters?"

"Hardly. Take a look. They're all about the clubs he's playing. The famous musicians he's hanging out with. He's responding to letters of hers, but I bet she sent a dozen for every one she got in return. Later she would spin me her romantic fairy tales about how terrific he was."

Devon joined her on the sofa and picked up the letters. Her grandfather's handwriting was cramped and spindly. He omitted some words and misspelled others, like *foregn* and *pospone*. Devon could see why Ruby might have wanted to stop reading; when he mentioned her at all, it was perfunctory. *What grade was she in? Would Camille send a photo when he had a permanent address?* Except he never seemed to get a permanent address. The letters were short and impersonal. Devon wondered why he took the trouble to write at all. It was like someone who calls you to vent his complaints. Maybe it was all about the complaints. His health, the fact he couldn't get work, the corruptness of the music business. He didn't ask Camille to lend him money, but not so subtly inquired if she knew anyone who could. He usually signed off with his full name, nothing else. Unfolding the last letter, Devon stopped short.

"This one's from someone else, Mom."

"A letter to him?"

"No, a letter to your mother about him. Recent."

Ruby's interest was momentarily piqued. Devon handed her the letter, typed on business stationery and dated July 2, 2010. The letterhead read:

EMMETT BROWNE

167 MADISON AVENUE

NEW YORK, NY 10004

A calling card was stapled in the upper corner; under the name and address was this:

DEALER IN VINTAGE INSTRUMENTS & MUSICAL RARITIES

Dear Ms. Broussard:
I have a matter of importance to discuss with you
concerning the late Valentine Owen. It could be
beneficially rewarding. Please call me at your
convenience.

The signature was florid, and his name on the card was printed in brown ink.

"What do you think?" Devon said.

"He doesn't really say much."

"He says it's important."

"That could mean anything." Ruby shrugged. "It is weird that he sent this twenty years after my father died."

"I think so, too. 'Musical rarities'—that's right up my alley. I'd like to find out if your mother ever contacted him. If it's okay with you."

"Be my guest. I doubt she acted on this: she was fading fast over the summer. I'm surprised she even filed it away." Ruby became irritated. "Why are we even discussing this as if it's important? Valentine Owen was never connected to anything important in his life."

At six A.M. Devon made the first of several calls to Browne's number, but even during business hours, she got nothing but a ringtone. No secretary, no answering machine.

"You can look him up when we get to New York," Ruby said to her that evening. She was wearing a gold kimono, applying matching polish to her fingernails. Whatever the invitation to speak at the conference meant to Ruby, the trip itself—requiring the better part of two days in an automobile rather than three hours on an airplane—had taken on an importance of its own, paralleling the inner journey she had undertaken, whose destination was not yet clear.

"Maybe you'll come with me when I meet this guy," Devon said.

Ruby kissed her cheek. "Of course I will. You know, Devon, you haven't told me about your tattoo. I hadn't seen it until you put on your bathing suit."

"It's new. I had it done last year." Devon realized it was the tattoo, centered between her shoulder blades, that mesmerized Ruby when she was in the pool, not her swimming. "What do you want to know?"

"Everything," Ruby said, holding her hand out to study her nails. "I want to know everything."

Alice Bolden called her son Charley from the day he was born to the day she buried him. The crowd knew him by other names. Buddy, of course. Then they called him Kid Bolden, and finally they crowned him King. She took pride in hearing others call him King Bolden, but it made her uneasy, too. Kings get knocked off their thrones; the same people who cheer them on bring them down. She was afraid for him—the adulation, the women, the money flowing in and flowing out. In the winter of 1906 her worst fears were realized.

Charley was on fire—not with his music, but with demons like she'd never seen. All his sweetness had turned bitter. He said he had enemies waiting on him. He accused her of letting them into the house and hiding them. He kept a knife under his pillow. Then he began sleeping on the floor, against the wall, so no one could come up behind him. He had a foul temper, and when he fed it alcohol, it could flare up and swallow him. She'd watched her husband waste away, and then her mother and father died, and her daughter Lottie, who was only five. But this was worse. Charley hollering in the night, like someone had him by the throat. Stumbling home filthy at dawn. Sometimes just making it back to the neighborhood, blind drunk, and passing out in the gutter where one of the neighbors—when they still cared—picked him up. Often with his pockets turned out by his bum companions, but still clutching his cornet, even if he hadn't played it all night.

Charley, you better stop before there's just enough of you left to kill off, and nothing more.

But he couldn't hear her, not a word of it, even if he wanted to. He could rave and shout, but he had trouble hearing any voices except his own, and sometimes there were so many of those that it sounded like a chorus, every singer working a different key. For a while, when he was still playing, that roar was way in the back of his head, a constant, ebbing and flowing, and he was able to draw a single line of sound out of it and make it into music. But that didn't last long.

When everything collapsed on him, it happened so fast that for the rest of her life Alice could barely make sense of it. The previous year, Charley was still on top, raking in the big money, wearing expensive suits and alligator shoes and custom-made hats. Some days he played seven or eight engagements, from the saloons in Back-of-Town to the biggest halls in New Orleans, where people lined up to get in. For four years running, he brought her enough money so that she didn't have to work at all, his sister Cora, too. He himself was living in a white house with yellow shutters on LaPierre Street with Nora and their daughter, Bernedine, and making his rounds, as everyone knew, of the hotels and apartments where he kept those other

*women in style. He was paying rent all over town. His house
was two stories high with indoor plumbing and brass fixtures
and a wide widow's walk on the roof where he could see clear
to the river. He used to lounge up there with Cornish and
Lewis, drinking good whiskey. Once, when Nora was out, just
to see what would happen, he played his horn loud and, sure
enough, people gathered, ten, twenty deep and called out to
him, frightening Bernedine inside, so he never did it again. He
had been spending more money in a week than Alice would see
in an entire year, but then he got erratic, drinking heavily, missing gigs, disappearing for days at a time, until he was nearly
broke, and Nora left him and went to live at her mother's house
with Bernedine, and Alice herself was back at Morton's Laundry on Quillon Place, scrubbing and ironing. She would tell the
story of her famous son to the other women in that steaming
room, she needed to hear herself tell it, because by then he was
disappearing before her eyes, and the story was all she had left,
the unfinished story he would remain for the next three decades.*

*Alice told them how Charley started out, learning the cor-
net from her onetime beau, Mr. Manuel Hall. She was still a
pretty widow then, and Charley was eight years old. Her husband, Westmore, whose good looks and charm Charley inherited, had died of a heart attack two years earlier, age twenty-nine.
Nearly all the men in that family died young. Not Charley,
who would suffer a long living death. Manny was a cook at
Nelson Quirile's Café on Royal Street. He often had sawdust
on his shoes from the kitchen. A widower himself, a big man
who worked the night shift, sweating in a low-ceilinged kitchen
with two coal stoves. He smelled of shrimp and shallots and
the West Indian lime cologne he splashed on Sunday morning*

that stayed with him till Tuesday. After she took Charley and Cora to church, and served them all lunch, ham hocks and beans with yellow rice, she and Manny would stroll along Marin Street, past the St. Jacques Shipyard, to a riverfront bar for a pitcher of beer. Then they'd go back to Manny's house, Number 2359, five doors down from her house. Sometimes Alice felt sure Charley and Cora saw them return from the bar. But they never once came knocking at Manny's door or questioned her when she came back home alone at dusk. Later, Charley told people that Manny was the only real father he ever knew.

Manny said to Alice one night: The boy is a natural—he can already hear the music in his head. I give him the rudiments, and two months later, he's ready to teach me. Must've come into this world with the instrument in his hands. You would know.

Charley took his lessons in Manny's house, down the street. It was the only house on the street that had a small porch, where Manny sat most nights, no matter the weather. Charley liked that porch. All the rooms in the house were painted blue, including Manny's bedroom, which Charley peeked into more than once: the hard bed with the thin blanket, the low bureau, the mirror big enough to hold a man's face, no more.

On Manny's cornet he practiced scales and arpeggios, learned marching songs, and then one day, from memory, played note for note the hymn "Yes, He Is on His Throne," which he had heard at church that week. Two weeks later, he began improvising around other hymns as well as the work songs he heard from the stevedores on the levee. At which point Manny took him to Brooker's Music Store and bought him a proper new brass cornet, better than his own.

Manny never went to church. I don't believe much in sin the way they teach it, *he told Charley on the way home that afternoon, his collar dark with sweat.* For me it's like this: there are things you do that others forgive, but you can't never forgive them in yourself. Like being born with a special gift and not using it right. Don't let that happen to you. And don't listen to anyone who doesn't have the gift himself. Just blow that horn the way you hear it in your head. Keep it pure.

That was Manny's most important piece of advice to Charley. A month later, he was gone to Louisville, Kentucky, where his brother had opened a restaurant. It took Charley some time to grasp that he would never see Manny again. Manny hadn't made a secret of the fact that he didn't want to marry again, Alice or anyone else. Yet, the previous Christmas, he had given her a topaz ring—his mother's ring—as a keepsake, and she kept it for the rest of her life. It was the closest she would come to remarrying, she told Cora, though it wasn't really that close at all.

Charley discovered soon enough, sooner than most, that there was a lot more to sin than what Manny had told him. But he never forgot Keep it pure *as he brought forth an entirely new kind of music. Others would give it a name, but he wouldn't know about that.*

Devon drove across the state line with Ruby dozing beside her in the passenger seat. She told herself she was accompanying her mother on this journey because she had grown protective of her. If that was so, why wasn't she calling Ruby on her meltdown? Did she think her own recent history denied her credibility? Was she getting off on watching Ruby lose control? Or had she rightly concluded that Ruby's denial was impregnable?

Trash picking eight hours a day for sixty days had focused Devon's mind in a way peyote never could. In an orange jumpsuit she had roamed the highway shoulders with a taciturn Jamaican girl named Giselle, on probation for dealing weed, who handed her a card on her last day, imprinted with a single sentence: INSTEAD OF TRYING TO CONTROL OTHER PEOPLE, CONTROL YOURSELF. "Another girl give that to me in jail," Giselle said. "I made it my motto—to maybe keep me from getting busted again." Self-control had never been Devon's strong suit, but keeping her mother from running off the rails might help her gain some measure of it.

Ruby coughed and raised her head. "How long was I asleep?"

"About twenty minutes."

"It felt like hours," she yawned, flipping down the visor and examining her makeup in the vanity mirror. "The red meat knocked me out."

"But you didn't eat it."

"Dessert, then. Meat, sugar—it's all the same. Look at that!" She sat up suddenly and pointed at a billboard. "That's what I'm talking about."

It was an ad for a flashy wristwatch. A model wearing only briefs, heels, a man's tuxedo jacket, and the watch was eating blackout cake with whipped cream. The open jacket revealed her long hair curled over her breasts.

"Overt message," Ruby said angrily, "is somebody just fucked her. Subliminal message: somebody just fucked her. She's fuckable, and the watch keeps perfect time."

"Yes, Mom. Sex sells watches, cars—"

"And why is she eating?" Ruby demanded.

"Because eating is sexy."

"Since when?"

Devon realized this was another of those instances when her mother was going to be right, no matter what. In the last week, she had learned to keep her mouth shut when Ruby went on a rant: a chance remark might ignite an entirely new grievance. Her tossing around four-letter words was also something new.

"Did you see the televisions in that restaurant—and not just in the bar," Ruby said. "Four flatscreens. You can't get away from them anymore, on airplanes, in terminals, even in taxis.

The other doctors in my wing all have them in their waiting rooms. The other day I was crossing the street and there was a kid wearing a T-shirt that read WHAT THE FUCK. He was telling passersby, 'Everybody's putting thoughts out into the world. So I try to put out good ones.' Is there a preacher or guru on the planet who can top that? But none of us can compete with the daily avalanche of bullshit. Are you ready for me to take the wheel, dear? You must be tired."

"I really haven't been driving long." Devon flipped open her cellphone. "I think I'll try this guy Browne again."

"Who?"

"Emmett Browne. The music dealer."

This time a man answered on the second ring. He had a clipped, precise voice that occasionally wavered, as if he were catching his breath.

"Mr. Browne?"

"This is Emmett Browne."

"My name is Devon Sheresky. My grandmother, Camille Broussard, passed away this month. We found your letter."

There was a long silence. "We?" he said finally.

"My mother and I."

"Your mother the doctor."

Devon was surprised. "That's right."

"My condolences for your grandmother."

"Thank you. Did she respond to you?"

"No, she never did."

"Well, I'm curious about your letter."

"I can appreciate that. Your call is very unexpected."

"I'm actually driving to New York right now."

Another silence. "Even more unexpected."

"My mother has business there."

"I see."

"Can you tell me what the letter is about?"

"I'd suggest we meet to discuss it. This is very fortuitous. When will you arrive in New York?"

"In a couple of days."

"Can you come by my office then?"

"I'd like to."

"Good."

"You said it was something important."

"It is. Thank you for calling. Call again when you get into town." And he hung up.

"Pretty strange," Devon said.

"What did he say?"

"He knew you were a doctor. How would he know anything about you?"

"My mother must've told him."

"He said he never spoke to her."

"Who knows?" Ruby said impatiently.

"He wouldn't say what the letter was about."

"My god, why all the mystery? He's probably just some creep who was mixed up with my father. You're still going to meet with him?"

"I want to know what this is about."

Ruby turned away and gazed out the window as a horse farm—thoroughbreds snorting mist, stables, a barn—slid by. "I said I'd go with you. And I will."

NEW ORLEANS—SEPTEMBER 3, 1906

When King Bolden made his last public appearance, Willie Cornish was playing beside him. The Labor Day parade, 1906. The Bolden Band used to lead this parade. Now they were nine bands back, second from last. And that was only because the band behind them, the Plaquemine Brass Band, had shown up without a bass player or a clarinetist. Except for Cornish and Frank Lewis, the Bolden Band had experienced a complete turnover: Mumford, Warner, Johnson, and Tillman either quit or were fired. Frankie Dusen, a fast-talking trombonist who doubled on clarinet and had ingratiated himself with Bolden, was in fact running the band: setting rehearsal times, booking engagements. Cornish thought him dishonest and dirty. To his face he called Dusen a chiseler. "Four-fingered" Henry Zeno was playing drums, and the second clarinetist was a little fellow named Mack Jones whom Cornish had never heard of.

Bolden had enlisted him the previous night in a dive on South Ramsay Street, without ever hearing him play.

You didn't hear him play because he can't play, *Cornish said to Bolden after listening to Jones tune up at Elks Place that morning. But it didn't matter anymore. None of it mattered. Bolden hadn't even remembered who Mack Jones was when Jones showed up in a horseblanket suit, smelling of bourbon. Bolden himself was wearing a rumpled brown suit and a derby. The silk vests were gone, and the bright shirts. For a pair of hobnailed boots he had traded the pocket watch engraved with a mermaid that Nora had given him. He wandered the streets at night, often all night, and the boots were good for that. He would go as far as the city limits, sometimes north, to Spanish Fort, where he gazed at Lake Pontchartrain, a dull green even in the dark. The roads there, around the big houses and hotels, were paved with crushed oyster shells that crackled underfoot— as if he was stepping on firecrackers. Most nights he headed south and rode a ferry across the river, to Gretna, where he had once played before packed houses at the Palm Grove. Sometimes he returned on the ferry, hunched alone in the stern, always looking back to land; sometimes he stayed on that side of the river and found a bench in Marais Park, never sleeping, just staring up at the elm branches swaying.*

One night he went to his mother-in-law's house on First Street. Nora was waiting tables again, working ten-hour shifts in a dive across town. She was only twenty-six, and though still pretty, looked much older after her years with Bolden. He lurched in carrying a bottle of rye. His hands were shaking, his shirt was soiled. I want to take you to Mexico, *he said.* Get you anything you want. *She replied,* I want you gone. *He was*

*downing the rye like it was beer. He collapsed onto the sofa,
tried to stand up, and passed out. Her mother came home and
recoiled at the sight of him.* Just until morning, Mama, Nora
said. Won't happen again. *At two* A.M. *Bolden woke with a
start, knocked over a chair, and crashed into the table. He
clutched his head. His throat was on fire. The two women
rushed in.* You poisoned me, *he shouted at his mother-in-law,*
but I ain't dead. *He grabbed a pitcher and threw it, grazing her
temple. Nora screamed, and he bolted out the door. A policeman arrested him on Jackson Street and booked him at the
House of Detention.*

*When the Labor Day parade started, people were lining the
sidewalk ten deep, waving sparklers, tossing confetti. The air
was heavy. Mist was boiling off the river, pinpricked with
lights. On poles jutting from buildings, the Stars and Stripes
were flapping. Dozens of flags. Twice the band launched into
"Sugar Blues" and twice Bolden veered off into jumbled scraps
of hymns, the music of his childhood from the Nazareth
Church. When the band reached St. Charles, he drifted away
without a word, concealing his cornet beneath his coat. Cornish looked around and he was gone. The band hesitated, then
kept marching. Bolden melted into the crowd, expecting people to shout* King Bolden, play for us! *But no one had shouted
to him for many months, and no one did now. Men, women,
and children seemed to be looking right through him—as if he
were already a ghost.* Maybe I am, *he thought, glancing down
at his hand to see if it was transparent. Then he pressed a finger
to his chest, because if he was vapor maybe the finger would
slide right into his heart. And if that was so, could he just disappear into the mist? Instead he found himself jostled, pressed,*

in a sea of flesh. A pounding, sweating, full-throated crowd
that left him in its wake as it swarmed around the corner, fol-
lowing the parade to South Rampart. The music faded, the
shouts died away. He was alone suddenly. All he could hear
was those flags flapping. They seemed to have grown bigger
than the sails on a schooner. The next morning, he woke up
again in a cell in the House of Detention, his right sleeve stiff
with dried blood, his pants torn. His Conn cornet was dented
and the mouthpiece was missing. He sat on an iron stool star-
ing at the cornet for an hour. When a policeman walked down
the stone corridor and asked him his name and address, he re-
plied, I'm not from around here anymore.

Willie Cornish kept the cylinder recording of "Tiger Rag"
in his wife's Indian chest with the maharajah on the lid. Even
after National Phonograph and Indestructible settled their suit
and new and improved cylinders were being reproduced at the
rate of one hundred a day in St. Louis and New Orleans and
Chicago, Cornish didn't think it would be right to give them
Bolden's cylinder. King Bolden had wanted a contract, cash up
front and royalties, and he wasn't in a position to get any of
that now. Not in the East Louisiana State Asylum in Jackson.

It had been one year and four months since a deputy sheriff
had transported him there in a dogcart on June 4, 1907, with a
commitment order signed by Judge T.W.C. Ellis. It stated that
the cause of his insanity was alcohol and noted that Charles
Bolden's own mother and sister had requested his commit-
ment.

Cornish would not touch that cylinder until Bolden got out
of that place. Maybe it would take a few months, maybe a year.
But the cylinder would be waiting for him. And maybe then

Bolden could get some of that money he was due. Revive his music. Record it. Maybe they could bring him back from the dead in that house of the dead.

In his heart Cornish wanted to believe that.

But he knew whiskey had soaked so deep into Bolden's brain that he was drunk even on days when he didn't drink. And in the end there weren't many of those. He had fallen as fast as he had risen. Even faster. And now it was over.

Cornish and four members of the old Bolden Band joined the Eagle Orchestra. Bunk Johnson's band. A solid band. They were making good money and getting offered more engagements than they could take. Bunk drank, but not like Bolden. Bunk wanted to be king now that Bolden was gone, but everyone agreed the new king was Freddie Keppard, who could blow hard and sweet and draw the big crowds. He and Bunk were playing the "new" music Bolden had created. Every time they performed, Cornish saw Bunk try to duplicate Bolden's sound. He couldn't. Not the slow blues and not the improvisations—Cornish called them "inspirations"—that came out of nowhere and kept on going. Bunk did attract the best musicians, picking them off from the Imperial Band, the Olympia Orchestra, the Peerless Band.

A couple of months earlier, an ace clarinetist had joined the Eagle Orchestra. He came from a Creole family, the son of a onetime cornetist who had become a shoe manufacturer. He was only eleven years old, a prodigy. He called himself a musicianer. His name was Sidney Bechet.

WASHINGTON, D.C.— DECEMBER 20, 10:00 P.M.

Though Ruby wanted to drive straight through to New York, Devon put up a fight and they stopped for the night in D.C. Not on the outskirts, in a motel in Maryland or Virginia; if Ruby was going to stop, it had to be in the city proper, and nothing less than a five-star hotel would do. They had driven into a blizzard in North Carolina, and by the time they reached Newport News, the visibility was two hundred feet. In the capital, the streets were deserted. The Washington Monument was invisible through the swirl of snow.

Checking in to the Hay-Adams, Ruby was distracted by a man who looked out of place: a salesman, down-at-heels, with a battered suitcase and a rumpled coat. He had been stranded in the neighborhood by the storm, and rather than brave the cold to find a cheaper hotel, he was trying to bargain with the desk clerk for a lower rate. It took Devon a moment to regain Ruby's attention.

"Come on, Mom," she said, leading her to the elevators.

Their suite was spacious and silent. Pine logs were burning in the fireplace. There was a vase of white roses and a basket of fruit. They were one floor down from the presidential suite, in which the Portuguese ambassador currently resided after a fire in his embassy.

"Ever been to Lisbon?" Ruby asked Devon, as she picked up the phone for room service. "I went with your father when we were in medical school. We sailed on the Tagus River. We drove into the mountains and drank the wine. I thought I was happy then. I didn't know anything."

The Hay-Adams had a 1988 Chateau Latour on its wine list. Ruby ordered a bottle along with another steak, whipped potatoes, and a double order of lemon Jell-O. She ate only the Jell-O and drank the wine while Devon had an omelette and orange juice.

"This wine is delicious," Ruby said. "Like some dessert?"

"I'm going to shower and turn in, Mom. We were on the road for fourteen hours."

When Devon came out of the bathroom twenty minutes later, wrapped in a terrycloth robe, Ruby was sprawled out on the couch, still fully dressed, channel surfing, alternating between a Japanese sitcom and a jai alai match in Brazil, with two announcers shouting in Portuguese.

"I wonder if the ambassador is watching this," Ruby said.

Devon shut the door to her room and put in a pair of earplugs. The sheets were cool. She had been prepared to answer questions about her tattoo, but Ruby had apparently lost interest. Which was fine with Devon. On her back, four inches in diameter, there was a tattoo of Saturn with fiery rings, the outermost ring a serpent with turquoise eyes.

This was a symbol she had salvaged from a peyote trip and preserved in a sketchpad. It was inked on her by a tattooist in Miami Beach named Ahmed. She had been introduced to Ahmed by her former boyfriend, Josef. Ahmed was from Kashmir. Posters of the Himalayas covered the walls of his parlor. He had a white beard and a ponytail. He wore brightly colored caftans and yellow horn-rimmed glasses. While he applied his needles, his soft voice lulled her to sleep.

"In the *Rig Veda*," he said, "the goddess Night is a tattoo artist, painting stars on her own body as she travels through space. That is why I work at night."

Devon met Josef at a club in Miami. Not the place where she tended bar, but a smaller, darker club across town that she frequented. He was thirty years old, compact and wiry, his curly hair prematurely gray. He was sitting at the bar wearing a black T-shirt, his laptop lit up before him. He said he was a cyberspace security expert who encrypted databases and designed firewalls. He lived in Chicago, in a loft by the old stockyards. After drinking shots of tequila, Devon took him back to her apartment. He was good in bed. He had powerful muscles for someone who sat in front of computers all day. They spent the weekend together.

When she visited him in Chicago two weeks later, she found that his loft was more like an office than a home. There was a kitchenette, a tiny bathroom, and a futon, but the room was dominated by two long tables lined with computers, monitors, and elaborate gadgetry. The small refrigerator contained a dozen cans of Red Bull and a bottle of vodka. There were three cans of soup in the cupboard. "I eat out or order in," he explained. He took her out for an expensive Japanese dinner. He told her his parents had defected from East Germany.

"My mother worked for the Stasi, tapping the phones of Party members. That's what got me interested in electronic security. Keeping people like her locked out." The next morning, he asked Devon if she would shave him with a straight-edge razor.

"I've never used one," she replied.

"You can do it." He showed her how to hold the razor and angle the blade, using short, sure strokes. "I've never had anyone shave me before."

She applied the lather with a soft brush, then shaved him without a nick. The next day, she asked if he would like her to do it again.

"No, I just wanted to experience it once."

She was dubious. "You haven't had your other girlfriends shave you?"

"Never."

"So this was your way of making me feel special."

"Not really."

That was Josef. She soon discovered that, like the other guys she had been involved with in recent years—especially the fellow band members she had made the mistake of dating—Josef's favorite place was inside his own head. For a while, he let you join him there, showed you the sights, took you down some interesting byways. Then one day he stepped back and you realized you, too, had become part of the landscape. This was her pattern—unbreakable, apparently.

In her room at the Hay-Adams Devon drifted to sleep. Two hours later, someone shook her shoulder gently. She opened her eyes, and there was Ruby, sitting on the edge of the bed. She was wearing a bathrobe now and her eyelids were heavy, her voice subdued. Her wineglass was on the bedside table.

"I need to tell you about Dad," Ruby said.

Taking out her earplugs, Devon assumed Ruby was referring to her own father, Marvin Sheresky. Until Ruby added, "You said you wanted to know. This would be a good time."

Maybe for you, Devon thought, trying to wake up. She reached toward the lamp.

"No, leave it off. It's better this way."

※

Devon knew some of the larger story, of course. That Camille Broussard had three childless marriages, but conceived Ruby with a guy she barely knew, a jazz musician named Valentine Owen. That Camille and Ruby became gypsies—Baton Rouge, Gulfport, Mobile were just a few of the pit stops. They lived in crummy apartments with Camille's various husbands. The Three Stooges, Ruby called them: Number One a drunk, Number Two a letch who hit on her, Number Three a worse drunk.

Her mother had a thing for truckers and oil riggers—the sort that couldn't hold their jobs. Valentine Owen was the most dashing man Camille Broussard ever met. She glorified him as she never could her husbands. In reality, their longest stint together was a week, but in her imagination Valentine Owen lived on for years. She constructed a private mythology around him.

"Supposedly he showed up again when I was born, to name me," Ruby said. "This was a story my mother made up for herself. When I asked why she could count the number of his visits on one hand, she got all weepy. Instead of answering the question, she said that he burned out young, like so many great musicians. Like who, for instance? I asked, and she couldn't name one. In fact, he wasn't so young. And he wasn't great."

Ruby only met her father twice, briefly, the first time ugly, the second unforgivable. For a while, Ruby had bought into the legend her mother had made of Owen. She wasn't the kind of kid who cried into her pillow at night, but as a teenager she mooned over his photo, feeling sorry for herself. She carried around a shot of him in a white suit and fedora until she was fifteen. Until she met him finally for the first time, on a July night in 1975.

Ruby was home with Camille, who was between husbands. Home was a three-room fourth-floor walkup in St. Louis. Camille was waitressing at a pancake house, dating a guy named Buzz, a mechanic. His standard (and apparently only) line was "Let me give you a buzz," as he poured his personal version of his favorite drink, a whiskey fizz: Five Roses, club soda, a teaspoon of sugar, a dash of bitters, and a squeeze of lime. He was proud of his inventiveness, substituting lime for lemon and adding bitters. He always had so much alcohol in his system that two of these drinks got him drunk, and by number four he was blacking out. That particular day he had given himself one buzz too many by three o'clock and passed out at the kitchen table. Camille left him there, sleeping on his crossed arms. He was still there when she came home from work and announced to Ruby, reading a magazine by the open window, that she had a big surprise for her. She needed her to put on her best dress, the yellow one she'd bought her in Tulsa, comb her hair, and ask no questions. A half hour later, they rode a bus across town to a nightclub called Flamingo Road, a low drab building on a brown street, which tried and failed to live up to its name with an assortment of anemic potted palms, a murky carp pool, and a wall lined with cardboard standups of flamingos.

The Flamingo Road marquee read TONITE ONLY—BILL GRAY'S DIXIELAND BAND.

Ruby didn't know what to expect. She had tagged along to neighborhood bars with her mother, but never a place like this. Camille grabbed a table up close to the small stage, but off to the side. She ordered a bourbon on the rocks, lit a cigarette, and absently popped peanuts from the bowl on the table. The only time Ruby saw her that nervous was when she couldn't get a drink. Though the club wasn't full, there was a decent crowd.

The lights dimmed and the band came out to scattered applause. Conversations trailed off only after the musicians had launched into "Bayou Rag." It was a brisk, upbeat tune that they managed to make dreary. The pianist was pretty good, and Bill Gray played a serviceable clarinet, but that was about it. And then Ruby took a closer look at the trumpeter.

"Surprised?" Camille said, throwing back half her bourbon.

Ruby couldn't believe her mother was doing this to her.

After the set, Camille hurried over to the stage and called out to the trumpeter, waving her arms. If *he* was surprised, he didn't show it. He kept a poker face. He followed Camille to their table and froze at the sight of Ruby.

"This is your daughter, Ruby," Camille said, a little too loudly, with a self-satisfied smile.

Valentine Owen just stared at her for a moment. "Hello, Ruby," he said, finding his voice. She nodded. Any shock he may have felt had seemingly evaporated, as if meeting his daughter for the first time in fifteen years was the most natural thing in the world. "Pretty dress. Thanks for coming tonight."

Ruby cringed. The fact he hadn't laid eyes on her since she was a baby didn't seem to inhibit him. Maybe women like her mother would fall for his glibness. But he was no longer the dashing young man in the white suit in her photo. He was middle-aged, with thinning hair, a soft gut, and a hollow look behind the languorous pose. There were smudges beneath his eyes, his lips were pursed. Maybe it was the cheap stage lights, but to Ruby his skin looked gray, almost bloodless. And he continued to study her closely, not like Husband Number Two, the letch, but not in a way she liked, either.

"Will you join us for a drink?" Camille said.

He cleared his throat and forced a smile. "I'll do better than that. I'd like to take you both out to dinner."

The way Ruby remembered it, she knew at that moment that he was lying, but it may be that she had forced herself to remember it that way. For after Valentine Owen left them with a smile, promising to return shortly, she and her mother waited, and waited, watching a roadie disassemble the drum set and pack up the microphones and carry off the amps. It was a good twenty minutes before Camille collared the stagehand dousing the lights and asked if she could go back to the dressing room to talk to a member of the band.

"They left on their bus five minutes ago."

"All of them?"

"That's how it usually works."

"The trumpeter . . ."

"They're gone, lady. Show's over."

Show's over. Ruby walked out of the club, into the night.

Camille caught up with her at the bus stop, but Ruby rushed to the rear of the waiting bus. She sat eight rows back from her mother. When Camille tried to approach her, she waved her away. Ruby had never felt emptier. She was trembling. It was a hot night, and the bus wasn't air-conditioned, but she felt cold. She hurried off at their stop and walked the streets alone for nearly an hour, trying to calm herself.

Back at the apartment, Ruby found that Buzz had revived himself and mixed several more rounds of whiskey fizzes, which Camille had drunk with him before passing out herself on the sofa. Camille never said anything to Ruby about what had happened at Flamingo Road that night.

The next year, Camille was out of work, and things got so grim around that apartment that even Buzz moved on. Camille sent Ruby to live with her second cousin, Marielle, in New Orleans. She said it was high time Ruby got a taste of that city. "It's your birthplace, after all. And Marielle's agreed to put you up. She was always kind to me. There was a time we were friends as well as cousins, but we fell out of touch long ago. She never left New Orleans. Meanwhile, I need to get back on my feet again. Change will do us both good."

Ruby knew Camille just wanted her out of her hair.

"You have always wanted to know about that part of my life," Ruby said to Devon, sipping her wine. "I hate to admit it, but maybe it's something I didn't want to share because it was good, not bad. The one part of my life I kept all for myself."

Marielle was a witch. She was Creole. She practiced white magic, not voodoo.

"Voodoo is a religion," she told Ruby, "and I am not religious."

But she was sober and disciplined and introspective—everything Camille was not.

Marielle was paid to keep spells off children and exorcise houses and heal the sick. She could also cast spells herself. She carried an alligator bag filled with herbs and tonics: bitterroot shavings, tamarind powder, oleander sap. In their four months together, Ruby learned a lot from her, including things she maybe never should've learned, she realized later. For example, that a few grains of arsenic dissolved in kerosene can trigger a heart attack without leaving a trace. And a cup of columbine broth with tamarind can make someone do whatever you ask: swim an icy river, put a gun to his head, pick up a hot coal. And a handful of wolfsbane pollen tossed into a haunted room can make the ghosts glow. Ruby saw some of these things with her own eyes.

Marielle made a very good living. Her most lucrative jobs were weddings. She wore a black dress, velvet gloves, and a veil. Before the ceremony, she prowled the premises, warding off wicked spirits. She prepared charms for the bride and groom and brewed them a special red tea laced with herbs to ensure fertility and longevity. When someone was dying, she'd be enlisted to help guide his spirit through its final days—and beyond. Then, at the funeral, she'd accompany the family to the cemetery and give them herbs to ease their pain.

The day Ruby arrived, she found Marielle taking a mud bath in a clawfoot tub in the garden. "From the Cougar River, honey," she said, her face masked by the stuff. "Turns your skin to butter." She was thirty-nine and quite striking, tall and slim, with amber eyes and long hair so dark it was blue. Her hands were flawless, smooth as marble. At the end of her bath, she stood up, unselfconscious, beautiful, and her housekeeper,

Theodora, an old black woman who was the only person she really trusted, rinsed the mud off with buckets of warm water. Then Marielle slipped into a gold bathrobe and beckoned Ruby over to a cedar bench. She had a sexy walk, a soft voice. She was centered—not New Age centered, but the real thing. She could read people—literally—intuiting your thoughts even before you were fully aware of them.

Her house was Gothic on the outside—mansard roof, baroque balustrades—and modern within. Sparsely furnished. Mirrored hallways. A greenhouse off the kitchen in which she grew strange flowers and herbs. Her bedroom was painted sea blue. The bathroom had an onyx sink and tub. She was crazy about onyx. Her jewelry box was filled with it: triangular earrings speckled with diamonds, a panther brooch with diamond eyes, a skull ring.

Ruby never ate so well in her life. She was amazed at Theodora's cooking. She could prepare shrimp ten ways, stewed okra, dandelion soup, crawfish gumbo. Three times a day, she brewed Marielle a pot of hibiscus tea. When Marielle served it, she added a teaspoon of sugar and a squeeze of lime to each cup. Occasionally she and Ruby rode the ferry to Algiers for dinner. Marielle liked the outdoor restaurants on the harbor. People came over to pay respects. She seemed to know everyone: artists and socialites, but also tough guys and cops. One night, she introduced Ruby to a famous tap dancer. As he walked away, she said matter-of-factly, "One night he and I figured out that we'd known each other long ago, in India, in another life. Except he was an old woman and I was a young man."

When Ruby asked her how that could be, she told her some people live many lives. To find out if you're one of them, you

place an object important to you, like a ring or a watch, under
your pillow and see if you have a dream in which that object
appears. If so, it's actually a glimpse into a previous life.

Of course Ruby tried it. She put an ivory comb, a gift from
Marielle, under her pillow. She dreamed she was in a house by
a river, combing her hair. There was a baby crying in another
room and a man chopping wood outside. She never saw their
faces. Later, she tried it with other objects, but it never happened again.

Ruby learned that Marielle could operate in several worlds
at once. Marielle would round a corner beside her and seem to
disappear, only to reappear an instant later some distance
away. Sometimes Ruby thought she saw sunlight pass right
through her, as if she were made of glass. One day when Ruby
was to meet Marielle at a restaurant, she smelled her freesia
perfume ten minutes before she arrived. Another time, Ruby
was in the greenhouse on a rainy afternoon when for an instant
her name, letter by letter, appeared briefly on the glass pane
before her, *Ruby*, as if it were being traced on the vapor with a
fingertip.

When Marielle arrived home, Ruby said, "How do you do
these things?"

"Optics. The power of suggestion." Marielle smiled. "And
magic."

Ruby began to see that there was a lot more to life than
stumbling around with her mother. She met other witches, and
people a lot stranger than witches: a Cuban sorcerer who
claimed to be two hundred years old, and three Malaysian sisters who said they were mermaids from the Delta, and a
self-styled Doctor of Telekinesis from Macao named Qi, who

had a watch tattooed on his left wrist that kept the time, he said, as accurately as any three-dimensional watch.

Ruby also got to know the city. She worked alongside Marielle in the greenhouse and stargazed beside her on the widow's walk. Ruby was roughly educated, having changed public schools annually, but Marielle gave her books to read, on alchemy, numerology, Egyptian amulets, Caribbean mythology. Ruby wished she could stay in New Orleans with her forever, and she sensed that Marielle wouldn't object if she did.

Ruby hadn't needed to be reminded by Camille that she was in the city of her birth, where her parents had spent what her mother called "their week" together during Mardi Gras. Marielle was one of several cousins Camille Broussard had in the city. The two of them were nearly the same age, but they moved in different worlds. Camille's father was a construction foreman. Having left home at seventeen, with no prospects and no real interests other than seeking a good time with a succession of good-time Charlies, she quickly found her way to the nightlife. She lived alone, restless, on the verge of becoming the drifter she would remain until old age.

Marielle's father had been born into an old Creole family. He was a doctor with a solid practice when he died of cancer at forty-five. He left Marielle a decent inheritance, but his brother, serving as executor, lost most of it on bad investments, forcing her to drop out of college in her first year. She inherited her psychic powers from her mother, who grew up on Martinique. After being widowed, her mother told Marielle that she would have to fend for herself eventually, and she taught her all she knew about witchcraft, divination, and what she called "medicinals."

Camille and Marielle crossed paths at large family gatherings—weddings, funerals, Christmas dinners—and they spent one summer month when they were children at another cousin's house on the Gulf. That was as close as they ever got. There was one occasion in their twenties when Marielle had a chance encounter with Camille outside the family, which she remembered well and related to Ruby.

"I met your father," she told Ruby one night, lighting up a clove cigarette. "It was in February 1960, and I was walking in Jefferson Park with a girlfriend. And there was Camille, all dolled up and grinning, on the arm of a man. She waved to me, and I could see right away that she was crazy about him and that he didn't give a damn about her. He looked my friend and me up and down, real quick, but he couldn't once look me in the eye. He smiled, but I didn't feel it was connected to anything inside him. Then, just a couple of years ago, I was at a private party in a nightclub when I saw Valentine Owen again. There was a crowd. Cops, gangsters, politicians. He was in a corner, deep in conversation with two large men who happened to be detectives. He didn't see me. He was too busy trying to talk himself out of a jam. He had been stupid enough to try to extort a drug dealer who happened to be the son of a city judge. Owen had done some business with this guy, helping to arrange for cocaine to be smuggled in from Saint Croix. He got his cut, then turned around and demanded more money. He had no idea who he was messing with. They could have knocked him off on the spot, and no one the wiser, but they decided to use him instead. That's how the police operate here. The police chief, Mathias Beaumont, really runs the city. He took over the largest crime syndicate and directs it from the police department. He answers to no one. He's untouchable.

He's corrupted half the force and killed anyone who crossed him, hoodlums and politicians alike. His MO is tossing them into the Mississippi chained to anchors. For a while, I went out with his half brother, Wick, who was nothing like Beaumont. He had a weakness for cards, but he was a decent man. Still, he'd seen and heard plenty, just because of who he was. He explained to me later what was going down when I spotted Owen at that party. He told me those detectives were giving Owen a choice: he could go to jail and wake up with a knife in his gut, or he could do them a service and then get out of town. It was a dirty piece of work, helping to set up an honest cop they wanted out of the way, as in shot dead. It wasn't a complicated plan. They showed Owen a photograph of the cop. They said he ate lunch every day at one o'clock at Morel's Café on Antille Street. Owen was to go there the next day at twelve forty-five, order a meal, pay his check at one-fifteen, and walk out, making sure the cop noticed him. A minute later, he was to run back in and shout that there was a robbery in progress at the jewelry store across the street. When Owen asked, 'Why all the theater, why aren't you just icing him outright?' the detectives said, 'Because we need him to die a hero. The chief needs it. This will square you with him, so don't fuck up.' Owen did as he was told, and it went as planned: the cop ran into the street and was shot in the chest and Owen walked away. The one thing they hadn't told him was that the shooter was supposed to shoot him, too. But he missed twice, shattering a store window and wounding another man. When Owen got on a bus for Houston an hour later, he felt he had used up more than one of his nine lives. Wick said that as far as he knew, Owen never returned to New Orleans. That was the last time I heard anything about Valentine Owen."

In addition to this portrait of her father that was so at odds with everything her mother ever told her, what Ruby took away was that Marielle was the first (and last) person she ever met who encountered her parents together around the time she was conceived.

Ruby had her mother's old address, an apartment house on Cassandra Street. She rode the Gentilly streetcar there. It was a backstreet in a poor parish. The bar, the grocery, the Chinese laundry looked as if they had been there for centuries. The panhandlers, too, all of them on crutches.

Her mother had relived that week of hers many times over the years. She had accompanied a friend to a jazz club called the King Cobra. The crowd was raucous. The band was hot. Her friend was dating the drummer. During a break, he and a tall man in a white suit joined them. The man introduced himself as Val. They drank bourbon, and after the last set Camille took Val home. She scrambled them eggs and they drank some more. Every night after that they went club hopping until dawn. She was impressed that he had played with some of the musicians they met. He wore lizard boots and a Stetson and rolled his own cigarettes. She became pregnant.

Then he left.

Ruby's own time in New Orleans, seventeen years later, also ended abruptly. It was a hot day, and she and Marielle had been working together all afternoon in the greenhouse. As they sat down to dinner in the garden, Ruby finally got up the courage to ask Marielle if she could stay in New Orleans with her for good. "Of course, honey," Marielle replied, taking her hand.

Ruby should have known that nothing good ever comes that easily.

The following week a man broke into the house and came into Ruby's bedroom. She was asleep, and suddenly he was on top of her. A big guy with rough hands. One of them was clamped over her mouth. He was tearing at her clothes and trying to push her legs apart. He stank of booze. She bit him. She screamed. Then the lights came on and he froze. Marielle had come up behind him and stuck a pistol in his ear. Ruby never knew she had a gun.

"Get off of her," Marielle said.

She walked him down the hall with the pistol in his back. She opened the front door. "Hands up, and clasp them."

"What?"

"Squeeze your hands together, you son of a bitch!"

As he stepped outside, she raised the gun and shot him through the hands and slammed the door on his screams.

Ruby was in shock. Marielle calmly wrapped her arms around her. "I'm so sorry, honey. Did he hurt you?"

"I'm all right. You shot him."

They could hear him howling down the street.

"I know him," Marielle said. "His name is Fawkes. And he's not done paying for this."

Two days later, on a warm autumn evening, Marielle disappeared without a trace. It had been a day like any other. A man brought his sick daughter by for some herbs. Marielle visited a client in the hospital, then drove to Metairie and cast a spell to protect a woman from her ex-husband. Later, she dined alone at her favorite restaurant, Ciro's. The waiters said she received a phone call from a man. They spoke briefly, and five minutes later she went out to the parking lot. No one heard from her after that or saw her blue Cadillac.

Theodora told Ruby that Marielle had made plenty of enemies. In Ruby's time with her, she had met so many of her friends and admirers that it never occurred to her that Marielle had enemies. Theodora said, "You do work like hers, you make enemies." That's why she had a gun, Ruby thought. Ruby mentioned Fawkes, but Theodora shook her head and said Marielle had more dangerous enemies than him. The local police chief, for example.

"Mathias Beaumont," Ruby said.

"She told you about him?"

"She also told me that she dated his half brother."

"That she did. For a while, Wick and Miss Marielle was tight. Then they broke off. Wick was all right at first, but then he began drinking heavy, and she don't care for that. Later he shot himself. It was on account of his gambling debts, but the chief blamed Miss Marielle. At Wick's funeral he said he would take her down one day. But she can watch out for herself. I'm hoping it's like those other times."

"What other times?" Ruby asked.

"When Miss Marielle lit out without a word about where she was going. She used to have a cabin upstate, in the Girardeau Woods, but she sold it a few years back. And after a few days, she would call to check in."

This time there was no call. Two weeks passed. Theodora and Ruby contacted everyone they could think of who might know something. They visited the woman with whom Marielle spent the afternoon and the restaurant where she disappeared. They talked to the maître d', the waiters, the busboys, and came up empty. They went over her calendar for that entire month, but there was nothing unusual. Going to the police, of course, was impossible.

Though Theodora remained hopeful, Ruby had the sick

feeling Marielle wasn't going to return. She couldn't stay in that house any longer. It was too painful. The first person who had really loved her for herself, and she was gone.

She returned to her mother in Mobile. Camille had hooked up again with Buzz. When Ruby told her what had happened with Marielle, it didn't really register. "Oh, she'll turn up," her mother said, then gave Ruby a hundred dollars. "Go to Panama, honey, for your birthday." Ruby's birthday was two months off. There just was no room for her in that cramped apartment where Camille and Buzz and their drinking pals were chugging Gallo. Camille said she had a lady friend in Panama City who owned a hostel where Ruby could earn her keep working as a maid.

That was it for Ruby. She was desperate to escape. She hardly knew her grandmother in Miami—she and Camille hadn't spoken in years, and her grandmother had only met Ruby once, when Camille and her first husband paid a surprise visit, drunk out of their minds. Her grandmother was disgusted by their antics in front of the child, and she and Camille had a terrible falling-out. After that, Camille remained incommunicado, which meant that Ruby, too, had no contact with her grandmother. Now when Ruby got hold of her phone number and asked if she could come live with her, her grandmother didn't skip a beat. "Get on a Greyhound today," she said. Ruby bought a one-way ticket and never looked back.

Ruby was lucky to have been with Marielle, and luckier still to end up with her grandmother. Her grandmother saved her. Her name was Theresa Cardillo. She had given up the name Broussard after her husband died. "We were only married six years," she explained, "we weren't happy, and when it was over, I wanted to put it behind me. I wanted my name back."

Ruby wanted to put things behind her, too. She also gave up Broussard and legally took her grandmother's name. They lived at 6591 Hyacinth Drive, a long street lined with stucco houses and coconut palms. It was the first place Ruby ever lived for more than a year. A safe neighborhood. Girls could go out alone at night. Kids played in the street. They had a cat named Tuxedo, rescued from a fire, who lived to be eighteen. No dog or cat had ever survived long with Camille. Therese Cardillo was a seamstress who saved enough to start her dry cleaning business. She put in twelve-hour days, six days a week. Her Spanish was better than her English, but she pushed Ruby to study, got her to school, paid for whatever her scholarships didn't cover. She lived to see her graduate from college and medical school. She traveled to New York for Ruby's wedding.

"When she died the next year, after you were born, a part of me went with her," Ruby said to Devon, who, even after her eyes had adjusted, was glad to have heard all this in the darkness. The only other sound to reach her in the late-night stillness was the occasional rush of snowflakes against the window. "I felt lost. Another part of me had gone with Marielle, and somehow that was worse. I knew Grandma would never come back, but I kept hoping Marielle would. And she never did.

"Meanwhile, soon after I arrived in Miami, Buzz went down with liver failure. My mother moved to Tulsa and started waitressing at a barbecue joint. She bleached her hair and wore a red dress with longhorns stitched on the back. Another waitress took her to a Seventh Day Adventist congregation. She joined and quit drinking, cold turkey. She started phoning me all the time. She spouted a lot of bullshit, no better than her drunken bullshit, including a plea for forgiveness: 'For the worst thing I ever did.' Meaning, sending me away. But that wasn't the worst thing she did." Ruby shook her head. "You want to know the worst thing my mother did to me? She lied about the kind of man my father was."

BATON ROUGE—JUNE 1, 1909

After his wife's second miscarriage in as many years, Oscar Zahn moved her and their four-year-old daughter out of New Orleans. He had come there to make his fortune, but they were three months behind in rent and a week from eviction when they slipped out of their house in Algiers in the middle of the night. Because Zahn was an honest man, he left the landlord half his remaining cash—twenty-one dollars. He packed what little they owned, including his recording equipment and three boxes of Edison cylinders, into a hired truck whose owner, a mechanic, drove them north to Baton Rouge on the dirt turnpike named after Jefferson Davis. Zahn's brother Gerald lived on a farm east of the city with his wife and three children. They grew corn and rye and cured the tobacco their sharecroppers picked. They invited Oscar and his family to stay on as long as they liked. Zahn stored his equipment in their barn and bought himself a third-class ticket for Kansas City on the Southern

Railroad. He checked in to a cheap hotel, ate one meal a day, and set out to find a job so he could send for his family.

He had gone broke in the second year of the National Phonograph–Indestructible lawsuit. For a while he recorded more cylinders—of Manuel Perez and Lorenzo Tio, among others—but was unable to distribute them. He kept hoping the suit would be settled, but finally he couldn't afford to rent an office or book a recording space or pay the assistant who had succeeded Myron Guideau.

Guideau himself had dropped out of sight one week after the recording session with the Bolden Band. Zahn hadn't believed Guideau's story of how the first cylinder disappeared, but all he could do was threaten to fire Guideau if it didn't turn up. Outside the Mix Saloon on Perdido Street, they had an argument so heated that a policeman interceded. Zahn never saw Guideau again after that night, and he never recovered the first cylinder.

In Kansas City Oscar Zahn wasn't thinking about the cylinders. Or Buddy Bolden. Or Bunk Johnson. Or anyone else in New Orleans. He was eating a crab apple on a park bench, down to his last dollar and with time running out on him. He had been walking the streets in ninety-degree heat. His feet were calloused. His head was pounding. It had taken him eight days to hit bottom. First he had gone to the Mirabell recording studio, where they didn't need another engineer; then the Kansas City Mirror, where he tried talking his way into a typesetter's job; then a clerical position at McKay's department store, for which he was deemed overqualified. And so on, until he lowered his sights to night watchman, factory packing clerk, waiter, and finally assistant janitor at the gas company, where the foreman told him to come back in a week.

But that night he caught a break. He was in a crowded saloon near his hotel where there was no cover charge, listening to a ragtime band. The band played staples like "Hyacinth Rag" and "Pine Apple Rag." They were terrible. The rags sounded like dirges—or maybe it was just him, Zahn thought, nursing the one beer he could afford. He was about to leave when a short, stout black man in a top hat and bow tie sat down beside him at the bar.

Mister Zahn? I'm Cyrus Picou. Buy you a real drink? You probably don't remember me from New Orleans.

The man had the largest head Zahn had ever seen. His four front teeth were gold and he wore a hoop earring in his left ear.

I was there, back room at Gabriel Hall, when you recorded my brother Alphonse.

Zahn remembered that Alphonse Picou had brought a bunch of people along when the Onward Brass Band cut two cylinders. They treated the session like a party. Even bringing their own bartender, a case of rye, and two kegs.

Sure, *Zahn said,* I remember you.

Cyrus Picou smiled and the gold teeth shone. I can see you don't, but good enough. There is no proper studio in New Orleans. Is that why you left?

One reason.

Whiskey? *Picou signaled the waiter.* I thought I seen you the other day at the Mirabell studio. My band, the Moonlight Brass, cut a cylinder of "High and Low" there. I'm the bass man. I used to play trombone, but I lost my teeth, and that was the end of that. You still be lookin' for a job?

I am.

I need someone.

Zahn's face lit up. To record you?

To run this saloon. Not the bar, the music.

What?

I own this place. Didn't you see the sign?

He hadn't. It was called Cyrus' Place.

The waiter brought a bottle and two shot glasses. Your health, *Picou said, throwing back his.* I need someone to book bands, good bands, someone that knows music.

Zahn sipped the whiskey and watched the band launch into "Syncopation Rag," then looked at Picou.

You can say it, *Picou grimaced.* They're shit. My band and I been up in Chicago, making some real money, and my brother-in-law's been watching over the place. That's fine, except he's been bringing in the bands and he don't know jack shit about music. It's embarrassing, me being a musician myself. So, you be interested?

I am, *Zahn replied without hesitation.*

Ten dollars a week. Starting tomorrow.

They shook on it.

Picou advanced him a week's pay, and Zahn found an apartment and bought himself a new suit. He sent for his wife and daughter. His wife brought along most of their personal possessions. They gave his brother the Kaiser Wilhelm chest, but the boxes of Edison cylinders Oscar Zahn recorded in New Orleans were placed in a storeroom adjoining the barn. Zahn would never see them again.

On the outskirts of Philadelphia, negotiating an icy cloverleaf, Ruby turned to Devon and said, "I want to go by the medical school."

"What?"

"Where I met your father. Just for a minute."

The storm had abated. It was 18 degrees. In Maryland, beneath a bright sun, the fields and forests had been uniformly white. Ruby had slipped on her mirrored sunglasses even before she blow-dried her hair. Though she had slept for four hours—longer than usual—she was subdued as they checked out of the Hay-Adams. Her outfit du jour was anything but: red slacks, magenta sweater, purple scarf, and white boots. At first, she switched on the car's air conditioner so she could wear her electric-blue faux fur coat, but within a few blocks, Devon, in her customary jeans and turtleneck, insisted she take off the coat and turn up the heat.

Devon had gotten even less sleep. After Ruby's bedside visit, she kept going over what she had heard about her mother's youth. It gave her a new understanding of her mother's ambivalence about her own musical career. Ruby was proud of the talent Devon showed in her music lessons as a child. But when Devon began hanging out with other musicians and jamming at clubs as a teenager, Ruby discouraged her, suggesting she focus on a viable profession. "So you never have to depend on anyone." Devon had assumed this was a simple matter of Ruby's oppressive practicality. Now she realized it must have been anything but simple for Ruby to see her only child become a jazz pianist. It would have horrified her that Devon would follow in her own father's footsteps.

But what truly stunned Devon the previous night was the extent to which Ruby had kept the New Orleans chapter of her life under wraps.

"You never heard from your aunt Marielle again?" Devon asked, as they entered Philadelphia.

"No one else did, either, as far as I know. My mother didn't care one way or the other." She opened her window and the icy air blew against her face. "It hurt. It still hurts. If it hadn't been for my grandmother, I might've killed myself. Oh yeah, another few years with my mother and I would've been drinking right alongside her and screwing the kind of guys she was screwing."

"Hard for me to imagine."

"That's why I'm telling you."

"Did you ever tell Dad?"

"Not about Marielle. But I told him some of the rest. It embarrassed him. He had known I was poor, of course, but in a respectable sort of way. My official history, which began with my grandmother, was okay. But my real past was something else. And it sure didn't help any the second time my father popped up in my life. It was the spring of 1983. You were a few months old. Your father was doing a residency at San Francisco General, and I had taken a leave from med school. We only lived out there for a year, but I liked it. We rented an apartment in an old townhouse near the bay. It was a nice neighborhood. There was a yard in back. We could smell the ocean. Marvin used to play tennis every morning at a nearby court. One afternoon I had a lot of errands downtown, so I hired a babysitter. When I got home, I noticed someone was sitting in a car across the street. Then the babysitter told me a man had phoned twice, asking for me, but wouldn't leave his name. By the time I saw her to the door, the car was gone. The next afternoon I came outside and a man got out of that same car, up the street, and called my name. There were people around, a neighbor on his porch, a woman raking her lawn. I didn't feel in danger, but my first instinct was to go back in the house. Then I recognized him, walking toward me with a hitch, wearing a shabby suit and a jaunty Panama hat that didn't fit the rest of the picture. I couldn't believe he was there. He looked old now, pale and drawn.

" 'I've been sick,' he said, shuffling up to me. 'I wanted to see you.'

" 'How did you find me here?'

" 'I live in L.A.,' he replied, as if that was an answer. 'Ruby—'

" 'Don't say my name again. Just go away.'

" 'Maybe you could forgive me long enough to hear me out.'

" 'I can't believe this,' I said.

"His tone shifted. 'All right. I'll tell you straight out: I need money. Don't look so surprised.' He pointed at the house. 'You've done well. I didn't have anywhere else to go.'

" 'Actually, you can go to hell.'

"I went into my house and slammed the door. I was shaking. When your father came home, I didn't tell him what had happened. The next day, I answered the phone, and it was him again. His message had gotten even simpler.

" 'I need five thousand dollars. That's not a lot for you. I've checked out who your husband is, what kind of family he comes from. A bunch of rich doctors. Give it to me, and you'll never hear from me again, if that's the way you want it.'

" 'This is bullshit. I'm not giving you anything.'

"He was unfazed. He had his talking points. 'Your husband comes from money,' he said. 'If you don't give me the cash, I'm going to tell them who you really are and where you came from.'

" 'My husband knows who I am. And he knows what a bastard you are.'

"That night I told Marvin what happened. He was very cool. He didn't ask me any questions. He thought it through, then told me to ask my father to come over the next day.

" 'Tell him you'll be alone and he'll get his money. Don't say anything else. I'll take care of the rest.'

"I was worried Marvin would go after him—he always had a hot temper—and I didn't want him to get into trouble. But he was too smart for that. My father arrived, and when I led him into the kitchen, he found Marvin waiting for him. Marvin lifted the telephone receiver.

" 'I understand you want to speak to my mother,' he said.

"My father started back toward the door, but Marvin blocked his way.

"He dialed his mother's number in Connecticut. 'Her name is Estelle Sheresky. Tell her anything you like about Ruby. Hello, Mother. I have someone here who wants to speak with you.' He held out the receiver. 'Take it,' he said through his teeth.

"I could hear his mother on the line. *Marvin? Marvin, are you there?*

" 'Come on,' Marvin said to my father.

"But he wouldn't take the phone.

"Marvin waited another few seconds, then said, 'I'll call you back, Mother.'

"He hung up and took my father's arm, not very gently, and walked him out the front door and all the way to his car. 'If you ever bother Ruby again,' he said, 'I'll break your neck.' "

Ruby had pulled in to a gas station and removed her sunglasses. They were waiting for the attendant to come out of the office.

"I've never been prouder of your father than I was at that moment. Not when we dined with the governor, or attended award ceremonies, not even when he went into the ER and saved a kid the ER surgeons had given up on. When we first separated, I asked myself how the man who stood up for me like that could have betrayed me so badly. The only mystery is why I was so clueless as to consider the two things incompatible."

JACKSON, LOUISIANA — SEPTEMBER 6, 1911

Willie Cornish walked out of his house on Erato Street wearing a white suit and a Panama hat. A yellow handkerchief was forked into his jacket pocket. His brown boots were freshly polished. He was carrying a small suitcase. At the Illinois Central station, he boarded the seven A.M. local for Jackson. It was crowded and hot and it made all thirty-five stops on the line: Frenier, Manchac, Alligator, Ponchatoula, Arcola, Beauregard, Crystal Springs . . . The trip took four and a half hours. Cornish felt cramped on the hard straw seat, stretching his long legs into the aisle. In Jackson it was 94 degrees. At a stand-up bar outside the station he ate a chicken sandwich and drank a glass of beer. Then he set out along the road that led to the East Louisiana State Asylum, the fields crackling with insects and dust catching in his throat.

Willie Cornish first met Buddy Bolden in October 1894, leaving Louis Jones's barbershop with a cornet under his arm.

*Just turned seventeen, Bolden was slender and quick, wearing
a black fedora, a checkered suit, and two-tone shoes. Cornish
himself was only twenty, but to Bolden he seemed much older.
Bolden had just had a haircut and shave and paid extra for one
of Louis's imported colognes. Even in those days, when he was
on the make, he was careless with a dollar. A professional for
only two years, he'd already built up a reputation and was becoming better known than the bandleaders who hired him,
which didn't always sit well. Cornish had become a member of
the Superior Orchestra the previous year. He and Bolden hit it
off at once. They started playing the same gigs, and afterward
drinking and talking music into the night. When Bolden formed
his own band the following January, Cornish left the Superior
and become Bolden's trombonist and general enforcer, collecting fees from hard-assed promoters and keeping the rest of the
band in line.*

*By the time he arrived in Jackson that day, Willie Cornish
had known plenty of crazy people, some driven mad by drink
and despair, some just broken inside, but he had never been
inside an asylum. He imagined a hospital that was run like a
jail. He had only been locked up once, for disorderly conduct,
in a stinking cell at the Michaud Street Jail. In the army he had
been in a field hospital outside Santa Clara, Cuba, for a week,
lying in the darkness listening to other soldiers scream through
the chloroform as doctors removed shrapnel and sawed off
limbs. They operated by lantern light, and he never forgot that
smell of blood and kerosene.*

*When Cornish caught sight of the State Asylum, it con-
firmed his fears: a forbidding monolith with Greek columns,
the main building was ringed by smaller ones, including two
grim dormitories, one for white, one for colored. Weeping wil-*

*lows dotted the broad lawn. There was a gazebo and a band-
stand in a shady corner. On Saturdays chairs were brought out
and either a band of visiting musicians or the patients' own
band played ragtime for the other patients and the staff.*

*In his pocket Cornish had the official response to the letter
his wife Bella had sent the superintendent, requesting permis-
sion for William Cornish to visit his friend and former col-
league, Charles Joseph Bolden.*

Cross out "former," *Cornish had chided her.* You don't
know that we're not gonna play together again.

*Bella crossed it out, but she knew better. She had talked to
Bolden's mother Alice and sister Cora, whom Bolden had
barely recognized when they visited him the previous winter.*

*Cornish was admitted to the colored dormitory after pre-
senting the superintendent's letter to the uniformed guards. A
sullen orderly led him down a corridor of blue doors to No.
495, unlocked it, and ushered him into a dim, low-ceilinged
room with four steel beds, four wall lockers, four stools, and a
sink. An old man in a tattered robe was curled up asleep on one
of the beds. Another man, wearing a blue hospital gown and
canvas slippers, was standing at the barred window, staring
out. He was counting aloud softly, 1-2-3-4-5. Cornish realized
he was counting the sparrows on a wire fence. 1-2-3-4-5 . . .
The man's shoulders were slumped, his arms hanging down as
if his hands were iron weights.*

Charley, *the orderly called out.*

*After a long moment, Bolden turned. His sunken eyes were
dull. His head was shaved. In four years, the handsome face
Cornish remembered had become swollen and slack.*

*Bolden looked right through Cornish, then glanced back
outside as two of the sparrows flew off. 1-2-3,* he murmured.

Charles, *Cornish said.*

Bolden took Cornish in, but with no sign of recognition, just the tacit acknowledgment that someone was occupying that portion of space. Wearing white. Carrying a bag. The doctors who examined him wore white. They carried bags. How many of them had there been over the years? And for how many years? It didn't matter, because they spoke a different language that he didn't understand—not English or Creole, but with some English words.

It was Bolden's thirty-fourth birthday. That was why Cornish had chosen this date to visit. He looks closer to fifty, Cornish thought.

It's me. Willie.

Cornish remembered how, even when he was still playing well, Bolden would abruptly wander from one room to another. It seemed as if he was a thousand miles away. Now it was as if he had walked into one of those rooms and just kept going. The silence in that small space was more painful to Cornish than the bedlam he had feared. Seeing Bolden, of all people, rendered mute made him feel helpless in a way he hadn't felt since the war.

Cornish took off his hat and sat down on one of the stools. The orderly remained at the door. Bolden looked blankly from Cornish to the orderly. Cornish was wondering if this hadn't been a mistake after all. Bella had tried to warn him.

You're not going to find the man you played music with. He's going to be a stranger. It's not even like your father drinking himself to death, because this isn't just about drink, it's about crazy. Buddy hasn't had a drink in four years and every year they say he's gotten crazier.

None of this was news to Cornish, but a part of him resisted it. He told himself he must try to get through to Bolden. Charles would've done it for me, he thought. So he made a plan.

The particulars of Bolden's commitment—the police hauling him to the House of Detention, his mother petitioning the court, a judge signing the order, the deputy sheriff transporting him—had been scrambled by the time they reached Cornish second- and thirdhand. But one fact had stood out and bothered him no end: that Bolden, who for years carried his cornet at all times, eating drinking sleeping fucking, had not taken it with him when he left New Orleans. Bella had told him that Cora said Bolden was afraid of his horn, but Cornish didn't believe her.

After a long silence, Cornish said, I saw the bandstand here, Charles. You ever play?

Bolden just stared at him.

Play what? *the orderly interjected.*

Cornish looked at him in astonishment. Do you know who this is? *He snapped opened the suitcase.* Look what I brought you, Charles. *He took out Bolden's Conn cornet.*

Did you clear this with the superintendent? *the orderly said.*

Everything about Bolden was slowed down, leaden, but not his reaction to the cornet. He recoiled, shaking his head vigorously. No no no, *he said, and hearing it for the first time, Cornish didn't recognize his voice, high and shaky, not the baritone he remembered.* No! *Bolden repeated, his face contorted, and that knocked the wind out of Cornish.*

Charles, it's okay, you don't have to take it, *Cornish said, putting the cornet back into the suitcase.*

Bolden had backed into the corner. With his right hand he

touched the wall on his left, the wall on his right, the sink, the thin bar of soap. Then his left hand touched each thing again, in reverse order. And he closed his eyes.

Don't do that again, *the orderly drawled.*

No, sir, I won't, *Cornish said.*

Bolden opened his eyes but wouldn't look at Cornish. He walked back to the window. The sparrows were gone.

Charles, is there anything I can get you? *Cornish asked.*

Bolden started humming, not music, just a steady mechanical hum.

You better go now, *the orderly said.*

Cornish stood up. He took two steps toward Bolden, then stopped. I'm leaving, Charles.

Bolden kept humming, but turned around. Still not making eye contact, just staring at Cornish's chest. Then nodding.

It took Cornish a moment to understand. He pointed at his yellow handkerchief. You want this?

Bolden didn't speak, didn't nod again, but he stopped humming.

That okay? *Cornish said to the orderly, who shrugged.*

Cornish held out the handkerchief and Bolden took it and turned back to the window.

Come on, Mister, *the orderly said.*

Cornish put on his hat. Goodbye, Charles.

Bolden remained there after Cornish was gone. He strained to look far to the left, at the dormitory's exit. A few minutes later, Cornish's white suit flashed in the sunlight and then he was gone.

Bolden raised the handkerchief to his face. He sniffed it. Ran it along his cheek. Held it up to the light, shifting it this way and that. There were daffodils that sprouted by the main

building, and a freshly painted rocking chair outside the show-
ers, and a cat that walked across the lawn one day, but not on
them, not anywhere for many years, had Bolden seen a yellow
this bright and deep.

He looked back at the spot where Cornish had passed and
clutched the handkerchief tight.

Willie, *he whispered.*

Ruby knew her way around Philadelphia, and they soon reached the Penn campus and turned onto Guardian Street.

"This is it," she said, pulling up before the Anatomy-Chemistry Building and opening her door. "Let's go."

"Into the building?"

"Where else?"

"Mom, this isn't a parking space."

"Damn it, stop worrying so much."

It was a granite building with opaque oblong windows. The glass doors opened automatically. In the vestibule a security guard was sitting beside a turnstile.

"We don't have IDs," Ruby said. "I'm an alumna."

"Ma'am—"

"Call up to the dean's office. Tell them Dr. Ruby Cardillo is here. I donated fifty thousand dollars this year."

Eyeing her outfit, seeing his own image doubled in her sunglasses, calculating the risks he might be running, the guard reluctantly picked up his phone.

"Is that true?" Devon whispered to Ruby.

"Of course not. But your father has given them plenty."

The guard handed them passes and directed them to the dean's office on the fourteenth floor.

In the elevator Ruby pressed the button for the fifth floor. "That's where I met your father," she said.

"Forgive me for asking, but are you really sentimental about this place?"

"Are you joking?"

"Then why are we here?" Devon asked, as they stepped onto the fifth floor.

The air smelled of ammonia and sulfur. The marble tiles shone.

"Exorcism," Ruby replied with a grim smile. "There are places I need to revisit firsthand, not just in my head, in order to purge myself of your father. This is one of them."

"And you figured that out an hour ago?"

"What do you mean?"

"That's when you first said we were detouring into Philadelphia."

"It's not a detour. I planned it all along."

"Really. I wish you'd told me in Washington."

Ruby fished a comb from her purse and ran it through her hair. "What difference would it have made?"

Glass cases lined the long corridor. They were filled with specimen jars containing a variety of animal and human parts: an ox heart, a lemur's intestines, a human eardrum, a polar bear fetus.

Devon was transfixed by the conjoined stomachs of Siamese

twins until Ruby tugged at her arm. "Not here, dear. We want the lab on the other side of the building."

Lab No. 9 had a soundproof door with a circular window at eye level. There was a bench beside the door, where students could wait for their class to begin. The lab was a large room, gleaming with stainless steel and glass. The walls and floor were pale green. A lone student was at work, an Asian girl wearing a brown smock, a surgical mask, and latex gloves. She was bent over a dissection table under stark light.

"This is where you met Dad?" Devon said in a hushed voice.

"Early one morning. It was painted blue back then, and the equipment was clunkier."

Ruby reached into her handbag and took out a plastic lighter and a roll of incense sticks held together with a rubber band.

"Skullcap," she said, responding to Devon's stare, "is a Caribbean herb that dispels evil spirits and negative energy. You have to dry it out in the sun for three days and then powder it. It cleanses a place, and the people in it."

"Like sage," Devon said. After all these years, she understood the true significance of her mother's greenhouse.

"Compared to skullcap, sage is an air freshener."

"Marielle taught you this?"

"Yes." Ruby counted out six incense sticks and returned the others to her bag. "You wait here."

Ruby entered the lab and strode past the Asian student to the main counter. She placed the six incense sticks in a beaker and lighted them. Wisps of smoke rose slowly. The student was startled at the sight of this middle-aged woman in garish colors and oversized sunglasses. Transfixed at the window, Devon could overhear their raised voices.

"Excuse me," the student said, "you cannot do that."

"You can't smoke tobacco here," Ruby replied. "But this is skullcap. It's far safer than the fumes from the Bunsen burners."

"No, you cannot burn it here."

As the argument escalated, Devon was about to go in when she heard rapid footsteps approaching. It was another security guard.

After escorting Devon and Ruby downstairs, the guard threatened to call the Philadelphia police.

"Go ahead," Ruby retorted. "Is that supposed to scare me?"

"There's no need to call anyone," Devon said. "We're leaving as soon as we hit the lobby."

"Devon!"

"We're *leaving*, Mom."

The guards stood behind the glass doors watching the two women walk to the Mercedes. Ruby snatched the parking ticket from beneath the windshield wiper, crumpled it, and tossed it in the gutter.

"Why did you undercut me?" she said angrily, making a fast U-turn.

"I was trying to keep you out of jail."

"You can't even keep yourself out of jail."

"Wow. You know what, this is bullshit. You're out of control."

"You're no judge of that."

"That does it. Let me out. I'll catch the first bus, train, anything, back to Miami."

Ruby accelerated through a red light. "Devon—"

"Slow down! Look, you invited me on this trip. I had some

idea of what I was getting into. But I didn't sign on for these weird detours."

"What are you talking about?"

"Just let me out."

They were approaching the cloverleaf that fed back onto the interstate. Ruby pulled onto the shoulder. She cried out as if she'd been struck and, dropping her chin, began sobbing. "I'm sorry, honey."

"Mom."

"I really am."

Devon squeezed her shoulder.

"There's so much shit coming down on me," Ruby said. "You don't know."

"It's okay."

"It's not okay."

"You'll get through it. Just try to be cool."

Ruby wiped her tears. "Devon, don't go. If you really want to, I'll take you to the airport. But don't, please."

"I'm staying. Just let me take the wheel, okay? And let's not talk for a while."

They drove about ten miles in silence. Ruby was quiet, toying with the tanzanite ring that had replaced the wedding band she had flung into Biscayne Bay. Then she sat up with a rueful smile and slid the Joan Jett CD into the stereo. "That girl was dissecting a parrot," she said. "Beautiful feathers, orange and green. The girl's karma was so grim. I told her she needed all the skullcap she could get."

NEW ORLEANS—SEPTEMBER 6, 1911

The night he returned from visiting the asylum in Jackson, Willie Cornish sat in his living room and poured himself a shot of rye and lighted an Upmann cigar he bought on the train. Bella was putting the children to bed. Walking home from the station, Cornish had stopped in briefly at the Fayette Bar. He ran into Jimmy Moore, who played with him in the Tuxedo Band. They had steady work, making good money, but Cornish didn't think much of their sound. Frank Lewis, from the old band, was in the bar too, but Cornish didn't have the heart to tell him where he'd been or what he'd seen. Frank was among those who assumed Bolden would come back sometime and play again.

After pouring himself another shot, Cornish unlocked Bella's Indian chest and dug out the Edison cylinder of "Tiger Rag." He uncapped the gold tube and slid the cylinder out, turning it in his hand, examining the hair-thin grooves. He and

Frank and the others were in there. They were on fire that day, Bolden as close to perfection as he would ever get.

Bella came downstairs in her nightdress and sat down. She was a fine-featured Creole woman, tall, with small hands. Her eyes were sharp and she wore her hair long, pulled back in a bun.

Cornish held up the cylinder. This ain't going nowhere anytime soon. Not for the fifty dollars National offered. Not for a hundred. Not until there's real money to get Charles out of that place.

She was surprised. What are you saying?

You heard me.

Honey, I'm sorry, nothin's gonna get him out of there. Including that, *she added, pointing at the cylinder.*

You don't know that.

I do know, she thought. The moment her husband had arrived home, his suit rumpled, his boots caked with dust, and took that cornet out of his suitcase and laid it down beside his trombones without a word, Bella saw how much frustration he was holding in.

He's safe there, isn't he? *she said gently.* You must've seen that he's safe.

I seen that he's near dead.

And you think money's gonna bring him back?

Cornish set down the cigar. What I know is that no one's gonna get his music for nothin' just because he's locked away.

You call fifty dollars nothin'?

Indestructible gave fifty to Mutt Carey. He couldn't stand up to Charles.

You think Buddy would want it this way—holdin' out?

Damn right. I promised him. *He tossed back the rye.* And you're gonna promise me, in case it comes to that.

Me?

Something happens to me, I want you to carry on my promise.

It took her a moment to take this in. Willie, you talk like you've got a gold brick in your hands.

I do. *He leaned in to her.* Listen, the bands are recording left and right—the Imperial, the Onward Brass—hell, even the Tuxedo next month. But if—if—you're right, and he don't get out, and get his health back, this will be the only complete recording by the Bolden Band. By Charles. Maybe that don't mean much now, but someday it will. You understand?

She looked hard at him. All right, then, I promise.

Ruby had called in their hotel reservation from the J. Fenimore Cooper rest stop on the New Jersey Turnpike: a two-bedroom suite on the sixteenth floor of the Pierre that went for $4,200 per night. When the gold lamé drapes were drawn, there was a spectacular view of Central Park. The Jacuzzi was Carrara marble, the wet bar was stocked with four kinds of champagne, there were three flatscreen televisions, Bose speakers in every room, and the beds had Tempur-Pedic mattresses.

"Best sleep I've had in weeks," Ruby observed, gazing out at the mist rising from the trees in the park.

Maybe so, Devon thought, but by her calculations Ruby could not have slept more than three hours.

They had garaged the car and checked in late the previous night, and after the obligatory order of a porterhouse steak and a bottle of 1988 Chateau Latour, Ruby planted herself at the marble-topped desk in the sitting room, switched on her iPod, and tapped away at her laptop until four A.M. When Devon awoke at seven-thirty, Ruby had already showered and returned to the desk in a plush robe. She had a pot of coffee beside her and a large bowl of raspberries that she was popping like mints.

"How's the speech coming?" Devon asked, still wary about the prospect of Ruby's public speaking.

"Almost done."

"Can you read me some of it?"

"Here's what I just wrote: 'After surgeries requiring general anesthesia, forty percent of patients experience long-term memory loss. Most of you attribute this to factors beyond our control: low body temperature in the OR, postoperative inflammation, trauma. I'm in the minority who believe we might solve this problem by eliminating certain substances from our procedures.'" She looked up. "How's that?"

"Couldn't be clearer." How was it that this particular part of her mind remained so lucid? Devon wondered. No matter how upset she was, or how great the distractions she generated, did her professional knowledge simply remain off-limits?

"The technical stuff is secondary," Ruby went on. "What I'm getting at is a moral issue: knowingly destroying someone's memories."

"But it's a side effect, right?"

"Loss of appetite, dizziness, blurred vision: those are side effects. We're talking about erasing a chunk of someone's life."

"The memories never return?"

"Rarely. Amnesia by Anesthesia, I'm calling it." She glanced at her watch. "Anyway, who knows, I may chuck this speech and write a whole new one. I'm just spouting what most of these other doctors don't want to hear and a few others already agree with."

"You're joking about writing a new speech."

"I'm not. There's still time." She picked up the house phone. "I'm going to reserve a sauna. Apparently the saunas here are constructed of Sumatran teak, with polished stones from Swedish fjords. The toxins just flow from your pores."

For a few minutes there, Devon thought, we were moving along a straight line together—we were conversing—but we're veering again.

"Sounds relaxing," Devon said, flipping open her cellphone. "I'm going to call this guy Browne again."

Ruby shrugged.

"You're not even curious?" Devon said.

"About Valentine Owen? Why would I be?"

"But it's more than that."

"I know. 'Musical rarities.' So call him."

Another man answered this time. "Emmett Browne Company," he said in a gravelly voice.

"Mr. Browne, please. This is Devon Sheresky."

Browne came on the line. "Miss Sheresky, you're in New York? Welcome. Can you come by my office? Today, two o'clock?"

"All right. My mother will be joining me."

"I expected she would. 167 Madison, eleventh floor." And he hung up.

Devon turned to Ruby. "He wants us to come by today at two."

"Fine. My sauna is in a half hour. Now, what were we talking about?"

"Your speech. And the possibility that this won't be the speech you give."

"Oh, look, it's starting to snow again."

Flakes were falling slowly, far apart, over Fifth Avenue. Ruby thought they looked like the snowflakes she'd seen on a vintage kimono.

"Before you were born," she said, "your father and I came to New York for the holidays when his mother lived here. He took me to good restaurants. He even took me shopping. He's probably on his new boat now, sailing the Grenadines, with the new Mrs. Sheresky. Your stepmother."

"Don't call her that."

"Well, she is. But maybe I should stop blaming your father for everything."

"He was a cheater."

"Sure, but if I hadn't been so busy fooling myself, I might have saved us a lot of grief." Drumming nervously on the desk, Ruby ate the last of the raspberries. "My grandmother used to say that if you only see what you want to see, you're doomed— the word in Spanish is *condenada*, which sounds even more ominous."

CHICAGO—NOVEMBER 10, 1922

He was twenty-five years old and had been playing the clarinet professionally since the age of eleven. After leaving Bunk Johnson's Eagle Orchestra, he was a member of the Onward Brass, Superior, and Imperial bands. He had performed in St. Louis, Kansas City, and all around the South before he moved to Chicago at nineteen. During the First World War nearly all the prominent jazzmen came north from New Orleans. After seeing Buddy Bolden and Freddie Keppard self-destruct, he was careful with drink, but not with the ladies. He was a sharp dresser, free with a dollar, and he had a weakness for tall women. He had been jailed twice on trumped-up charges, in Galveston, Texas, and London, England. In August 1919, before his run-in with the London police, he gave a command performance at Buckingham Palace for King George V and a thousand of his guests. In the front row, the king tapped his foot discreetly. When the clarinetist launched into his solo on

"*Characteristic Blues,*" *the king stood up clapping and the rest of the audience followed. When he sat down again, everyone else sat.*

Now Sidney Bechet was playing for a packed house at the Dreamland Cabaret on State Street alongside another king, Joe Oliver, and his Creole Jazz Band. King Oliver had assumed Bolden's crown after Keppard's flameout. He was a barrel-chested trumpeter with a big sound who wrapped a bath towel around his neck when he began to sweat. Before sailing to England, Bechet had been Oliver's clarinetist. Bechet was alternating solos with the newest and youngest member of the band, Louis Armstrong, just up from New Orleans. They had known each other growing up, when Armstrong was a ward of the Colored Waifs' Home for Boys and Bechet was a member of a tightly knit Creole family on the prosperous side of town. Both had heard Buddy Bolden play at Lincoln Park and Funky Butt Hall, across the street from the apartment house where Armstrong once lived with his mother. Armstrong remembered Bolden leading a small parade up Perdido Street, playing loud enough to shatter windows, streetlamps, even a drinking glass filled with hootch. Before entering the dance hall, Bolden always performed a few numbers on the front steps for hundreds of his admirers who couldn't get in, including Armstrong, age six.

Bechet's brother Leonard, a failed trombone player who had become a successful dentist, was in the audience at the Dreamland that night in 1922. Sitting next to him was Willie Cornish, who had traveled to Chicago with Bella to visit her sister. Cornish had come to the Dreamland to hear his old friend Kid Ory, the greatest trombonist of the day, but it was the virtuosity of Armstrong and Bechet that gripped him. At forty-seven, Cornish was old enough to be their father. They were the next generation. Their faces were plastered all over town. People waited in line for their autographs. They performed for millionaires and royalty—something Cornish and Bolden could never have imagined when they were playing smoky bars in Algiers and juke joints in Plaquemine. Later that evening, in a speakeasy on Thirty-fifth Street, Leonard described to Cornish how Sidney, in a white tuxedo, had shaken the hand of the king of England.

Cornish and Leonard Bechet had become friends back in 1910 when Leonard tried to make a go of it with his short-lived band, the Silver Bells Brass. Leonard was an elegant man with a pencil mustache and a keen eye. He was short and bald like his brother, with a large head and delicate fingers; he had expected the latter to abet a career in music, not dentistry. He had a penchant for bow ties and alligator shoes. Famously generous to musicians, he fixed their teeth for free, lent them money, and helped them find lawyers. The satisfaction he derived from this had taken the sting out of his thwarted musical ambitions and his brother's tremendous fame since boyhood. Each year, Sidney seems to get bigger while I get smaller, Leonard thought. But I made my peace with that now. I'll even pick up the trombone now and then. For a long time, I couldn't do that.

Cornish had sought Leonard out that night because he wanted his advice.

It's about Bolden, *Cornish said, ordering a pint of gin.*

Willie, I've told you before—

It's not about that.

More than once, Cornish had asked Leonard to intercede on Bolden's behalf, to get him out of the state asylum. You're a doctor, they'll listen to you, *Cornish insisted, and though Leon-ard wasn't convinced, he agreed to drive up to Jackson one spring day in 1920 in his Model T coupe with Cornish beside him puffing a cigar. But after a conversation with the superin-tendent, and a visit with Bolden on the rear portico—during which Bolden managed to remain motionless in a rocking chair for twenty minutes, staring into the distance—Leonard had come to the same conclusion as Bella years before: Bolden was never getting out of there.*

It's about his recording, Leonard, *Cornish went on.*

What recording?

I got a cylinder. 1904 we set it down. The real Bolden Band. Charles when he was on top.

So Bolden did record.

Yes, he did. We did.

And you kept quiet about it all this time? *Leonard said, cleaning his spectacles with a handkerchief.*

I kept it close. I did try selling it to the companies, but the time wasn't right.

And you think now it is.

I do. It's a four-minute Edison cylinder. I was hoping you could help me get the music out there.

Willie, people are listening to records now, on the Victrola.

I know that. I got a Victrola. I hear Armstrong on it, and Sidney.

That's the future. You record a song and a hundred thou-sand people are gonna hear it.

They should hear Charles.

People don't know who he is. *He softened his voice.* Even in New Orleans, how many people truly remember? He disappeared overnight. Outside New Orleans—he never had the exposure. What's the furthest you fellas ever played from New Orleans? Arcola? Baton Rouge?

You don't have to know him to appreciate the music.

It's four minutes—one side. A record's got two sides, ten minutes to a side, four cuts. Willie, it's hard enough when a musician's out there playing every night. When did Bolden last play his horn? He himself couldn't tell you.

Cornish sat back slowly. I was gonna talk to Sidney about it, too. He heard Charles play.

He can't help you with this. I'm sorry. I know what those days mean to you.

I'm telling you, it's not the memories, it's the music.

Leonard poured them both another shot of gin. I have to tell you, this isn't the first I've heard of a Bolden cylinder.

What do you mean?

It was years ago, when Sidney played with Bunk Johnson in the Eagle Orchestra. On a night when Bunk was drinking particularly hard he told Sidney and me he once had a cylinder of the Bolden Band.

That can't be.

Well, he spun a whole yarn around it. Said he took the cylinder off a man in a sporting house. A white man. Seems this fellow tracked Bunk down and accused him of being a thief, riling him. We all know Bunk was on a short fuse when he felt slighted. Well, he and a couple of toughs waited on this white man one night outside a saloon, beat him senseless, trussed him up, and put him on a freight car headed to Saint Louis. No one in New Orleans ever saw or heard of him again. Bunk was proud of this.

And the cylinder?

He claims he threw it into the Mississippi a week after he snatched it.

What for?

He told us he hated Bolden because Bolden had crossed him. Probably he was also drunk as hell.

Did he say what music was on the cylinder?

Leonard nodded. The old "Number 2"—"Tiger Rag."

Cornish sat up.

Bunk said no one would ever hear it now, except the fishes.

That's it? *Cornish said.*

That's all I know.

Goddamn. It's "Tiger Rag" that's on my cylinder, too. The day we recorded it, Charles gave it that name.

Then Bunk wasn't lying.

Bunk was jealous of Charles. After Charles was gone, Bunk boasted that he played with us, which was a lie. When we started out, he was barely weaned. Later on, Charles wouldn't let him in the band. Son of a bitch just wasn't good enough. This was the payback.

The cylinder you have, who was the engineer?

Cornish thought about it. A German fella.

Oscar Zahn. I've heard other cylinders he recorded. He left New Orleans around the same time as Bolden. I heard he went to Kansas City. Hit hard times. Died a few years back.

Cornish was combing his memory. You know, we cut three cylinders that day. First two takes weren't as good. I figured they got destroyed. There was another white fella there that day, who worked for Zahn. It must've been him in the sporting house. Never knew his name.

Bunk's been livin' over in New Iberia the last seven years. He's got a new band. Been touring in Kansas and Missouri.

Had some trouble in Texas. Nobody plays with him long 'cause of his temper.

I never liked him, *Cornish said.* He was a liar, a chiseler. *He reached into his coat.* Anyway, I have something for your collection—your picture collection. I hear you got some rare materials from the old days.

He handed him a photograph of the Bolden Band. Leonard recognized Frank Lewis and Jimmy Johnson, who played with his brother in the Superior Orchestra, and a young Willie Cornish, and Bolden himself, dapper and at ease, cornet in hand.

1905, *Cornish said.* A fellow named Morgan took this at the Restoration Hall. Only picture of the band I know of. Only picture of Charles I've ever seen.

That's a pretty rare thing right there. I thank you for it, Willie. And I'm sorry I can't help with the cylinder. Maybe when we're back home, you can play it for me sometime.

Leonard would have liked to show his brother the photograph, but Sidney had already left Chicago by train for an engagement in Detroit, the beginning of a long tour. Leonard returned to New Orleans. When he next saw Sidney, four months later, it was at their brother Omar's funeral, and his conversation with Willie Cornish was the last thing on his mind.

When Ruby and Devon walked out of the Pierre, a white stretch limousine awaited them.

"What's this?" Devon said.

The driver came around in the falling snow and opened the rear door. He was a young Japanese man wearing a blue uniform with black gloves and boots. "Good morning, Dr. Cardillo. My name is Kenji."

As they slid into the car, Devon whispered, "We could take cabs, you know."

"Or the subway," Ruby said dryly. "This is better." She leaned forward. "Go up Madison, please, Kenji. I'll tell you where to stop."

The rear seat was equipped with a television and stereo system. Behind a sliding walnut panel there was a well-stocked bar and a miniature fridge with cheese, crudités, and fruit.

As they turned onto Madison, Ruby poured herself a glass of Moët et Chandon and Devon uncapped a Diet Coke.

"Where are we going?" Devon asked.

"I have some errands uptown."

"Remember, we only have an hour before our appointment with Browne."

"Plenty of time. Pull over, please," Ruby ordered Kenji as they crossed Sixty-second Street. "Come," she said, taking Devon's hand and leading her into the Hermès boutique.

It took Ruby five minutes to choose a purple silk scarf with green zodiacal symbols, a lizard handbag dyed purple, and a purple belt with an eighteen-karat gold buckle. The tab was seven thousand dollars and change. The cute French salesgirl had unfolded and laid out an assortment of scarves on the glass counter, and when she turned around and bent low to pick another off the shelf, Devon realized she could have pocketed any one of them in a flash, with no one the wiser. What's worse, she asked herself: blowing seven grand or swiping something worth a few hundred dollars? Pretending she didn't know the answer, even for a few seconds, made her queasy.

They drove another three blocks, to Valentino's.

"I'll wait here," Devon said, breaking off a cluster of grapes.

Ruby returned after ten minutes with a pair of purple patent leather heels. They rode up to the corner.

"Stop here, please," Ruby said. "I need your opinion this time, Devon."

They got out of the limo and went into Armani.

"I need a new outfit for tomorrow," Ruby said. "I don't like the one I brought from Miami. It doesn't feel right anymore."

A smiling salesgirl approached them, her heels clicking rhythmically.

"Let me guess," Devon said. "You want a purple dress."

"No. A pantsuit." Ruby shrugged. "Professional concession."

Devon knew she wasn't joking. "How can you be sure they carry purple pantsuits?"

"Because I called ahead. And they have one in a six."

When Ruby stepped out of the changing room, Devon nodded. "Looks great."

And it did: a sleek fit, meticulously tailored, in the deepest purple Devon had ever seen.

"They call it Tyrian," Ruby said.

"Because the finest purple dye was produced by sea snails in ancient Tyre," the salesgirl chimed in, pronouncing it *Ty-ah*.

"Good to know," Devon said.

Ruby studied herself in the three-way mirror while the fitter pinned the cuffs on the pants and jacket. Then the salesgirl took her Amex card.

"Send it to the Pierre by tonight," Ruby said. "Suite 16-02."

Next she bought a box of chocolates at Neuhaus on Seventy-third Street, then directed Kenji four blocks north, to Alain Mikli. "Last store, Devon. These sunglasses are giving me a migraine."

Devon remained in the limo and watched a stream of pedestrians duck into the icy wind, slipping and sliding. Their hats were pulled low so as not to blow away. Some had scarves knotted over their faces, like bandits. The engine purring, the windshield wipers ticking, Devon put away Ruby's empty

champagne glass and made a mental note to hit a meeting
ASAP. It had already been too long, and spending all this time
around her mother made it feel even longer.

When Ruby emerged from the optician's shop, Kenji jumped
out and took her arm on the slippery sidewalk. She was wearing her new glasses: retro purple frames, wraparounds, with
lavender lenses.

"Ready to go?" she said to Devon.

They continued up Madison another dozen blocks, and following Ruby's directions, turned east on Eighty-sixth Street,
went up Park, and turned left on Eighty-seventh.

When they were halfway up the block, Ruby leaned forward. "Stop here, on the left."

They were in front of the Park Avenue Synagogue, a high
building of ochre stone.

Ruby took a deep breath. "Wait here."

What now? Devon thought.

Stepping out of the limo, Ruby was buffeted by the wind as
she walked up the broad steps to a pair of enormous doors. She
didn't attempt to open them. Snowflakes swirled around her.
First she bowed her head to the temple. Then she reached into
her handbag and took out a leather pouch. She squatted and
poured the contents into a nook beside the door frame untouched by snow and shielded the spot with her back. Cupping
her hands, she struck a match and lit what Devon recognized
was a ball of skullcap.

"Jesus," Devon muttered.

Kenji was intrigued. "Incense?" he asked politely.

"Yes, incense."

The skullcap flared and burned quickly and the wind swept
up the ashes. Ruby stood there for nearly a minute, the snow

collecting on her shoulders. Finally she returned to the limo, trailing a wave of frigid air. She brushed away the snow, but smoke clung to her coat.

"This is where your father and I were married," Ruby said. "That was the last of the skullcap." She leaned back against the leather headrest and closed her eyes as they drove downtown to meet Emmett Browne. "And that was my errand."

BATON ROUGE—MAY 12, 1930

When he discovered he had lung cancer in the summer of 1919, Oscar Zahn and his family returned to Louisiana. Their years in Kansas City had been hard on them. His job as a nightclub manager hadn't panned out. Booking bands, handling staff, tracking receipts, dealing with an often raucous public—it wasn't for him. The worst part was the commotion: he was a recording engineer, accustomed to nuanced work in soundproof rooms. A clamorous saloon was the last place he wanted to be.

He stuck it out until he found a job selling men's shirts at the Parrish Department Store. His wife worked part-time as a waitress, to make ends meet. They felt crushed by money worries. They could barely afford proper clothes for their daughter. He himself simply did without—and that included proper medical care. A heavy smoker, he endured two bouts of pneumonia and developed a hacking cough. He began drinking on the sly.

He toyed with taking his family to Chicago or Detroit, but with the Depression taking hold, he couldn't see how his prospects would improve in those cities. Finally, after years of trying, he landed a job as an assistant engineer at the Mirabell recording studio. The big drawback was that he was given no autonomy. The chief engineer was covetous of his turf and preferred cowboy bands to jazz. By the time the chief engineer moved on and Zahn was offered a shot at his job, his health was failing.

Zahn's brother took him to a doctor in Baton Rouge who confirmed the cancer diagnosis and told him he had a month, maybe two, to live. Wrapped in a blanket in eighty-degree heat, Zahn spent the next five weeks and four days rocking on his brother's front porch, watching shadows cross the lawn, humming tunes. His wife recognized the tune he had been humming the afternoon she found him slumped over in his chair. It was "Tiger Rag." After his funeral, she and her daughter set out for Colorado, where she had family. All she took of her husband's were the few keepsakes he had refused to hock when their money ran out: a pair of pearl cuff links, a Hohner harmonica, and his father's pocket watch. The Edison cylinders remained in his brother's barn where he had left them nine years earlier. They were still there when his brother died in 1930 and his sister-in-law moved to a retirement home in St. Petersburg, Florida. Her daughter, Bennie, Oscar Zahn's niece, sold the farm, and with her new husband, a doctor, bought a house in Baton Rouge. They had three acres, a separate two-car garage, and a storage shed in which Bennie placed certain keepsakes from her family's farm.

By then, the same journalists and critics who had dubbed the previous decade the Jazz Age were starting to write about

*the actual music and the men who invented it. Early jazz histo-
rians like Bill Russell interviewed Louis Armstrong and Earl
Hines, Johnny Dodds and Jimmie Noone. Scholars from LSU
recorded the oral histories of famous musicians like Jelly Roll
Morton and failing ones like Bunk Johnson. One name kept
cropping up, a murky figure who had influenced all of them,
lost his mind, and disappeared. Few of his contemporaries
knew that Buddy Bolden was still alive, and fewer still that he
was in his twenty-third year as a patient in the East Louisiana
State Asylum. They tried to describe to critics Bolden's explosive sound, the lightning riffs that ignited crowds and the slow
smoldering numbers that made women cry out to him as they
danced. They tried to explain how Bolden invented the cornet
as a solo instrument. How he had been inspired—by whom or
what no one knew—to merge ragtime, blues, Cuban rumba,
and the jagged African rhythms that freed slaves once played
in Congo Square on drums, stringed gourds, and hand-carved
flutes. Archimedes Robinson, a florid young writer from Parade magazine, called this amalgam a "Delta confluence," a
musical stew that Bolden was the first to serve up. Robinson
titled his article on Bolden "Whiskey, Women, and Wild
Nights," but the facts of Bolden's personal life were still so
scarce that the article never lived up to its title. Robinson found
only a single fleeting reference to Bolden in the newspapers of
his day: in March 1906, the crime blotters of the Daily Pica-
yune and the New Orleans Item reported that Charles Bolden
had attacked his mother-in-law and was locked up in the House
of Detention. That was it.*

*Not surprisingly, the more frustrating the search for clues,
the more curiosity Bolden aroused. In one short year, he went
from forgotten man to mystery man. Later critics, aided by*

technology, filled in some of the blanks in his personal history. But despite extensive searches in libraries and archives, no one could locate a single recording of Bolden's band. A lost, undamaged Edison cylinder was rumored to exist, and a handful of true believers searched for it in vain. In 1977, an established music dealer who had been searching for years discovered that a man named Oscar Zahn had engineered Bolden's one recording. The dealer even knew the time and place of the recording session. He tracked down Zahn's only living relative in Louisiana, Bennie Jay Zahn, and explained to her what he was looking for.

Throwing up her hands, she replied that she would not be able to help him. Over the years, she explained, as she and her husband prospered and raised three children, they expanded their home. They added two wings and built a solarium. In June 1967, they decided to level the yard and put in a swimming pool for their grandchildren. Their old storage shed was demolished. Before the workmen started in with their sledgehammers and bulldozer, Bennie removed her father's tools, her mother's Singer sewing machine, a Royal typewriter, and her Uncle Oscar's Edison phonograph. She realized later that she had forgotten all about the two boxes of her uncle's Edison cylinders, which had been placed in a crate atop a high shelf.

They were surely destroyed and carted away with the rest of the rubble, *she told the dealer,* and I'm sorry for that.

The dealer sat down in her yard, tapping the ashes from his meerschaum pipe, and drank the iced tea she served him. He looked as disappointed as a man could be, she thought, and she felt bad about it. But he recovered quickly and surprised her, offering two hundred dollars for the Edison phonograph.

She hesitated, saying it was all she had left of her uncle's.

He upped his offer to five hundred, just like that. I promise you, that's top dollar, *he told her.* I wouldn't cheat you.

His name was Emmett Browne, and he traveled all the way down from New York City, *she told her husband when he came home from the office that night. She spread out the ten crisp fifty-dollar bills on the kitchen table.* How Uncle Oscar could've used this, *she added, shaking her head.*

NEW YORK CITY—DECEMBER 22, 2:10 P.M.

One hundred sixty-seven Madison Avenue was a gloomy brown building, twelve stories high, with a copper roof. Its name was carved on a marble slab over the entrance: THE GARFIELD BUILDING.

Before getting out of the limo, Ruby said to Kenji, "We shouldn't be here long."

Ruby had fallen silent during the drive downtown. Except for the lavender glasses, she seemed to have lost interest in her purchases, piled helter-skelter at her feet. When they were stuck in traffic at Fifty-ninth Street, she opened her window and breathed in the icy air. She watched the Christmas shoppers laden with packages lurching out of Bloomingdale's. On the corner, the Salvation Army Santa was ringing his bell. A pretzel vendor with fingerless gloves was stamping his feet. Snow blew through the window and melted in Ruby's hair. She fixed her gaze on a woman in a fur coat and hat. The woman had stepped from a taxi and turned up Lexington Avenue, walking purposefully, sure of herself in the snow.

"Marvin's mother," Ruby said matter-of-factly.

"What?" Devon strained to look out the rear window, but saw only the woman's back.

"That's the way she walked. Ahead of everyone else. It could have been her. That's happened to me a few times lately, seeing people who are so much like people I once knew. If you let your eye go, you pick up on them."

A lane opened and Kenji nosed the limo forward.

Ruby shut her window and again lapsed into silence. Devon had grown accustomed to her withdrawing abruptly. What baffled her was that Ruby, an empiricist who had always been so grounded, could now slip in and out of different worlds with such ease. Nothing seemed alien to her, nothing surprised her. And this made Devon uneasy. That's what it was like when I was high, she thought. Personally and professionally Ruby had always been fiercely focused, viewing reality through clear lenses, assessing it with precision instruments. The kaleidoscope was not one of them.

In the manual elevator of the Garfield Building, the cage door rattled and the ceiling light flickered. The stooped operator and his uniform had over time undergone osmosis until they were the same pale gray. He resembled one of those fully attired, semitransparent ghosts in an old movie. Ruby removed her gloves and ran a comb through her hair.

On the eleventh floor they walked down a dim hallway, past the darkened offices of the Franco-Bulgarian Chess Association and an outfit called Narzowski & Wu, Cartographers, to a black door with a plaque that read ♪EMMETT BROWNE COMPANY♪.

They were greeted by a balding young man with a paunch, a slouch, and a slack jaw. He was wearing a cheap brown suit and brown tie to match. That his brown eyes, beneath heavy lids, were sharply alert made the rest of him seem all the more sluggish.

He introduced himself as Emmett Browne's assistant. "Fallon," he said in a gravelly voice which Devon recognized as the one that answered her second phone call.

They followed Fallon through two rooms, the first filled with boxes, crates, and all the paraphernalia of a mailroom, the second nearly empty apart from a framed photograph of a bald, bearded man of the nineteenth century. Then Fallon opened a door padded in green leather and ushered them into a huge inner office.

Emmett Browne was sitting behind his desk in a circle of blue light by the far wall. Fine yellow dust filled the air. Except for a brass lamp and a marble statuette, the desk was bare. An inkwell, manual typewriter, rotary phone, and two stacks of books and papers were arranged on an identical desk behind him. He was in an electric wheelchair, his bony fingers hovering over a control panel on the arm.

The office was a maze of tables, cabinets, and display cases cluttered with carefully labeled memorabilia. Devon grew increasingly excited as she and Ruby wended their way to Browne's desk, passing an original flat-top Victrola, a Scott Joplin player piano roll, Gene Krupa's black drumsticks, Duke Ellington's top hat, Benny Goodman's spectacles, Gene Autry's ukulele, Django Reinhardt's lion-headed cane, and a music box that once belonged to Amelia Earhart. There was a vibraphone Lionel Hampton played at the Cotton Club and a silver dobro an admirer had sent to Hank Williams. Except for a stretch of floor-to-ceiling bookshelves, the walls were hung with every imaginable instrument: trombones, saxophones, flutes, banjos, mandolins, fiddles, and even a washboard used in Bill Monroe's first bluegrass band. These were the "vintage instruments and musical rarities" Browne advertised on his calling card, and they were rare indeed.

"Look," Devon whispered excitedly as she and Ruby came upon a pair of of Artie Shaw's clarinets on a small table. She wanted to reach out and touch them. "I'd give anything to have one of those."

But Ruby wasn't interested. She had taken off her glasses and was peering at Emmett Browne. He was in his eighties, clean-shaven, with a full head of white hair and clear blue eyes. With her trained eye, she saw at once that he was suffering from MS—at least twenty years into the disease, with two years left to him, tops. His neural circuits had been misfiring for so long that when they fizzled out, it would happen fast. She knew this meant his legs had turned to matchsticks, his olfactory system was gone, and he was short of breath. She imagined he had been a tall, dapper man before his disease began eating away at him. His nose was long and thin, his lips pursed. He was wearing a black suit with pink pinstripes, a pink shirt, and a wide black-and-red-striped tie.

Browne kept a private investigator named Nate Kane on retainer. After reading Kane's report about Ruby Cardillo and her daughter, Browne had expected the musician daughter to be a flamboyant dresser and the physician mother to look straitlaced. Instead, the mother had on an electric-blue coat, purple cashmere sweater, gold pants, and gold boots, while the daughter was wearing a black turtleneck, jeans, and black boots.

"Good afternoon," Browne greeted them. "Dr. Cardillo, Ms. Sheresky, I'm Emmett Browne. Welcome."

As she and Ruby sat down in a pair of chairs before the desk, Devon admired the marble statuette. It was a young woman playing a lyre, her long hair and the folds of her gown so lifelike they seemed to be stirring in a breeze.

"Terpsichore, the muse of dance and song," Browne said to her. "I found her in a pawnshop in Montreal."

Ruby put her glasses back on. Browne's easy, courtly manner, Devon thought, was in contrast to his clipped voice on the phone.

"Thank you for coming," he said. "Again, my condolences on your mother's passing. I will discuss with both of you what I would have discussed with her and hope that, indeed, it will turn out to be mutually profitable. But, first, I want to tell you about myself. I have been a collector and dealer for fifty-three years. I search out rare items for my clients, buying and selling on commission. I guarantee the authenticity of every item I handle. I don't travel anymore. My agents travel for me. I enjoy working in this office. I have been here since 1958. This building has special meaning for me. It was posthumously named for James Garfield after being constructed in its entirety during the six months of his presidency."

Devon realized the bearded man in the photograph must be President Garfield.

"Do you know anything about James Garfield?" Browne asked.

Ruby just stared at him, but Devon replied, "I know he was assassinated."

"In 1881. He was the twentieth president, the only one ever elected straight from the House of Representatives. A war

hero, an inspired mathematician, he had unusual talents outside of politics. Most interesting to me is the fact he was the
only ambidextrous president. When posed a question in English, he could simultaneously write his answer in Latin with
one hand and Greek with the other. And the year he died was
palindromic, which happens only once a century. Just four
months after his inauguration, a madman named Charles Guiteau shot him in a railroad station. Afterward, surgeons
couldn't locate the bullet, which was lodged in his spine. They
scanned his torso with a metal detector specially invented by
Alexander Graham Bell. When it failed, the surgeons probed
the wound with unsterilized instruments, causing a fatal infec-
tion."

Ruby was thinking, Why are you telling us this?

"He was my great-grandfather," Browne said. "On my
mother's side. Her father was Abram Garfield, the president's
sixth child. He was a violinist, as was my mother. She attended
the Boston Conservatory. Then she eloped with my father, a
sailor named Julian Browne. Her family disowned her. A friend
took my father into his business, importing European wines.
He began collecting wine himself and started his own business.
My mother introduced me to music. I had no musical talent
myself. But I knew something about collecting. What you see
all around you: that's been my life. I never married, I have no
children."

Devon was enthralled with the artifacts and fascinated by
Browne himself. But Ruby was growing impatient, and he
sensed it.

"Now, let's get to Valentine Owen," he said, "and my
long-standing unfinished business with him. Messy business,

I'm sorry to say. What do you know about your father's musical career, Dr. Cardillo?"

"Not much. I'm here because my daughter's interested. You should tell her."

"Do you know about his life in New York?"

"I know he was born here," Ruby said.

"No, his later life."

"Look, I know very little about his life, period."

"I thought that might be so."

"How do you know anything about us? How did you know I was a physician?"

If he was taken aback, he didn't show it. "Research is a crucial part of my business."

"You mean, you check people out?"

"Sometimes. Objects, rare and otherwise, belong to people. And it's people who determine what happens to them: they change hands, they're lost, and sometimes," he paused for emphasis, "they're stolen. I'm not a voyeur. And rest assured, I did not invite you here to mystify you. Quite the opposite."

Ruby wasn't satisfied. "Meaning?"

Devon was surprised. Her mother was seldom rude. "Why don't we hear what Mr. Browne has to say," she said gently, "and take it from there."

Ruby sat back with a sigh. "Fine."

Browne nodded. "Please bear with me. Devon—may I call you Devon?—you've heard of Buddy Bolden?"

"Of course."

"Who?" Ruby asked.

"In 1900 Charles Bolden was the greatest cornet player alive. He was the father of all jazz trumpeters, including your father, and he changed the course of American music. I'll tell you some things about Bolden that only a few people know. And some things about your father, Dr. Cardillo, that nobody knows. Fallon!"

Fallon reappeared, laid a trumpet and a cornet on Browne's desk, and left the room again.

"The differences between the two instruments are often blurred," Browne said. "You see that the trumpet is larger. By 1930, jazz musicians preferred it to the cornet. The cornet possesses a mellower tone, but the trumpet has greater range, a crisper timbre, more subtlety." He tapped the stem of the trumpet. "The key is here, in the vibrating tube. In the trumpet the tube is cylindrical. In the cornet it's partly conical and much thicker. The cornet also has a deeper mouthpiece. It's pitched in B-flat, with a practical range of three octaves—four for virtuosos like Bolden. At twenty-nine, Bolden was declared insane and institutionalized. Today they would say he was schizophrenic and treat him with drugs. Back then, they just locked him away. While many early jazzmen cut wax cylinders, for decades it was an accepted fact that Bolden had left behind no recordings. Rumors sprang up occasionally—a New Orleans gangster owned a cylinder, or a collector in Chicago, or a distant relative in Florida—but they were always debunked. However, the truth is often embedded in rumors, in small details that overlap. There were enough of these to convince me that Bolden and his band had produced a recording. At least two musicians who played with Bolden attested to it: Alphonse Picou, the clarinetist, and more significantly, Willie Cornish, Bolden's trombonist and also his closest friend and confidant. And there was Picou's brother, Cyrus, who claimed to know the engineer who had made the recording." Browne leaned forward. "If it existed, I had to have it. It would be rarer and more important than anything in this room. So I started looking for answers. I'm a patient man. I followed dozens of false leads. I came up against a lot of walls. But I got lucky, too, and discovered that in 1904 the Bolden Band produced three Edison cylinders. Actually laying my hands on them would be more difficult. I gained access to the National Phonograph Company archives in a warehouse in Orange, New Jersey, but the earliest files had turned to dust. I paid researchers in New Orleans to scour public records and newspaper morgues. I tracked down the widows and children of various musicians. I interviewed archivists. I pored over memorabilia collections and searched the stacks at LSU and Tulane. I paid bribes, put out feelers, you name it, and I came up empty. What evidence I uncovered indicated that the three cylinders had only been in the same place together once—the day they were recorded—and afterward were each apparently destroyed in different ways. I couldn't be sure, because when it comes to Bolden, basic facts are in short supply, distortions are plentiful. For example, of more than sixty musicians who claimed to have played with Bolden, at least forty never even met him. Such 'witnesses' spun a lot of tales. A whole mythology grew up around Bolden. Everything was a mystery. It felt as if the more you knew, the less you understood. After coming very close to finding one of the cylinders in 1981, only to learn it had been destroyed, I gave up. I just couldn't go any further. Then, in 1983, I met your father, Dr. Cardillo, and though he lied to me more than anyone else, it was through Valentine Owen that I learned the truth."

JACKSON, LOUISIANA—JUNE 4, 1931

He walked along the colonnade, touching the columns one by one. Starlings swooped by. A chicken hawk was cutting circles in the sky. A patient named Mister Henry, who had fat hands, told him starlings sound like children because they were humans in another life. He wanted to reply that if there was another life there wouldn't be people in it. But he couldn't speak. He stopped trying after he realized that another patient, Deaf Al, was teaching him sign language from afar. That must be how you learn it best, he thought, so he never allowed himself to get close enough to Deaf Al to discover that he wasn't deaf at all and that his name wasn't Al, it was Ray.

He crossed the lawn toward the bandstand. The black trees behind it turned bright green as he approached. The air was humming with bees and flies. Mosquitoes that he waved away. If the grass was allowed to grow another inch, it would catch fire. The fire would spread. The buildings would empty. Some patients would drop to their knees, others would try to scale the wall. To run where? Often his vision was blurred, but not today. And for the first time in weeks his head didn't hurt—a crackling pain so constant it took him a while to realize it had lifted.

One of the nurses wore a canary-colored smock. White stockings. Gloves. She had long legs. Her brown hair was knotted in a bun. She was carrying a pitcher of ice water to a table beneath the trees. Some guards were sitting, smoking. Only guards and doctors were allowed to smoke. Wooden chairs had been set in rows before the bandstand. Seven rows, sixteen to a row. Who had known there would be someone for each chair and no one left standing?

There were men like him, but not like him, waiting to sit. They all wore baggy blue pants and blue shirts. Five buttons on the shirts. No pockets. The women from the women's building over the hill wore yellow gowns. He didn't like to look at those women. It was bad luck. Once he talked to the doctors about girls he'd known: They betrayed me by letting me lie to them. But that was maybe one hundred twenty years ago and now some of those girls were looking down on him from heaven and most were looking up from hell. He wouldn't know them anymore because in hell they take away your name and give you a new face. Like this place. No names. And somebody else's face in the mirror. Ella was in heaven, eighteen years old, wrapped in a yellow sheet. He would know her face. One hundred eighteen years ago he lay beside her in a silent room. Her breathing soft. Her perfume a cloud of spices.

People took their seats. Doctors in front. Then patients. In the back row: orderlies, nurses, groundskeepers, cooks. The cooks had sawdust on their shoes, like Manny. The sun was

*beating down. The air green with pollen. Clouds sailing over-
head, like ships. He sat in the sixth row, on the end. So he
could leave when he liked. The fellow next to him was wring-
ing his hands, wheezing, front teeth gone. He himself still had
all his teeth. Every night he rubbed his gums with salt.*

*On the bandstand the patients' brass band was setting up to
play. They played the same stuff every month, note for note,
including the wrong notes. Quadrilles. Marching songs. Old
downtown Creole music that had no bite. And one or two
numbers they called jazz. Jazz. What was that? It was like what
he used to play, but without the blues. Where was the blues?
Eleven patients playing music, and none of them blue? When
he couldn't listen anymore, he would wander back across the
lawn and around the big house.*

*None of the patients knew who he was. One of the doctors
did, but he had gone away. He himself knew, but not in the
way he used to.* I was Charles Bolden, *he once told a startled
orderly, accustomed to his silence.* I was born two hundred
years ago on Howard Street and Erato and I died many times
since.

*The band started in, playing "Moon Glow." Terrible, he
thought. Too slow. Like it was being dragged by a chain. Clarinet flat, bass out of sync. But there was a new trumpeter, recently arrived. Just a kid, from Plaquemine. Quiet, didn't look
crazy, but they said he tried to shoot his own father, so here he
was. Playing hard, he pulled away from the others, their dead
weight. But he could only go so far before they yanked him
back. Dragged him by that chain.*

*He knew the kid had something, and he wanted to hear
more.*

They played "Rocking Chair," which sounded awful, and

"*Coming Home,*" *which was worse. He was thinking maybe he ought to leave. Then that kid stood up and played a riff to open "Get Out of Here"—a song he had written, that his band used to play at the end of dances at the rougher joints, in Algiers and in Arabi by the slaughterhouse. The kid almost hit it, but stopped, and the others got that one wrong, too. Played it too slow and too long. You're supposed to play it fast and loud and then get out, just like the song says. They followed that with "Lord, Take Me," and then, finally, laid down their instruments and filed off the bandstand.*

There was clapping. Everyone stood up and drifted toward the lawn. He didn't follow them. Instead, he did something he had never done before and would never do again. Maybe it was that kid. Remembering how he himself used to play in Plaquemine. The prettiest girls came from there. There was a big loading platform by the railroad station where bands played in the open air. All afternoon, drinking beer from buckets, while hundreds of people danced, kicking up a world of dust. And every so often a train steamed in and passengers leaned out the windows clapping and shouting.

He walked past everyone, not looking at any of them, straight to the bandstand, up the steps, keeping steady. The cedar planks creaked. He touched the railing with his left hand and his right, so that he could know this was happening now, outside of him. He touched each musician's chair until he reached the kid's chair, with the trumpet. He looked at the trumpet, catching reflections, his own face elongated, his hand—huge—reaching for it. It was a cheap instrument, tarnished and dented, the valves worn. He had not touched a cornet or trumpet in twenty-five years. He picked it up. It was heavy—nothing like his old Conn cornets, so perfectly bal-

anced. *He turned to the rows of chairs. A few people stood watching him, most were still shuffling away.*

He drew in his breath and pressed the mouthpiece to his lips and blew. That first note nearly split him in half. He blew it again, and the next note came, and the next, and then the notes were flying away from him. Up and out over the trees, the wall, the big house. The riff emerged smooth and clear, as if he had been playing it every day—those opening bars he had snatched out of the air at the Hotel Balfour one hundred twenty years ago. Climbing, peaking, exploding.

Now everyone turned to look. After twenty-four years of isolation, Patient Number 7742, who had never listened to a radio or seen a vinyl disk, never heard of Louis Armstrong or Joe Oliver, was playing jazz that sounded contemporary to the doctors and orderlies who left the grounds at the end of the day, went to nightclubs, and heard the latest music on their radios. One orderly asked a nurse, How the hell can he play like that? *The piece of music he played had become a staple of bands from New Orleans to Chicago, but no one on the lawn of the state asylum that afternoon had ever heard anyone play it like this. In 1931 Charles Bolden picked up where he had left off in 1906, just that once stepping back into real time by way of his music, which had thrived in the outside world while he himself was wasting away. It was as if, for a few minutes, without being remotely aware of it, much less imagining the possibility in such grand terms, he had been allowed to participate in his own immortality.*

The piece was "Tiger Rag."

He stopped playing at the reprise, and before he opened his eyes felt all those eyes on him, the last notes still reverberating. Many of the patients, and nearly all the caretakers, were stunned, ready to applaud, but he avoided that, placing the trumpet back on the chair and hurrying down the steps, not even touching the railing and never looking back as he crossed the lawn.

In his room he lay still on his bed. He pulled the woolen blanket over him despite the heat. His hands were shaking. A moth was ticking against the overhead light. A fan was whirring in the corridor. His headache had returned, those red-hot splinters swarming the base of his skull. And he was thinking it was true about the starlings. They didn't sing like birds, they sang with children's voices, insisting nobody was going to leave this place alive if they couldn't fly.

If you can't fly, you're gonna die.

That was their song. A song he wished he had written himself a long time ago.

If you can't fly, you're gonna die.

※

Five months later to the day, November 4, 1931, Charles Bolden died in the asylum's general hospital, age fifty-four. His death certificate listed the cause as "cerebral arterial sclerosis," which explained the vicious headaches and blurred vision. A Baton Rouge undertaker picked up his body and transported it to New Orleans in his truck. Bolden was embalmed and laid out for viewing for a single day at the Geddes-Moss Undertaking Company on Jackson Avenue. His mother and sister attended with a few of their cousins. Bankrupted by Charley's incarceration, living in a cramped two-room house at 2338 Philip Street, Alice and Cora Bolden would both be dead within a few months. There was no notice of Bolden's death in the newspapers, no formal wake, no church service, no pall-

bearers. A musician of his stature was customarily given a large, boisterous wake, after which a band of his peers performed at the funeral. The great clarinetist Alphonse Picou, who played with Bolden in his youth, lived into his eighties and was accompanied to his grave by three brass bands and twenty-five thousand people. But Charles Bolden had been forgotten. The only musician to show up for the viewing was Willie Cornish. The other surviving member of the Bolden Band, Jimmy Johnson, no longer rode a bicycle with his bass strapped to his back; stricken with tuberculosis, he was touring for the last time, with a pickup band, in Alabama.

Willie and Bella Cornish didn't recognize Bolden's body. Shriveled, greenish-brown, bald, he looked a hundred years old. As if he was just dug up, Willie remarked, rather than about to be buried. The undertaker had dressed Bolden in the brown suit his sister Cora brought. The jacket was tight, and he had to tear open the seam down the back. The previous night, Cora had patched a hole on the sleeve and sewn on two buttons. Bolden had bought the suit for twenty-five dollars in a haberdashery on Dauphine Street on a spring day in 1905. After he was sent away, Cora kept it in a trunk with his other clothes. Cora was a laundress, like her mother, earning three dollars a week. When it became clear Charley would not be released anytime soon, if ever, she sold his silk vests and English derbies and velvet gloves to a secondhand shop. She gave his shoes and shirts to relatives even poorer than her. That was in 1917. She saved two articles of clothing for Buddy's funeral, whenever that might be: the brown suit and his favorite yellow shirt. Time had bleached the shirt white, so she bought a bright yellow tie for twenty cents, and they put that on him, too.

He would have liked that, *Cornish said.* That is, if that's really him.

It's him, all right, *Bella replied,* and tomorrow for the funeral you bring your horn and play something, 'cause there ain't gonna be no band or nothin' else, from the looks of it.

And he did. Bolden was buried in a potter's field called Holt Cemetery, beside an abandoned railroad depot. Before the undertaker lowered the pine box, Cornish took up his trombone and played "Ride On, King," a spiritual Bolden was partial to. Then, after Alice and Cora left, and it was just him and Bella and the two boys filling in the grave, Cornish let loose and played "Careless Love," the low slow blues Bolden wrote for that girl Ella who ended up working at Mrs. Vance's sporting house after he was sent away.

He near lost his mind for her, *Cornish said to Bella as they walked home along the river.*

Lost it before that, honey, all by himself.

※

The following night, in Rayne, Louisiana, one hundred fifty miles west of New Orleans and halfway to Texas, the Black Eagles threw themselves a party at Durand's Saloon to celebrate an upcoming tour of Mexico. They were a successful band. Their leader was the cornetist Evan Thomas. He had risen fast in hard times. His father was a white man he never knew, his mother a black prostitute on Lafayette Street. He was handsome, something of a dandy. That night he was feeling especially ebullient. He had the band play an extended set for a packed house. He had just hired a new cornetist, Bunk Johnson, who at forty-two was an old-time New Orleans mu-

sician. Bunk had led bands of his own, and made good money, but those days were behind him. Flat broke, he felt lucky to be joining the Black Eagles. Most of their jobs were in western Louisiana and Texas, never in New Orleans. Bunk was still lying about having played with Buddy Bolden in 1896 (when he was eleven years old) and tutored Louis Armstrong in 1903 (when Armstrong was three). Bad-tempered and fast-talking, as a bandleader Bunk had become notorious for reneging on engagements and shortchanging musicians. Blackballed by the best clubs, he had been reckless enough to double-cross a Mardi Gras krewe, who promptly put out a contract on him, and he had to flee New Orleans altogether. Evan Thomas didn't care about any of this: like King Oliver before him, he wanted to expand his band with a second cornet—a bigger sound—and he knew Bunk could still blow his horn.

It was a lively crowd and the band put on a good show. Whiskey was flowing, and at ten o'clock the barkeepers broke out six kegs of Jax beer. Drinks on me, Thomas shouted, and a cheer went up. Getting off work, girls drifted in from the sporting houses, followed by a wave of crashers. These included the members of a rival band, the Pyramid Brass, and the Black Eagles' former manager, Mickey Vincent. There was a double dose of bad blood between Mickey Vincent and Evan Thomas: Thomas had caught Vincent skimming, and Vincent had learned that Thomas was sleeping with his wife.

Among the few white men in the crowd was a bearded stranger wearing a brown duster, a Stetson, and cowboy boots. He entered flanked by a pair of large black men in raincoats. He was darkly tanned, with deep crow's-feet and dusty gray hair. He walked with a limp. Plenty of Texans passed through Rayne, but this man was from Provo, Utah. He had arrived there penniless from St. Louis over twenty years before, ragged and badly beaten, his left leg fractured, his jaw broken. For the next fifteen years, nursing his resentments, he scratched out a living as a field hand and truck driver. At the age of forty, he gambled his meager savings on a prospecting stake in the Uinta Mountains, and for the first time in his life caught some luck, sharing in a massive silver lode with ten other miners. Even divided that many times, the spoils were huge. In addition to his share of the mine, he bought a hotel and a cannery. He built himself a big house on a nine-hundred-acre ranch. For a while, he enjoyed his prosperity. But rather than cooling those old resentments, each passing year fueled his desire to settle scores. He was in Rayne that night to settle the biggest of them.

As the music grew louder and the crowd rowdier, he drank rye at a table in the rear and never took his eyes off the band. By midnight, five of the beer kegs were empty. Tempers were flaring. Scuffles were breaking out—over women, money, insults real and imagined. Things escalated when some jostling by the bar turned ugly. Knives flashed. Chairs were thrown. The Pyramid Brass drummer clubbed the Black Eagles guitarist, and someone in turn sucker-punched him. One of the barkeepers was slashed ear to ear. Another was cut up with a broken bottle. A girl spattered with blood tried to climb out a window.

The man in the duster couldn't believe his luck. He had expected to wait half the night for an opening. Now he could take care of his business in the open and no one would blink. He and his companions muscled their way through the crowd to the stage. He was only interested in one of the Black Eagles, and even when they were just a few feet apart, he saw that Bunk Johnson didn't recognize him.

Remember me? *he shouted at Bunk.*

Bunk shook his head apprehensively and clutched his cornet close. He had made far more enemies than he could remember.

My name is Myron Guideau. *He slipped his hand into his pocket.* Last time we met I was hog-tied in a freight car.

Bunk's eyes lit up with recognition, but it was too late: Guideau whipped the pistol from his pocket and smashed Bunk in the mouth and his teeth flew out like corn in a cloud of blood.

Goddamn you, *Bunk cried, choking, and dropped to his knees.*

One of Guideau's men snatched away his cornet and crushed it under his boot. As Guideau headed for the door, he realized he might have gotten away with shooting Bunk, as he had originally planned. But this was better, he thought: without teeth, Bunk wouldn't be able to play worth shit, and for him that would be worse than death. At that moment, Guideau had also learned something about himself: he wasn't his uncle. He wouldn't shoot an unarmed man, and he sure as hell wouldn't shoot him in the back. When he hit this bastard who had jumped him in the dark, he was looking right into his eyes.

In fact, Guideau might not have gotten away with shooting Bunk. Moments later a shot rang out and Mickey Vincent settled his own score, putting a bullet into Evan Thomas's heart. Now there was a lot of screaming, and people swarmed the exits. Before Myron Guideau lost himself in the crowd, he saw three policemen rush in the rear door and drag Mickey Vincent away.

Spitting blood, Bunk Johnson was on all fours, scrambling

to gather up his teeth. He realized at once—just as Guideau hoped he would—that he couldn't play the cornet anymore.

Two months later, Bunk got a job as a field hand for the Magnolia Fruit Company in New Iberia. For the next ten years, he worked long hours for low wages. Cutting sugarcane, packing rice, driving a truck for the Louisiana Hot Sauce Company. His lone respite, courtesy of President Roosevelt, was giving trumpet lessons in local schools for the WPA. He and his wife and children lived in a ramshackle cottage. He seldom picked up a cornet unless he was drinking, alone, at night. He would press the mouthpiece to his lips and close his eyes and finger the valves without blowing. But even when he hit each note correctly, and could hear the music in his head, it didn't sound good.

Emmett Browne poured Ruby and Devon tea and relit his pipe. They had listened without interruption to the story he spun. While Ruby remained fidgety, preoccupied, Devon immediately felt drawn to these long-gone musicians and their music, not because of her grandfather's career, but her own—if she could call it that. Some of this music had vanished forever, some had survived and evolved; that Buddy Bolden's had apparently exerted its influence by way of secondhand descriptions, rather than actual recordings, amazed her. She was more curious than ever to learn what information Emmett Browne had wanted from her grandmother.

"During the Depression," Browne continued, "Willie Cornish gave trombone and trumpet lessons to children. He tuned pianos. On occasion he played in a parade. That was his greatest pleasure. In 1939 he suffered a stroke. He was sixty-four years old. Bill Russell, the jazz historian, told me Cornish's left arm was nearly paralyzed, but he refused to give up the trombone. He rigged a sling that enabled him to support the instrument while he fingered the valves. In a music collection I bought at an auction in St. Louis, I discovered a cache of letters written to Sidney Bechet's brother, Leonard. Except for the previous owner, I know of no one else who has read them. One was a long letter from Cornish, dated February 1940. The moment I started reading it, I knew I had struck gold. It was the link I needed: a concrete, eyewitness report about the Bolden cylinder. Cornish wrote that he had traveled to New York and visited various record companies to pitch the cylinder—Decca, Columbia, Bluebird. Now that Bolden was dead, Cornish felt a new urgency. But none of these record people were interested in Buddy Bolden. Most had never heard of him. One asked what he could be expected to do with a single cut. When he offered sixty dollars for the world rights, Cornish stood up and walked out. He was still convinced he was holding a valuable commodity, of historical importance, and he wanted real money for it, to honor Bolden's memory. And also to help his wife Bella when he was gone. In the letter, he stressed to Leonard Bechet that he would've helped Bolden's family, too, but Alice and Cora had died, and Nora and Bernedine had left New Orleans in 1909 and disappeared up north. He didn't know of any other relatives. Cornish ended the letter on a touching note. He wrote how honored he felt when he listened to the latest jazz—Hawkins, Ellington, Waller—and heard just how much the Bolden Band had shaped this new generation of musicians. The proof of it was in that Edison cylinder.

"In January 1942, there was a parade for local army recruits shipping out to the war. Ten bands were marching through New Orleans. Cornish's old friend Alphonse Picou had become wealthy in his old age investing in a string of bars and restaurants, but he never stopped playing music. He invited Cornish to play along with his New Tuxedo Band during the parade. In a taped interview with Bill Russell, Picou recounted how he ordered two of his young musicians to walk on either side of Cornish and watch out for him. As they turned onto South Rampart from Julia Street, playing 'Limehouse Blues,' Cornish suffered another stroke and was taken to the Veterans Hospital at Alexandria. Now his left side was entirely paralyzed. Upbeat all his life, he grew bitter and depressed. He made Bella promise that no music would be played at his funeral. It was the only promise she ever broke. Willie Cornish died on January 12, 1942. At the cemetery, Picou played a spirited version of 'Perdido Street Blues,' because for most of their marriage, Willie and Bella had lived at 1423 Perdido.

"Cornish was the last member of the Bolden Band to go," Browne concluded, tapping the ashes from his pipe. "Bella lived on his veteran's pension and conducted the girls' choir at the First Baptist Church. For the next seven years, until her own health began to fail, she kept the Bolden cylinder under wraps, just as she had promised Willie she would."

NEW YORK CITY—JULY 28, 1949

Sammy LeMond walked out of Pennsylvania Station on a steamy summer night and hailed a taxi. It was one A.M., *but he had barely slept during the twenty-hour trip from New Orleans. Smoking and sipping rum, he had sat in the bar car of the Gulfstream Special gazing out at the dark countryside, the trees in silhouette, the occasional lights of distant towns whirling by. He was a tall, handsome man, twenty-six years old, with a broad forehead and a thinly clipped mustache. His father was Creole, originally from Trinidad, and his mother was Jamaican. He had her beautiful black skin and his father's pale eyes. LeMond's tan suit was well cut and his blue shirt crisp despite the heat.*

LeMond was a trumpet player. He had been in New Orleans for a week, playing three gigs at the Crystal Palace, one of the best clubs in town, with Red Lanier's Iberian Band. Red wanted him to move back to New Orleans and join the band full time, but LeMond had settled in New York for good after the war. He played swing and bebop, but always revered the early New Orleans jazz. And he worked with some of the best bands in both cities: Ben Webster, Johnny Hodges, Cab Calloway's orchestra at the Cotton Club. Eventually he formed a band of his own, the Eclipse Sextet, and achieved some real fame.

The highlight of his recent trip to New Orleans had been an invitation to dine at the home of Dr. Leonard Bechet. LeMond had first met Leonard in 1945 while visiting his brother Sidney backstage at the Domino Club on Lennox Avenue. Max Roach and Ray Brown were there, and Sidney was pouring his favorite champagne, a prewar Dom Pérignon, which he had brought back from Paris by the case. Sidney was barrel-chested and boisterous, but Leonard was quiet, observing and listening. At first, he took notice of Sammy LeMond, an up-and-comer, only because his brother—no easy critic—admired the kid's style, his passion for the music and its roots. "He's a real musicianer," Sidney had said, and that was his ultimate compliment. In subsequent meetings, Leonard came to like LeMond personally as well as professionally, to respect his character as well as his musicianship.

It was those qualities that Leonard had in mind when he invited LeMond to New Orleans. Also the fact that LeMond's father, like Leonard's, had been a craftsman, a tailor, with a shop on Esplanade Avenue and a nice house in the same Creole neighborhood as the Bechets.

Leonard had told LeMond to come by his dental office before dinner. And so, as evening fell, Sammy LeMond climbed the same oak stairs to the third floor of 3166 Marais Street that

Bunk Johnson and Bella Cornish had climbed two years ear-
lier, four hours apart, on a rainy March afternoon.

Bunk arrived at two o'clock to be fitted for dentures. By
1947 Leonard was one of the two remaining friends in New
Orleans that Bunk could count on. They had known each
other for over thirty years, from the days when Leonard started
the Silver Bells Brass with Sidney on clarinet, their brother Joe
on guitar, and Bunk on cornet. When Sidney became famous,
the band broke up. Bunk joined the Eagle Band and Leonard
began his dental apprenticeship. Bunk's other remaining friend
was Bill Russell, who had taken up a collection to pay for his
dental work. The donors were mostly younger musicians on
the West Coast who had heard of Bunk but never met him, and
thus never been antagonized by him. Bill wanted Bunk to join
a revival band he was organizing to record authentic New Or-
leans jazz from the days of King Bolden. Like everyone else,
Russell believed Bunk's lies about playing with Bolden. Now
Bunk went so far as to assert that, even after all those years, he
could emulate Bolden's style note for note. I can educate people, *he said,* who cannot hear King Bolden directly, since of
course he never did record nothing. *Bunk was so confident of*
the job Russell promised him that he gave notice at the Louisi-
ana Hot Sauce plant and swore he would never drive a truck
again.

While working on Bunk's teeth under the examining light,
Leonard saw how leathery the sun had left his face and neck.
His hands were rough, too, and scarred from his days cutting
sugarcane.

When the dentures were in, Leonard gave Bunk his stan-
dard lecture. Take care of your remaining teeth or the dentures

won't hold. I've always watched out for Sidney's teeth. The only musician I know who took care of his own since he was a boy is Louis Armstrong—a miracle when you consider his childhood. His teeth are straight and white as piano keys. He gets them cleaned every three months. He'll die with those teeth in his head. Other horn men? Forget it. King Oliver: first thing that went was his teeth. Buck Clayton, the same. Even Bix Beiderbecke, who grew up white and well-to-do. Bix had a single false tooth in front he used to stick in when he played. Couldn't play a note without it. Then he'd take it out. You should be all right now. Just don't let anyone belt you again.

I'll kill that fella if I ever see him.

You ain't never gonna see him. And you're too old now to kill anybody but yourself.

Bunk stood up to leave.

Stay a moment, Bunk, *Leonard said.* I need to ask you something. It's gonna take you way back, to when you and Sidney were playing in the Eagle Band.

That's maybe too long, *Bunk said lightly, lifting his Panama hat off the coatrack.*

It's about Buddy Bolden. Some Edison cylinders his band cut.

Bunk just looked at him now.

You told Sidney and me you had one of them.

I must've been drunk.

You were. You also told us you threw the cylinder into the river.

What?

I'd like to know: did that happen?

Did what happen?

Come on, Bunk. I helped you out today. Now you help me.

Bunk shook his head and looked away. I don't know nothing about it. If I told you that, it was just drunk talk. Stupid talk. We were kids.

Leonard knew then that it must be true.

Why are you asking me this now? *Bunk said, putting on his hat.* Bolden—he must be long dead.

You know he is.

So?

Everyone in his band is dead. That's got nothing to do with it.

I was in his band. And we never cut no cylinder.

All right, then, *Leonard said, showing him to the door.* Willie Cornish was in the band and he told me otherwise. His widow is coming to see me.

When did Willie die?

January. He'd been sickly.

I'm sorry to hear it. She's coming about her teeth?

No. I need to see her about some business.

And what's it got to do with me?

Not a thing. Goodbye, Bunk. Take care of those teeth.

At quarter to six, Bella Cornish got off the Number 5 trolley on LaSalle Street and walked the short distance to Leonard's office. She carried a blue umbrella and walked with a cane. Her hair was white and her shoulders stooped, but some of her youthful beauty still shone through the wrinkles and shadows of her face. You could see she had been a spry, spirited woman. But by the late forties, unable to get by on her own, she had moved out to Gentilly to live with her daughter Charlene. The doctor said she was doing all right, and Charlene was encouraging, but Bella knew her heart was growing weaker. She could feel it when she climbed stairs or woke short of breath in the night. Sometimes when that really scared her, she called out to Willie, and it was taking her longer now to remember he was gone.

As her condition worsened, Bella wanted to make sure she honored her pledge to Willie and passed the Bolden cylinder on to someone they both trusted. Willie had told her he intended to approach Leonard Bechet again when the circumstances were right. Willie wanted the cylinder to stay in the hands of musicians or their kin—the only people he trusted. Bella sent Leonard a letter to that effect, and he responded immediately, inviting her to meet with him. He had been searching for her in vain in New Orleans for over a year. Jazz had become wildly popular, and Bolden's name was frequently invoked by critics and musicians alike. Leonard had come to regret his rebuff of Willie Cornish in Chicago twenty-five years earlier. He wished he had shown more faith in Willie's judgment. Now Leonard felt an increased urgency because, like Bella, he too was gravely ill, recently diagnosed with stomach cancer. The cylinder might not be in his hands for long, but he knew he was in a better position than Bella to find a young, trustworthy caretaker. Someone who would cherish the cylinder the way Willie Cornish had, and if the opportunity arose, put it before the public in the proper way.

When Bella walked into Leonard's office, he had just finished up with his last patient of the day. He was still wearing his white medical jacket over a white shirt and black tie. The jacket looked large on him; he was naturally a big man, but he had lost a lot of weight in the last two months. Rain was tapping at the windowpanes. Bella remembered Willie telling her that Leonard had been a fair trombonist on the slide but never did master the valve. She was impressed by the size of his of-

fices, *the bright cleanliness, the furniture in the waiting room. Leonard seated her beside his desk. Poured her a glass of water. Saw how hard she was breathing. And the twitch in her right eyelid.*

Thank you for answering my letter, *she said.*

Of course. How are you, Bella?

How does it look.

Getting headaches?

Not like Willie.

But you're getting them.

I am. Doctor gave me these. *She took a pill bottle from her handbag.* For blood pressure.

Leonard examined the label. Dr. Franks. Don't know him. This is a strong dose. Would you like to see my doctor, too?

What for?

Another opinion.

I don't need no other opinions. I know what's happening. That's why I wrote you. That's why I'm here. *She reached into her handbag again and took out the leather pouch Willie had stowed in her Indian chest all those years ago.* On account of this, *she said, placing it on his desk.*

He opened the pouch and carefully removed the cylinder. He read the white lettering inked on the rim in Oscar Zahn's hand: CHARLES BOLDEN — "TIGER RAG" — 5 JULY 04.

That cylinder meant the world to Willie, *Bella said.*

I know it did. I'm sure you listened to it.

Many times. I never heard them play better. Now it's all that's left of them. I still don't know that anyone's gonna want to buy it.

There's a good chance that will happen.

Well, if it does, I know you'll see it happens right. If not, you pass it along to someone else who will do the same. *She shrugged.* It's gotta end somewhere.

Yes it does. Willie told me there were three takes.

Yes, and this was the best of them.

Leonard slipped the cylinder back into the pouch. I'll take good care of it. I promise.

Bella died two months later.

And in July 1949, as he opened the pouch for Sammy Le-Mond, Leonard knew he himself had only a few months to live. He was fast losing his battle with cancer, just as Bunk Johnson had lost his three weeks earlier.

After listening to Leonard recount what he knew of the cylinder's history, LeMond was astonished when Leonard handed it to him.

But why do you want me to have it? *LeMond said.*

Same reason the Cornishes gave it to me: because I can trust you. And I know what the music means to you.

But what about your brother?

What about him? Sidney is living in France year-round now. He has a new wife. A big house in Marseilles. He's a celebrity. He can barely keep up with all the gigs and recordings they want from him. The government's pinned medals on him. They write about what he eats and wears and the cars he drives. He wouldn't be watching after this. He never paid notice to the memorabilia I collected, including his own. I'm giving most of it to my daughter Ruth. She can sell it, donate it, whatever. Sidney can be careless, and he doesn't much care about things, old or new, outside of his instruments. I love him, but I know him well. Anyway, this is something special. Bill Russell and these music critics are writing about Bolden now. People are learning who he was. *He shook his head.* These fellas are putting together books about jazz. To me, it's a swirl of memories: dance halls, saloons, juke joints, and all the musicians that came and went. To other people, it's serious history now, and I suppose this is a piece of it. *He opened a drawer.* This, too. Willie Cornish gave it to me a long time ago, when he tried to give me the cylinder.

He held up the photograph of the Bolden Band and ran his finger from figure to figure: Frank Lewis, Willie Warner, Cornish, Brock Mumford, Bolden, Jimmy Johnson. Looks like somebody nailed a sheet up behind them. I knew them all, one way or another.

When he was riding high, Bolden was a customer of my father's, *LeMond said.*

I didn't know, but I'm not surprised. He always dressed sharp.

LeMond's father had told Sammy he made Bolden two suits—one white, one black-and-blue striped—and a yellow silk vest, specially cut so Bolden could get down low when he performed. LeMond would never know that this was in fact the vest Bolden had been wearing when he recorded "Tiger Rag." It was enough for him that his father had been up close to Bolden, fitting him before a full-length mirror.

LeMond looked back at the photograph. What happened to the rest of the band?

Mumford put down his guitar and took up barbering. He had a photo collection of everyone he played with—Bolden, Keppard, Perez—but after he passed away, it disappeared. Frank Lewis moved across the lake to Mandeville and died of TB. Jimmy Johnson played in Fate Marabale's band on a riverboat. Willie Warner joined Sidney in the Eagle Orchestra, then took off for California. He was the youngest and he died young. For the few years they were together, these fellas blew down some big doors. They were jamming onstage before anybody called it that. Bolden invented improvisation on the cornet. The band would be playing fast and hot and he'd just take off, like he had a stick of dynamite in his gut. Some people thought that was why he went crazy, blowing so hard, but it wasn't. His music was what kept him going. After Sidney's old teacher, George Baquet, sat in with Bolden, he said he never played the same again. And George was a serious man, he didn't speak off the cuff. Bolden liked to get down and dirty in the dives on Cherokee Street. The clientele was rough and they liked their music loud. But he made his money in the big dance halls, playing the slow blues, deep and low, for the ladies. He was the first jazzman to play the blues for dancing. Those were his specialties, *Leonard chuckled,* ladies and blues. *He passed LeMond the photograph.* Take this, too, Sammy. And keep that cylinder safe.

✳

Sammy LeMond invited Valentine Owen to sit in with his Eclipse Sextet on the Fourth of July, 1959, at Club Tunis on Forty-sixth Street. At that time, LeMond was thirty-five, six years younger than Owen, though LeMond seemed like the older man. Owen was less accomplished, less sophisticated, and until that evening operating on a far lower professional level. He had been doing session work, recording instrumental tracks for radio jingles, and at night performing with pickup bands in New Jersey clubs. While Clifford Brown and Miles Davis were taking the jazz trumpet into new terrain, Owen was one of the hundreds of technically capable but uninspired professional musicians who could play popular standards.

Sammy LeMond wasn't a prodigy like Brown, but he was a gifted player with a devoted following. RCA had just signed him to a recording contract. He had a large, lush sound. He had grown up listening to his father's soca and calypso records, and his earliest musical roots were as much Caribbean as New Orleans. His later models were Roy Eldridge and Mario Bauza, the virtuoso from Havana. After playing swing and bebop for a dozen years, LeMond was steering his band toward a cooler, more adventurous sound. He worked in the middle registers, playing brisk, exuberant solos, improvising smartly in and around the melodic line. In the mid-fifties, during the calypso craze, he enjoyed a celebrated run, forging the sound critics dubbed "Tropical Cool," which was so widely imitated over the years that LeMond realized this was the label that would stick to him no matter what else he did.

The Eclipse Sextet boasted a Coleman Hawkins protégé on saxophone, Stan Getz's former bassist, and a samba guitarist from Rio who alternated on flute. A journeyman like Valentine Owen found himself in this company for one reason only: his ability to ingratiate himself with people who, out of vanity or generosity, put aside their better judgment. In the case of Sammy LeMond, it was his generosity.

He met LeMond at a jam session at Lou Hayes's basement studio on Fifty-sixth Street. Hayes was Dizzy Gillespie's pianist. Owen used to go to the racetrack with him and his brother, and he got Hayes to introduce him to LeMond. After a couple of drinks, Owen complimented LeMond on his playing—not too fulsomely—and asked where his sextet would be appearing next. Two nights later, Owen was sitting at a front-row table at the Blue Note. He went backstage. He returned four nights in a row. By week's end, he joined LeMond, his girlfriend Mo-

*nique, and a party of friends for dinner at the Mermaid Room.
Then Owen was invited to a party at LeMond's apartment in
Harlem, six spacious rooms on 111th Street, overlooking Central Park. Owen was mightily impressed by the teak furniture,
African sculptures, and white Steinway grand in LeMond's living room. And the view clear across the park to the tall buildings on Central Park West. Within a month of meeting LeMond,
Owen made his move. He and LeMond were having lunch at a
coffee shop on Columbus Avenue. LeMond ordered ham and
eggs, Owen a bowl of bean soup he barely touched. It was 96
degrees and humid. The air was heavy. The city seemed to be
operating in slow motion. Stores were closing early. Bus fumes
lingered long after the buses were gone. The customers lining
the counter were hunched over, quiet. On the radio the an-
nouncer at Yankee Stadium was calling the play-by-play in a
languorous monotone.*

I have a chance with a band out of Miami, *Owen said.* Ever
hear of Tex Mayeux?

LeMond shook his head.

His band, the Hurricanes, plays Dixieland.

You going to audition?

Tex wants more than that.

LeMond was buttering his toast. Like what?

Like hearing me live with a band. He's in New York next
week for some Cajun music festival.

So you're playing with those boys in Jersey City, right?

Owen sighed. I am. But they're a pickup band. And it's a
lousy club. Bad acoustics, a noisy bar. I can't bring him there.

LeMond signaled the waitress for more coffee. Can you get
some other gig?

I don't know. *He fidgeted as if he was nervous, but he wasn't really nervous.* I thought maybe you could help.

How's that?

See, it's got to be a special gig. *Owen hesitated.* Oh hell. I can't ask you this, man. Forget it.

What?

Owen stubbed out his cigarette. Look, if I'm out of line, stop me. I wondered if I could sit in with the sextet for a couple of numbers, with Tex in the house.

LeMond sat back, and misreading his gaze, Owen was afraid he had offended him. In fact, LeMond's mind had wandered far from that place and time, and it had nothing to do with Valentine Owen, but with a stranger who had entered the coffee shop, lingered for several seconds, then changed her mind and walked out. LeMond was back in his father's shop, age twelve, practicing Fats Waller's "All My Life," the number one hit in the spring of 1936—All my life, I've been waiting for you—when the bell affixed to the door tinkled and a young girl in a green coat walked in out of the rain. The wind was blowing her hair over her face, which he never did see. Whether she had chosen the wrong address, or thought to duck out of the storm and changed her mind, she immediately stepped back outside. LeMond laid down his trumpet and rushed out after her, with no idea of what he would say or do, looking up and down the street, but she was gone. Several times in the ensuing years he thought he glimpsed her again—on a steamboat, in the Mardi Gras crowd, riding a streetcar on Canal Street— always in a green coat or dress and just out of reach, so that he knew it would be futile to chase after her. He didn't believe in magic, or fate, or God, and he thought coincidence was just another word for luck, good or bad. He didn't believe in spirits, either, but he didn't have to in this case: though her appearances were fleeting, whatever else she was, this girl was flesh and blood, and very much of this world.

Realizing that LeMond had been distracted, Owen glanced over his shoulder. Someone you know?

What?

At the door.

LeMond focused on him again. What were you saying?

That I could sit in and play off of you. Second trumpet. Just one night, Sammy.

That's what you want? We can do that.

You're sure?

If it gets you the job, why not.

What Owen didn't reveal was that he had already told Tex Mayeux he was playing with the sextet, implying that it was not for the first or last time. The only reason Mayeux was interested in Owen was his supposed connection to LeMond's band. Owen had gambled that, good-natured as he was, LeMond would say yes.

And so it was that Valentine Owen found himself standing under the blue spotlights at Club Tunis as the sextet launched into "XYZ" before a full house that included Tex Mayeux, impressed as hell with himself for auditioning a musician who played alongside the great Sammy LeMond.

That's how Valentine Owen got invited to join the Hurricanes, whose repertoire of "Sweet Georgia Brown," "When the Saints Go Marching In," and the like were more his speed. After the performance, Tex Mayeux, wearing a seersucker suit and alligator boots, walked into the dressing room, doffed his

*hat, and shook LeMond's hand. Unbidden, LeMond offered
up a sterling recommendation of Owen.*

*Eddie Dawson, the sextet's drummer, witnessed all of this.
When he was alone with LeMond, he said,* Sammy, who was
that other guy tonight?

I told you.

I mean, who *was* he?

A friend.

Eddie shook his head and uncapped a bottle of beer.

You had a problem with his playing? *LeMond said.*

What do you think.

I think you oughtn't to trouble yourself—or me. *LeMond's
voice softened.* It was just this once. Don't you remember when
you were hungry, Eddie?

I'm still hungry. But hunger ain't the same as talent. *He
squeezed LeMond's shoulder.* You're a soft touch, Sammy.

*Valentine Owen didn't actually join up with Tex Mayeux
and the Hurricanes for another three months, when they
started touring again in the Deep South. Living in a dingy hotel
on Howard Street in Chinatown, he used the time to practice
the Hurricanes' repertoire until he could have played it in his
sleep. He also tried, with less success, to cut down on his drinking. LeMond lent him fifty dollars to buy a white tuxedo jacket
and black pants with a satin stripe down the sides, the Hurricanes' uniform.*

*Owen expressed his gratitude, but felt only contempt for
LeMond. He believed that, by definition, anyone you could
game was unworthy of your respect. Previously he had coveted
LeMond's good fortune; now he hated him for it. The more
helpful LeMond was, the more Owen resented him. He was*

motivated as much by envy as ambition; and even as he accepted the fact that his ambition exceeded his talent, he began to realize his envy was boundless.

※

In the 1960s Sammy LeMond continued to prosper. At forty, he was still youthful, dapper, with a full head of hair. His health was good, though like his father he had been born with a heart murmur and a faulty valve in his right ventricle, which he knew could only worsen as he grew older. But while his father had helped his condition along with cigarettes and bourbon, dying after a heart attack at fifty-five, LeMond was a nonsmoker and light drinker. He never touched drugs at a time when many of his peers were doing whatever came their way.

The Eclipse Sextet cut three LPs. One of them hit number 7 on the Billboard *jazz* chart. They all got a lot of radio play. The band toured the States, Scandinavia, and England and played some major festivals in France and Italy. They made very good money for their day. But LeMond didn't like to travel. The grueling schedules exhausted him. And he didn't like living out of hotels. By 1970 he was only playing gigs in New York. He bought a run-down nightclub on 124th Street, near Mount Morris Park, and converted it into a fine supper club, beautifully appointed. He hired an experienced manager, a prizewinning chef, and a booking agent. Musicians coming into town coveted a gig there. Local notables like Coleman Hawkins and Art Blakey stopped by to jam. At the same time, LeMond expanded his home, purchasing the adjacent apartment, gutting it, and constructing a soundproof studio where he and the band could rehearse and record. He got a reputation as a recluse; not only didn't he tour, but he began bypassing the RCA *recording studios. He built up an extensive jazz library, thousands of 78s, 45s, 16s, LPs, and reel-to-reels and several dozen wax cylinders. He even owned a large selection of rare 76 rpm vinyl recordings that Victor produced in the twenties before they cut a deal with Columbia—whose recordings were 80 rpm—to split the difference and set 78 rpm as the industry standard. And of course there was the secret prize of his collection, the rarest recording of all.*

He kept it locked in a hidden cabinet, with controlled temperature and humidity, within the armoire that housed his oldest recordings. He had acquired an Edison cylinder phonograph in mint condition. The oak casing was highly polished, without a scratch. In the first years after Leonard Bechet entrusted him with it, LeMond listened to the Bolden cylinder many times. Except for Louis Armstrong's Hot 5 recordings, produced two decades after Bolden recorded, LeMond had never heard anything comparable. He was astounded by Bolden's technique—the impeccable phrasing, incendiary improvisation, and plaintive, passionate solos in which the cornet's complexities rivaled the human voice. He had heard all the top-flight trumpeters play "Tiger Rag," live and on records, but never like this. From this singular sample, LeMond understood Bolden's enormous influence, fusing so many kinds of American music that preceded him into something new. Fifty years later, it remained unique.

Determined to preserve the cylinder, LeMond eventually restricted himself to playing it once a year, on Bolden's birthday, September 6. He would sit alone in his study, sipping cognac, attach the fourteen-inch brass horn to the phonograph, and turn the brass crank. By then, Monique was long gone, and there was no woman to speak of in his life. He only shared the cylinder with two men who understood its significance and whom he trusted implicitly: his longtime engineer, Felix Girard, and his bass player, Isaiah Wells. Felix helped LeMond preserve the cylinder by brushing it lightly with a solution of tannic acid and aluminum oxide that prevented mold and ensured the integrity of the grooves. He also made two tape recordings off the cylinder, using the most sophisticated acoustical devices available in the mid-fifties. LeMond stored the tapes in a safe deposit box at the Chemical Bank on Eighty-sixth Street. He kept the key to the armoire cabinet in a small drawer at the base of his humidor, behind the matchboxes and cigar clippers.

LeMond was one of the least selfish men imaginable, yet for all those years he had chosen not to share the contents of that cylinder with the rest of the world. He was aware that at a time when jazz musicology and history were being studied in universities, and the early musicians' lives chronicled, Buddy Bolden was no longer a forgotten figure. In fact, Bolden had been so mythologized that the cylinder would be hailed as a major discovery that put to rest a great musical mystery. But still LeMond could not part with it. When he had qualms—and he did—he rationalized that, having always been generous, sharing his good fortune, he wanted this one thing for himself. At least for a while—or maybe even until after his death. It was not a rationalization he found altogether convincing, or took pride in, but he was willing to live with it, telling himself that for all the critical interest the cylinder would arouse, there were people whose sole interest would be to exploit it. With Bolden's legend growing, the same record company executives who had ignored or insulted Willie Cornish would see dollar signs and start jockeying. LeMond wanted no part of that. He respected how loyal Cornish had been to Bolden's memory, and he was still amazed that Leonard Bechet had entrusted the cylinder to him rather than to his own brother. LeMond would see to it that the cylinder took its place in the world, shining a light on Bolden as the inventor of jazz, but it would be done properly, respectfully, and to maximum effect.

But not just yet, LeMond thought on September 6, 1978, as he sat in his study and was thrilled once again listening to King Bolden play his fierce opening solo before Willie Cornish's trombone joined in on the ninth measure. His joy was such that he felt sure he was about to get lucky in a way he never had before. He just didn't know what that was.

The following night, the city sky velvety blue, the trees in the park fresh with rain, he met Joan Neptune for the first time.

⁕

She walked into Sammy LeMond's club at nine o'clock wearing a dark green dress. He was sitting at his customary table, with a clear view of both the stage and the front entrance. She scanned the room—for a moment he thought she might leave—and then asked the maître d' for a table for one.

Though she had yet to look at him, LeMond was certain this woman hadn't just walked into his club, but his life. He stared at her profile, five tables away. She was around forty years old. Tall and elegant. Her face unlined, unblemished, planed like one of his mahogany busts from West Africa, with a high forehead and full lips. A pleasingly symmetrical face. Her straight black hair was drawn back with an ebony barrette.

She ordered a Manhattan. As her waiter headed for the bar, LeMond beckoned him over. A few minutes later, the waiter brought her a 1964 Dom Pérignon. When she protested, he told her the owner had sent it and pointed out LeMond, who nodded, smiling. She thought about this, and then asked him to invite Mr. LeMond over, and to bring a glass for him.

The waiters and bartenders had known LeMond to order up drinks on the house for Sonny Rollins and Max Roach, and to send Duke Ellington's table a bottle of the maestro's favorite Scotch, twenty-year-old Talisker, but they had never seen him do this for an unattached woman.

Mr. LeMond, *she said, extending her hand.* I'm Joan Neptune. Thank you, and please join me. I know your music. I'm honored.

It was her voice that finished him, not her words. Soft but resonant. The honor is all mine, *he smiled.*

The waiter uncorked and poured the champagne, then took the pianist a request from LeMond.

He asked if you'd play "All My Life," *the waiter said.* In D.

❇

Joan Neptune was a psychic. By her definition that meant someone with exceptional powers of perception, sometimes extending beyond the five senses. If you wanted to call that "paranormal," it was fine with her. But she thought of it as perfectly normal, a highly developed sense of intuition, perhaps, coupled with a belief that the world is composed of more than three dimensions and time is measurable in units other than hours, days, and years when it is measurable at all. She operated in a realm far removed from the fortune-tellers and palm readers in seedy storefronts and the charlatans who spoke in tongues on late-night television. She had made a niche for herself, working on commission on her own terms. Some of her clients were well-heeled people for whom she was more thera-

pist than soothsayer, exploring their pasts in order to anticipate their futures. They were easy to deal with, and she only worked with people she liked. Other clients were executives, often young, the type who had made The Art of War their business manual. She offered them a simple concept: Learn how to think in the future. Not to imagine, but to inhabit, it, so you can arrive there before your competitors and make the terrain your own. Last, there was the New York City Police Department, who outsourced her for more esoteric—and grisly—work.

She brought no formal business background to her sessions with MBAs and no prior connection to crime detection to her dealings with the police. Her business clientele grew rapidly after one of her first clients, the CEO of a fiber optics company, credited her in an interview with giving him the tools—his "psychic tool kit," he called it—to outmaneuver two larger companies and land a contract laying cable in Brazil. Despite the praise, and the lucrative pay, she felt this aspect of her work was antiseptic.

With the police, the pay, when she accepted it, was meager, and the work was anything but antiseptic. It was not work she had sought. The city's chief of detectives, frustrated by an unsolved crime that was inflaming the public, heard about Joan from the deputy mayor's wife, who was a client. The chief had enlisted conventional psychics on previous cases, with mixed results, but never one who came so highly recommended. So he called Joan and then drove up to her apartment on Riverside Drive.

On its surface, the crime was not complicated. Four months earlier, the ten-year-old daughter of a Queens firefighter had disappeared on her way to school in Rego Park. The firefighter was a widower and she was his only child. Her smiling *face—blond, brown-eyed, with a gap in her front teeth—had beamed from newspapers, televisions, and posters plastered around the city. No witnesses came forward, and no trace of her was found. There was also no ransom demand, always a bad sign. The manhunt occupied hundreds of policemen in four states. A squad of city detectives worked overtime without pay. Dozens of sex offenders were hauled in for questioning. The fire department posted a $25,000 reward. A Mafia capo in Flushing let it be known that his soldiers would pass along any information they picked up. For two months, not a single lead surfaced. The papers stopped covering the case. All but two detectives were pulled from it. Then one afternoon a patrolman investigating a car theft at an outdoor parking lot found a size 4 sneaker caked with blood wedged into a gap in a brick wall. He pulled the sneaker out, and there was still a foot inside it. The missing girl had been wearing sneakers. And the parking lot was just ten blocks from her house. The cops were certain now that she was dead—but where was the rest of her? The newspapers jumped back on the story. Again there was a massive search, for a body this time, but after two more months, they found nothing.*

After relating the facts, the chief asked Joan for assistance.

She possessed certain abilities she was uncomfortable tapping for an assignment like this. She was aware there could be serious repercussions for her personally. She would need to channel at least two people, picking up traces of their thoughts, memories, emotions: the girl and her killer. And that wasn't a place she wanted to go. It would mean focusing on the girl's home and possessions, and the one object they knew the killer had handled, her severed foot, and the place where they had almost certainly been together, the parking lot. If she was suc-

cessful, it would be because she managed to enter a nightmare and remain there long enough to decipher its contents.

She agreed to help. Her only condition was that the chief promise to keep her name out of the papers, no matter how things turned out. She visited the parking lot, behind an old supermarket. The asphalt was cracked, and it was littered with trash. There were ten rows of parking spaces, nine spaces to a row. On that particular morning, there were only fourteen cars parked there. Joan examined the gap in the wall and studied photos of the sneaker when it was discovered there.

Then she went to the girl's house. She met the father, John Kelly, a broken man on indefinite leave from his job. He was sitting alone in his dining room. On the table, a plate, napkin, and cutlery were set at the girl's place, for the dinner she had never come home to. Her name was Frances. Joan went upstairs to her bedroom alone. She could hardly bear to touch the T-shirts and underwear in the dresser and the dresses in the closet, to pick up the doll propped on the bed and uncap the tiny bottle of Two Hearts perfume that smelled like roses. After placing several strands from a hairbrush into an envelope, Joan sat down on the bed and wept.

When she returned to the dining room, John Kelly was drinking a can of beer. A beefy man with a crew cut, he had lost fifty pounds. He hadn't shaved that week. Without looking up, he pushed two photo albums over to Joan. She studied every shot of Frances: Christmas under the tree, age four; riding a bicycle in the park, age six; first day at school; first communion; curled up on a couch with a gray terrier. There was no dog in the house now. The photos were arranged in reverse chronology, so Joan ended on a photograph taken in winter light, of a smiling young woman with fair hair and the same eyes her daughter would have, cradling a swaddled newborn in front of Queens Hospital.

John Kelly studied Joan. His eyes were not friendly or unfriendly. Something had struck him, and Joan picked up on it at once: he had never had a black woman in his house.

Your wife was beautiful, Mr. Kelly. And Frances was very special. Thank you for showing me these.

He nodded.

I'm so sorry.

He looked away. No pity, *he mumbled.*

I want to help.

So many times he'd been disappointed, but he believed she meant it.

I do mean it, *she said softly.*

He looked back at her, surprised.

We will find her, *she said.* I promise you.

Her voice was soothing, but he had also seen how hard her eyes were when she came downstairs.

Through the bay window, at the curb, two gold-shield detectives were sitting in an unmarked sedan. They had been specially chosen by the chief to accompany Joan everywhere, gain her access wherever she wanted, do whatever she asked of them.

They drove her downtown to Police Plaza and took her to the pathology lab. A technician gave her latex gloves. He brought the bloody sneaker to an examining table. It was torn and black. Once it had been pink, with red laces. She held it in her palm. It seemed weightless. The technician took a clear box from a refrigerator. The severed foot was at its center, in dry ice. It, too, was black. And the elements had done their work:

it looked even smaller than Joan expected, shriveled, two toes gone, the heel eaten away.

It was sawed off by hand, *the technician said,* just above the talus. Most likely a hacksaw.

Joan had seen her share of ugliness, among the living and the dead, but this was the worst. She went numb, her mouth so dry she couldn't swallow.

Can you leave me alone for a minute? *she said to the detectives, and they took the technician with them.*

She placed her fingertips on the clear box and moved around the table, studying the foot from every angle.

She returned to Queens with the detectives. They drove to the parking lot, this time with the patrolman who had found the sneaker. Joan stood at the wall alone, her back against the rough brick. Then she crisscrossed the lot, covering different ground each time. The third time she stopped in the fourth parking space in the second row. She stepped in and out of it. A cool shiver ran up her legs. She planted her feet and closed her eyes for what felt like an hour.

One of the detectives came over.

They were parked here, *Joan said.*

What did you see?

She shook her head. She felt light-headed. Her stomach was tied in knots. What she had seen was Frances's face flash by, then a blaze of blue light. Frances did not appear as she had in any of those photographs. She looked terrified.

It was a blue van, *Joan said.*

For the next three days the detectives did their work, cataloging every blue van in Queens, attempting in vain to find a match on the list of vehicles registered to sex offenders. They established which vans could have been in the vicinity of the parking lot the day Frances disappeared, then systematically winnowed that list down. Joan couldn't eat or sleep. She kept the strands of Frances's hair in a glass jar on her dressing table beside a photograph of the girl. It was the most recent photograph her father had, taken for the school yearbook two weeks before her disappearance. Sixty children had lined up and posed singly, one after the other, before a white screen. Frances was smiling, but looked not quite ready for the photographer to snap.

Joan took the F train to Queens and walked around for hours, on random streets. She returned home and ate some rice. It was all she could tolerate. That night, around nine, the detectives called. Gus and Frank. They had something. She got dressed and made a pot of coffee.

Frank Ramos lived in Brooklyn. He was married, with two kids. Gus Albanese was divorced. He lived in the Bronx, in the Italian neighborhood near Tremont Avenue. He was taken with Joan's looks, voice, the easy manner beneath which you sensed her intensity. He sat down in her living room, with its leather sofa and Moroccan carpets, and stirred his coffee.

We've narrowed it to three vans, *Frank said.* None registered to prior offenders. We have addresses. Before we obtain warrants or do forensics, we want you to check out the vans. Are you up for it?

The first van belonged to a laundry on Ditmars Boulevard. It was parked outside a two-family house in Jamaica. The driver was a Chinese kid, working for his uncle. He was petrified when the detectives asked him to step outside. Joan circled the van, laying her hands on it. She looked at the kid and shook her head.

The second van was driven by the owner of a hardware store. He was sixty-four years old, Polish, living in an apartment in Corona. The van was parked in the building's garage. Joan circled it and touched it. They knocked at the man's door, and he was bewildered at the sight of the grim detectives and the tall black woman. He was five four, maybe 120 pounds. His left arm was so arthritic he could barely lift it. His wife was in a wheelchair in front of the TV.

Their third stop was on a street of rowhouses in St. Albans, near Montefiore Cemetery. The houses were all on the right side of the street, facing a strip of woods. A blue Chevy van was parked in front of Number 40. The house was dark. A window on the second floor lit up when Gus pressed the doorbell. Then a second window. A heavyset middle-aged woman opened the door but kept the chain fastened until she saw Gus's badge up close. She had gray hair and doughy skin. A second woman, even older and grayer, ambled up behind her. They were retired nurses, sisters.

What is it? *the second sister said.*

They said they mostly used the van to travel to arts and crafts fairs. They were certain they hadn't been out driving that day.

How can you be so sure? *Gus said.*

The housepainters were here for two weeks in April, *the first sister said,* and we never left them in the house alone.

What's this about? *the second sister said.*

Does anyone else ever drive your van? *Frank asked.*

The sisters looked at each other.

Only my brother, *the first sister replied.* He borrows it sometimes.

Where does he live?

Linden Boulevard. But he wouldn't go to Rego Park.

How do you know that? *Gus said.*

What would he want there? *the second sister replied.*

Gus glanced over his shoulder at Joan, who was backing away from the van, edging toward the woods across the street. Her spine was stiff and her expression was frozen.

Gus squeezed Frank's arm and said, I'll go with Joan.

He had his flashlight out as he caught up to her in the woods. They have a brother who uses the van, *he said.*

Joan nodded. He has red hands, a flushed face, thick lips. Asthma, maybe, that makes him wheeze.

It was true, he had all of those things. And a temper that had gotten him fired from his last job, custodian at a technical school, where he had stolen the many tools discovered in his cluttered one-room apartment—and one tool that wasn't found.

Thirty minutes later, the forensics squad and four cops arrived in two vans. Two other detectives were dispatched to 467 Linden Boulevard, awaiting the go-ahead to make an arrest. At one A.M., *beneath portable floodlights, two of the cops began digging in a drainage ditch across the woods to which Joan had directed them. The scent of Two Hearts perfume filled her head as she threaded the trees. But Frances's screams, which had rung in her ears when she approached the van, stopped abruptly.*

The drainage ditch, dug months before, was still waiting to be lined with cement. Raymond Mullen had concluded correctly that additional digging would never be noticed before the cement was poured and the grave sealed. It didn't have to be a large grave for a girl Frances's size. Standing with Gus and Frank, Joan watched the wet dirt pile up beside the ditch. Then

*the diggers stopped abruptly and signaled the forensics chief,
who stepped into the ditch and squatted with his small rakes
and brushes. After fifteen minutes, there she was, four feet
under, the hacksaw on her chest. Her remains looked intact at
first. Then they saw that her other foot had been severed, too.*
Christ, *Frank muttered.*

*After Gus and Frank drove her home, Joan curled up on
the sofa in her raincoat. She didn't want to go to bed. Didn't
want to dream. She only wanted to blot out what she had
seen. And to detach from whatever it was internally that had
enabled her to find Frances.*

*She attended the funeral with Gus and Frank. John Kelly
embraced her outside the church. The fire commissioner was
there, and Kelly's squad, and the chief of detectives. They all
watched the hearse and the cortege drive away.*

Don't call me anymore, *Joan told the chief.*

She kissed Gus on the cheek, then Frank.

Want a ride home? *Gus said.*

She shook her head. I need to walk.

If we can ever do anything for you, *Frank said,* you know
where to find us.

✹

*Sammy LeMond and Joan Neptune had a two-month court-
ship. He asked her to marry him at his apartment. She knew
something was up when he insisted on dining there, ordering
up lobster, fried oysters, and grilled peppers from the club.
After a champagne toast, LeMond took out a two-carat diamond ring.*

*He was fifty-three years old, and she was thirteen years his
junior. His friends were astonished. A confirmed bachelor, he*

*hadn't lived with anyone in years, hadn't even dated seriously.
No one expected he would ever marry.*

*They were married by a city judge in his chambers on Cen-
tre Street. The members of LeMond's band and a few friends
were on hand. After a festive lunch at the club, the couple
drove to Connecticut. She gave up her clients. When she moved
into Sammy's apartment, she added her own touches: black
caryatids in the bath, a Japanese screen depicting court musicians, a mosaic of nightingales in the foyer. She had fine taste,
and an instinct for what pleased her husband, from honey-
colored bedsheets and towels to the dormant fireplace she refurbished, clearing the flue and installing a marble mantelpiece.
LeMond was happiest when they curled up before a fire and
listened to music. Ever since Joan entered his life, it was as if he
were approaching forty again, not sixty. She liked to drive him
out to the country in her sky-blue convertible. With her, he
began traveling abroad again. And he composed, recorded,
and dedicated to her what many considered his finest LP, Mountains of the Moon. It sold so well that RCA renegotiated his
contract. Joan had had lovers, but never lived with anyone, and
like LeMond, hadn't considered marriage. What set him apart
for her was his abiding faith in himself and his belief in the re-
demptive power of music. Whether they were alone in his studio
or he was onstage somewhere, she knew he was playing for
her—not just because he told her so, but because she felt it. Private, even shy, with most people, he never concealed his passion
for her. One night, soon after they met, when he took the Bolden
cylinder from the armoire and she heard "Tiger Rag" for the
first time, she knew he was sharing something sacred to him.*

※

On the other side of the country, Valentine Owen was back to doing session work. The long road he had taken was mostly downhill. After several fractious years with the Hurricanes—culminating in missed engagements and a barroom brawl—Tex Mayeux fired him. Owen had kicked around Kansas City before hooking up with another Dixieland band. They didn't tour or record. Local dives, Elks dinners, and smokers were their staple. It was the winter of 1967. Owen was forty-nine years old. When that band dissolved, he had to hustle pickup work at bars to make ends meet. Sometimes that meant playing pop with an electric band. He was back to living in a residence hotel, eating at diners, trying to keep to four drinks a day, spread out. But sometimes that didn't work out, and afterward he would drink beer, not bourbon, for a couple of weeks.

He went to Dallas to audition for the house band in a gentlemen's club named Diamond Jim's. It was a step up from a strip joint: they called the girls dancers. Owen couldn't stand the inland heat, the cement landscape and harsh light, the religious nuts. In the Deep Ellum district, doomsday prophets and soapbox preachers outnumbered hookers. And the cops were as crooked as any in New Orleans. But there was work to be had, and he was desperate.

He passed the audition and joined the band at a salary of forty dollars a week. He found a room with a kitchenette on Valero Street. He ate at taco joints and diners and after work hung out in a bar that served shots of mescal for twenty-five cents. The whorehouses were cheap, but after a couple of weeks he took up with the cashier at the club. Some women still saw something in him at that point, just as Camille Broussard had five years earlier. The cashier's name was Polly Moore. She had friends. She and Owen were invited to barbecues.

They went dancing. He hadn't danced in years. He got wind of the fact she was seeing another man. A guy named Ralph who worked at a radio station. She thought Owen didn't suspect. In fact, he didn't care. She had gone to El Paso for an abortion the previous year. A Mexican doctor who came over the border. Now she was pregnant again.

She and Owen were sitting in her small apartment having a drink. When she told him it was his child, he brought up Ralph for the first time. She was stunned that he knew his name.

It couldn't be him, *she said.*

Why not?

I just know it isn't. Women know.

Sure they do.

Well, I'm not losing another baby, *she said defiantly.*

That was it for Owen. He stood up to leave. Do what you like.

Val—

I don't want any part of this.

You what?

I'm gone.

She saw he meant it. You bastard.

Tell it to Ralph.

As he turned to the door, Polly grabbed at his coat. He wheeled around and slapped her. She lunged toward him, her hands up to scratch, and he slapped her again, and again.

By the time he stopped himself, she was bleeding, her mouth badly cut, a gash on her forehead. Jesus Christ, *he muttered.*

She curled up on the floor sobbing. You won't get away with this.

He opened the door and hurried out.

He had only hit a woman once before, and that was a

hooker who was emptying his wallet. This was different; he didn't like all that blood.

Anyway, he was sick of Dallas. Things had soured at the club. Except for the drummer, the other members of the band shunned him. They were tired of hearing what a big shot he'd been and how their gig was only a temporary bump in the road. The club manager had taken a dislike to him, too, after catching him cadging one drink too many. Owen was sure he was on the verge of being canned. This would ice it, if Polly came crying to them, or worse, brought the cops.

He decided to go back to Kansas City. He collected his paycheck at the club and borrowed fifty bucks from the drummer that he promised to pay back the next day. Then he got on the three o'clock bus.

This was the second time he had been reckless with some woman he didn't care about, and he promised himself it would be the last. Maybe Polly went back to El Paso, maybe she had the baby. Maybe it was his and maybe it wasn't. She had been two-timing him, after all, whether he cared about it or not. He never saw her again, just as he had never seen Camille. Camille had given birth to a daughter and named her Ruby. She would have been five years old at that time. He didn't think about her much, either. For several years, Camille sent him letters, and once in a while he wrote back. But he was cruising then; after he left the Hurricanes, he didn't bother. Then she wrote that she had left New Orleans and was getting married, and he didn't hear from her again.

Every so often he contacted Sammy LeMond, asking him to put in a good word with this or that promoter in Chicago or New Orleans, but nothing ever panned out. Owen attributed this to a lack of effort on LeMond's part, not to his own short-

comings. He resented the fact that LeMond had never invited him back to sit in with the Eclipse Sextet or introduced him to people with real clout in New York. Owen's anger was intensified by LeMond's continued success; because Owen had boasted about playing with him, musicians passing through Kansas City often shared bits of information.

As the years passed, LeMond didn't give Owen much thought one way or the other. He was just one of many musicians he had helped out. Some drifted in and out of his orbit quickly; others stayed in touch. Joan thought her husband could be overly open and generous, but also knew that those were two of the qualities that had attracted her. When she decided he was crossing the line—expending too much energy on someone who took it for granted or was somehow undeserving—she let him know. Valentine Owen had dropped out of LeMond's orbit long before Joan appeared, and she had never heard her husband mention his name.

In 1974 Owen moved to L.A. He had been hanging out in Kansas City with a drummer named Cal Perry who got a gig as a studio sideman for a small record label in L.A., a company that recorded second-rate vocal groups and crooners. Sick of Kansas City, broke again, Owen took a chance and joined Cal. He secured one last reference from LeMond and was hired. He moved into another furnished room, in West Hollywood, a pink stucco building with a dusty palm in front.

Work was steady and Owen liked the climate. After Kansas, L.A. felt like anything goes.

One night at a party in Alhambra, two musicians were shooting up in the living room.

Cal took out a vial and tapped some powder onto the coffee table.

Coke? *Owen said. He had smoked weed with Cal in Kansas City, but that was it.*

Smack. To snort.

Owen didn't want to go there. But he was drunk and he snorted two lines and a few minutes later lurched outside and threw up into the bushes. When someone drove him home later, the oncoming headlights on the freeway were like balls of fire.

He didn't touch drugs again, but he couldn't stop drinking. He managed to keep it to a six-pack a day.

He hated his job, but was able to hold it down for several years. He rented a two-room apartment. He bought a second-hand Pontiac. Then he developed bleeding ulcers. In three weeks he dropped twenty pounds. He had lost his looks; now suddenly he just looked old. Hollow cheeks, thinning hair, a trumpeter's teeth, which he had neglected. The doctor ordered him to stop drinking immediately. In fact, even if he could have kept it down, a single beer racked his insides so badly that he didn't want to pick up. Despite himself, he got sober. After a year, his ulcers healed, but his old resentments felt raw as ever—maybe worse now that he could pick over them with a clear head.

✳

In the fall of 1983, Owen decided to take his chances and move back to New York. He was sixty-five, the oldest guy in his circle of session men. The younger musicians called him "Pops," which he hated. Though his prospects had flatlined, in his own mind some promising gambit still lay ahead, out of reach but real. In the same vein, during the twilit moments between sleeping and waking he could imagine himself handsome still, and strong, and attractive to women, despite the fact he hadn't slept beside a woman in years and the only ones he touched cost him sixty dollars for twenty minutes. There were no more Camilles or Pollys in his life.

He was sick of the West Coast and convinced he was owed one more throw of the dice in New York. His savings were meager and he was terrified of dying broke in a state nursing home—or worse.

He bought a new black suit and the sort of expensive, splashy shirts he hadn't worn in years. He cleaned himself up: good haircut, shave, manicure. He dyed his hair himself: it came out coppery, unnatural, but he preferred it to gray. After flying in to Newark, he checked in to a prewar hotel off Times Square, the Lancaster Arms, and ate soup and crackers at a deli.

He had a plan of sorts. Step one: reintroduce himself to Sammy LeMond; step two: get into LeMond's good graces again; step three: get the lay of the land. There was still no step four. He had listened to LeMond's LPs with envy, but knew little about his personal life, aside from the fact he was married. He'd heard he was reclusive, rarely performing in public anymore, but was still generous with his friends. A clarinetist named Harry Madison attested to this one night in L.A., relating to Owen how LeMond had allowed him to eat off the cuff at his club. He knew my eyesight was goin', *Madison said,* and he done what he could. If there's a better man around, I don't know who he is.

Owen's second afternoon in New York, he worked up the nerve to telephone LeMond's apartment. A woman answered the phone. The new wife. She had a strong low voice. It unnerved him for a moment; it was not what he had imagined. He hung up on her. He waited until the next morning to call again, and this time the housekeeper took a message. That evening LeMond returned his call.

You're back, Val. Come by my club tomorrow night.

Though he had heard about the club's success, Owen was surprised to discover how ritzy it was, abuzz with well-heeled customers, limos in front, the sidewalk rope line managed by a pair of bouncers. There were eight-foot bronze mirrors behind the bar. The rows of bottles on glass shelves were lit mauve and magenta. Atop Doric columns, marble mermaids surveyed the room. The waitresses wore black pants, white vests, and red bow ties. They sailed out of the kitchen with trays of steaming crab platters, fried shrimp, garlic soup. A quartet of lean young musicians was burning up the stage with a double-time version of "Flying Home." In a green neon suit and yellow shirt, the handsome trumpeter was obviously their leader. To close the piece, he reared back beneath a gold spotlight and launched into a wicked extended solo. Owen hadn't heard anyone that good in years: the intricate phrasing at high speed, the tremendous volume. And he had presence. The stage was his.

Owen found LeMond holding court in a corner booth with three other men. Businessmen. Armani suits and Santoni shoes. The one sitting next to LeMond was the oldest and flashiest: tanned, his silver hair glistening, he wore a purplish suit and a diamond-studded Rolex.

LeMond himself was wearing a chalk-striped jacket and orange shirt. His brow was unlined and his thick hair streaked gray. He's gotten older, too, Owen thought, but he still looks younger than me. LeMond had just turned sixty. He was on medication for high blood pressure and arrhythmia. He was plagued by vertigo and insomnia. After an angina attack, he went in for weekly cardiograms, but everything looked all right. His wife put him on a regimen of vegetables, rice, and green tea. But that night, in high spirits, he was drinking more than usual. The champagne, he told himself, would help him sleep.

He beckoned Owen to join them. As Owen slid into the booth, LeMond introduced him all around. The silver-haired man, Jake Romer, turned out to be president of the jazz division at RCA.

This is a celebration, Val, *LeMond said.* Jake signed Lenny there to a three-record contract.

Lenny was the young trumpeter, just taking his bow.

Bravo, *Jake shouted, raising his Scotch in the direction of the stage.*

Lenny's conservatory trained, *LeMond said.* Knows every kind of music. *When the applause died down, he turned to Val.* What'll you have?

Ginger ale, thanks.

Val's a fine trumpeter himself, Jake, *LeMond said.* He's just in from the coast.

Jake smiled at Owen, then looked away.

Owen wished he could disappear at that moment. He was furious at LeMond for inviting him to such an occasion, setting him up for humiliation. His anger made it easy for him to forget that it was he who had called LeMond, fishing for just such an invitation. At the same time, Owen was dazed to find himself in such company—well beyond the realm of his recent fantasies—just two days after walking out of his run-down building in West Hollywood.

The band left the stage, and Lenny Marquet made his way to their booth. Trumpet tucked under his arm, he had a confi-

dent gait, smiling at friends in the audience, winking at girls. "Conservatory trained," Owen thought mockingly. He could barely look at him.

An hour later, they were all at LeMond's apartment, Lenny and his band, the record executives, and about seventy other people, including two of the girls who had caught Lenny's eye and were now planted beside him. Valentine Owen was glad to be among them, but at the same time felt even more uncomfortable than he had at the club. He recognized a number of guests: Keith Jarrett's sidemen, Gary Peacock and Jack DeJohnette—both older than he had imagined; Sonny Rollins; Emile Griffith, the former boxing champion; Eartha Kitt; Craig Toland, the jazz critic for Billboard; *and a couple of young film actresses whose names he couldn't remember. There was a sumptuous buffet, a bartender from the club mixing drinks, and three of those waitresses with the red bow ties floating around with trays of hors d'oeuvres and champagne. Owen could have used a drink, but he resisted. Even spruced up, in his new clothes, he was sure he stuck out. In reality, hardly anyone took notice of him.*

Mostly he stood against the wall, taking the place in. LeMond was flush, all right. The white Steinway was still there and the African sculptures, but plenty had changed in twenty years. The apartment felt warmer, more intimate. The furniture upholstered colorfully, the carpets more ornate, the track lighting soft. The wife's touches were everywhere: pale satin drapes, French mirrors, a collection of Haitian art. Gilt-framed photographs of the couple adorned a table beside the piano. In Paris and Tangier, on the Ramblas in Barcelona, tossing coins into a fountain in Copenhagen. She was certainly a beautiful woman, Owen thought.

He filled a plate at the buffet. The stuff his stomach could tolerate: bread, cheese, potato salad. He drifted around the room. The music on the stereo was Lenny Marquet's forthcoming album. The kid was more than good. He played his own compositions, some reconfigured Ellington, a samba, and two old New Orleans standards, "Riverside Blues" and "Weather Bird," that he'd made his own. Owen sat by the window and listened. One of the actresses came over for a smoke. She stood with her back to him, gazing at the impressive view. She had long hair, an hourglass figure. Owen could feel the heat off her body. He wished he could touch her.

At that moment, feeling a pair of eyes on him, he glanced up and there was LeMond's wife in a knot of people in the foyer, putting on her coat, staring intently at him. She was even more striking in person. He mustered a smile, but she didn't return it. Why the icy stare? Suddenly she was walking toward him. He stood up. There was nowhere for him to go. She stepped up close. He could smell her perfume. She was his height, looking into his eyes.

I'm Joan. Sammy's wife.

Pleased to meet you. I'm Valentine Owen.

She nodded, and he felt she was looking right through him.

Sammy's mentioned me?

No.

I'm an old friend. I met Sammy years ago. He helped me out.

He helps a lot of people.

Owen was sweating. Well, I'll never forget it.

She lowered her voice. Stay away from Sammy, you understand?

What?

You heard me, *she said sharply.* I don't want to see you here again.

Turning on her heel, she returned to the foyer and walked out the door with her companions.

Owen was shaken. He nearly left the apartment then, too, but thought better of it. His instincts told him that if he didn't stick around now, he might never get the chance to return.

Joan Neptune took a taxi across town to a friend's birthday party, and an hour later, sipping bourbon on top of all the champagne, Sammy LeMond acted on an impulse she surely would have quashed.

He invited Lenny Marquet, Lenny's bass player and cousin, Marvell Atkins, and Valentine Owen into his study and closed the door. Like the rest of the apartment, it had been made over: oak bookshelves, an antique desk, a plush sofa. On one wall there were inscribed photographs of famous jazzmen—Ben Webster, Stan Getz, Gene Krupa, Milt Jackson—each of them standing with LeMond. There were also photographs of early New Orleans bands, like Kid Ory's Sunshine Orchestra and the Excelsior Brass Band. A beautifully preserved cylinder phonograph with a brass horn sat on a shelf between a humidor and a bust of a fierce, mustachioed man.

As LeMond picked up the phonograph, he gestured toward the bust. That's Rafael Méndez, the Mexican cornetist. Recently passed away. He was trained classical—like you, Lenny—but he also played the cornet in Pancho Villa's army.

You knew him? *Lenny asked.*

I did. Some say he is the greatest cornetist of all time.

He placed the phonograph on the coffee table, then sat down and poured each man a tumbler of bourbon.

When LeMond toasted Lenny, Owen put his tumbler to his lips, but didn't drink.

Thank you for this party, man, *Lenny said.*

LeMond patted his shoulder. This is just the beginning for you boys. Isn't that right, Val?

Owen smiled, thinking, How the hell would I know? Fuck you, Sammy.

Lenny downed his drink. The fighter you introduced me to: is it true he killed a man in the ring?

LeMond refilled his tumbler. Never got over it. Pretty much killed him, too.

I remember that fight, *Owen put in.*

The other guy was out on his feet, but wouldn't go down, *LeMond said.* I was there.

Of course you were, Owen thought. Everything LeMond said was bothering him now.

Emile's a friend of Joan's, *LeMond said.* She helped him through a tough time.

She's a fine woman, *Marvell said.*

Yes, she is, *LeMond said.* Now, this is a special evening, and I've got a surprise for you, Lenny. Didn't plan it, but it feels right.

He opened the armoire in the corner. On one knee, wobbling slightly, he reached way in, inserted a key in a lock, and brought out a cylindrical box with a gold top. It was labeled EDISON GOLD MOULDED RECORDS, *beside an oval photograph of a young Thomas Edison.*

With due respect to Méndez, *he said,* the man I consider the greatest cornetist of all time recorded this cylinder. In 1904. There is no possession I treasure more. Only three people have ever listened to it with me.

LeMond took one of the photographs off the wall and handed it to Lenny. I expect you've heard of Buddy Bolden. This is his band. That's him, second from right on top. He was about your age then. This is the only photograph of him there is. *LeMond fastened the cylinder to the mandrel.* And this is his only known recording.

No way, *Marvell said.* My grandfather talked about Bolden. He heard him play in New Orleans.

Onstage, live, is the only way you could hear him, *LeMond said.* Until now. *He lifted the needle and placed it on the wax.* Listen . . .

There was a sizzle of static before the soaring version of "Tiger Rag" filled the room. Tilting his head back, closing his eyes, Lenny drank in the sound. He never forgot that Louis Armstrong said a real musician doesn't listen to the music, he listens to the notes, and that's what he did, astonished at the progressions he was hearing from the cornet.

Goddamn, *Marvell murmured.*

Valentine Owen had the same reaction, but his eyes were open and his mind was racing, trying to calculate the cylinder's worth. A hundred thousand, two hundred, more?

The music ended, and LeMond lifted the needle.

Was I right? *he asked.*

Lenny laughed. I never heard anybody play like that. Not Miles, not anyone.

No one, *Marvell agreed, turning to LeMond.* But where did you get it?

LeMond shook his head and poured himself another shot. Let's just say this cylinder traveled a long way before it came into my hands. One day I'll put it out in the world.

Somebody own the rights? *Marvell asked.*

LeMond smiled. A ghost. And he'll get his due. In the meantime, please keep this to yourselves—no questions asked. I need you to do that.

Lenny and Marvell exchanged glances. You can count on it, *Lenny said.*

That's right, *Owen put in.*

Good. *LeMond slid the cylinder back in its box, returned it to the hidden cabinet, and closed up the armoire.*

Thank you, man, *Lenny said.*

My pleasure. Now, I need to get back to my other guests. *He opened the door, and the noise of the party washed in.* You all run on ahead.

Thanks for inviting me in, *Owen said.*

LeMond patted his arm. My pleasure.

Lenny and Marvell melted into the crowd. Owen lingered by the door long enough to see LeMond tuck the key away in a drawer at the base of the humidor.

For ten days, Owen waited for an opening. He became a regular at LeMond's club, waiting for LeMond to turn up, dining there every night despite the strain it put on his budget. It was like the old days, trying to attach himself to LeMond, except LeMond's wife had ordered him to stay away. He spent hours lying awake in his hotel room, dredging his memory, trying to figure out why she would be so vehement about someone she'd never met, who hadn't been anywhere near her husband in years. Then, at the club, he heard she was a psychic: could she possibly have read his thoughts and intentions regarding LeMond? He had to be more than cautious. He certainly couldn't telephone LeMond again, or appear pushy in any way. He was in a quandary: if she had told LeMond to avoid him—and Owen couldn't imagine she hadn't—all bets were off. But Owen was desperate, with literally nothing to lose. He just had to make sure he didn't cross paths with her again.

During those ten days, LeMond only showed up at the club twice, both times accompanied by Joan Neptune. They dined alone in a corner booth, and Owen made himself scarce.

Finally, on the twelfth day, Owen got what he was waiting for: LeMond entered the club alone at eight o'clock, spotted Owen a short time later, and invited him over for a drink.

I thought I saw you here the other night, Val. *LeMond's voice was flat. He seemed preoccupied as he looked Owen over.*

It's a great place, *Owen said, slipping into the booth, trying to conceal his nervousness.*

That was quite a party we had, *LeMond said.* I had a few. By the way, I know I told you this, but not a word to anyone about that cylinder.

Of course not.

I don't want it to get around yet. *LeMond broke a roll in half and buttered it.* My wife told me that she doesn't want you coming around. She told you, too.

In the split second he had, Owen decided to play it straight. He didn't feign surprise. I didn't understand, Sammy. Why would she say that?

You tell me.

I don't know. I never met her before. And I've been away for twenty years.

LeMond looked at him closely, stirring the ice in his ginger ale. Maybe she thought you were someone else.

Could be. There's lots of trumpet players around. *Owen had a sinking feeling. He expected the conversation, and their meeting, to end at that point.* I'm sorry if I upset her.

LeMond himself didn't seem upset. In fact, he was calm.

Maybe it would have been different right after the party. But now, to Owen's surprise, he seemed to shrug off his wife's advice. Well, you're not the first person she's said that to. There are plenty of people in our business she hasn't cottoned to over the years. Plenty of people with troubles.

Sure, I understand, *Owen said, though he wasn't sure which particular troubles LeMond was referring to.*

A waiter brought LeMond a steak with a side of peas.

Been having some issues with my ticker, *LeMond said, taking out a pill container and picking out two pills, different colors, that he washed down with the ginger ale.* Haven't been out much.

You look good.

My wife has me on salads and fruit. I need a break. *He cut into the steak.* You want to order something?

No, thanks.

So you're back in town to stay?

Just a visit.

Got anything going?

Not really.

A few of the boys are coming by my studio tomorrow afternoon to jam. Why don't you join us?

I'd like that. *Owen was trying to come up with a tactful way to ask the one question he had.*

But LeMond did his work for him. My wife's upstate on business, coming home tomorrow night, so I want to start at noon.

I'll be there.

When Owen arrived the next day, the current members of the Eclipse Sextet were tuning up. LeMond was sitting on a couch, talking to the clarinetist. The engineer was testing his levels. Sandwiches, fruit salad, coffee, and beer were set out on a table. Owen had brought his trumpet. He sat down in a director's chair against the wall beside two other musicians who weren't in the band. He studied the room. The equipment was state-of-the-art. On the right-hand wall, there was a small kitchen and a bathroom.

The band was very professional, talking quietly as they took their places. LeMond invited Owen to join in when the spirit moved him.

The band launched into "Stardust," stopping and starting several times. LeMond wasn't happy with it. Then they jammed, improvising on a theme from "Scarlet and Red," switching keys and tempos and concluding with a long solo by LeMond. After a half hour of this, LeMond told the band to take five and huddled with the engineer.

The musicians gathered at the food table. One of them went into the bathroom. That was what Owen had been waiting for. He went and stood by the bathroom door. LeMond saw him.

No need to wait, Val. Use the one inside, down the hall.

Thanks, Sammy, I remember.

Owen went through the soundproof doors to the apartment. It was silent. The housekeeper was ironing in the laundry room. He walked down the carpeted hallway, past the bathroom, to the study. The door was ajar. He slid open the drawer in the humidor and took out the key. He opened the armoire and, on his knees, groped for the cabinet in the back. Minutes later, he walked out of the apartment and rode the elevator to the lobby. It was a cool sunny afternoon. He broke into a sweat trying to find a taxi. Finally one turned the corner. His ninety-dollar trumpet remained beneath his chair in the studio. The Bolden cylinder was in his raincoat pocket.

The lights of the city were coming on through Emmett Browne's windows. The dim roar of rush hour traffic was punctuated by car horns. His ancient radiators were knocking.

"Sammy LeMond misjudged Owen from the first," Browne said. "But this time it proved fatal—to both of them."

Ruby, whose attention had been drifting, looked up. "What do you mean?"

"Two weeks after the cylinder was stolen, LeMond suffered a heart attack." Browne hesitated. "And you know how your father died."

"My mother told me it was a stroke."

"No, that's not true. Your father froze to death, Dr. Cardillo."

Ruby was stunned.

"I'm sorry. I thought you knew," Browne said.

"You could be a little more sensitive," Devon said angrily.

She didn't think Ruby could absorb another shock. "You want the Bolden cylinder. It's obvious my mother knows nothing about it. And I certainly don't."

"I realize that now," Browne said.

"He assumed I would know, Devon," Ruby said evenly. Turning back to Browne, she shifted into her physician's voice. "Acute hypothermia—where was he, exactly?"

"In a car," Browne replied. "Parked in the woods near Sugar Hill, New Hampshire."

"What was he doing there?"

"I don't know. The state police declared it a suicide."

"I've never heard of a suicide like that."

"He was on a logging trail, a mile into the woods, two miles from a paved road. Not a place you would pull over to rest. The car had been rented here in Manhattan. The gas tank was full. There were no engine problems. No sign of foul play. And the autopsy revealed no evidence of a heart attack. The police concluded that he drove himself there after dark and turned off the engine."

Devon took Ruby's hand.

"Did he leave a note?" Ruby said.

"None was found."

Ruby picked up her teacup and set it down again without taking a sip. "When did this happen?"

"January 1984."

My final year of medical school, Ruby thought. A year after he tried to blackmail me in San Francisco. "So my father stole the cylinder. Tell me, how do you come to know all this?"

"Earlier that month, your father came to me with a business proposition: he wanted to sell me the Bolden cylinder. He'd found out I was after it. At first, I thought it was a hoax. He wasn't the first person to claim he had a Bolden recording. And he seemed nervous, jittery. He allowed me to play the cylinder—just once—on an Edison phonograph. When I heard 'Tiger Rag,' I knew the cylinder was the real thing. The cornetist was playing on a level I hadn't heard before and haven't heard since, except maybe from Louis Armstrong. Of course Owen wouldn't tell me how he came by the cylinder. I told him I needed to know, but he saw I was bluffing. I'm ashamed to admit it, but I was so eager to possess the cylinder, I didn't really care." He paused, choosing his words carefully. "He offered to sell me the cylinder for one hundred fifty thousand dollars. I said I would give him ninety thousand, no more."

"It's worth that much?" Devon said.

"It would be worth three times that now. He accepted my offer, but wanted cash. I told him I needed two days to put that together. We shook on it, and he left with the cylinder. I never saw him again. Only later did I discover he had stolen it."

"How?" Ruby asked.

"Sammy LeMond's wife came to see me. Because of their club, she and LeMond knew a lot of musicians. Someone had heard on the grapevine that Owen visited me. He wasn't the most discreet person. She asked me what I knew. I told her what I just told you. When she informed me that Owen had stolen the cylinder from her home, I was horrified, of course. She said her husband had been having heart trouble. He was recovering from an angina attack, and the shock of being betrayed and robbed had been too much for him. He complained of dizziness and headaches, and woke up one morning with chest pains. She called an ambulance, and he suffered a heart attack en route to the hospital. It was bad. She said he was so weak, another one like that would kill him. I assured her I didn't have the cylinder. I promised I would find out what I could. I put my private investigator, Nate Kane, on it. A week after visiting me, she became a widow."

"How awful," Devon said.

"When Nate picked up Owen's trail, all he discovered was how Owen had died."

"But what happened to the cylinder?" Devon said.

"If I knew that, I would not have written to your grandmother, or met with you today. Obviously it wasn't among Owen's possessions. I don't have many years left, and I'd like to have it. So I thought I'd try once more to search."

"Where is LeMond's wife now?" Devon said.

"She still lives in New York. The cylinder was never recovered. I think she lost interest." He paused. "She inherited LeMond's club in Harlem. I don't know if she goes there anymore."

"What's the name of it?" Devon asked.

Browne scribbled on a piece of notepaper and slipped it across the desk to Devon. "It's called Algiers," he said. "On 124th Street."

"One more question," Devon said. "If you had managed to buy this cylinder from my grandfather, would you have returned it to LeMond's wife?"

"I don't know," he said after a moment's hesitation, and Devon took that as a no.

※

Riding down from Browne's office in the ancient elevator, Ruby flipped open her compact and checked her makeup. She applied lipstick. "I'm okay," she said, anticipating Devon.

"I'm sorry I brought you here."

"It's all right," Ruby said breezily.

"You're sure?" Devon said, studying her warily.

"Devon, even if every word that man told us is true, I wouldn't trust him any more than I trusted my father."

"Neither would I," Devon agreed, as they stepped outside.

Kenji was waiting in front. Smoke was purling from the limousine's exhaust pipe. Snow was still falling fast.

"I need to work on my speech back at the hotel," Ruby said.

"Do you mind if I join you later, Mom? The cold air feels good."

"Of course." Ruby pulled on her gloves as Kenji opened the rear door for her. "You know, I always knew I fell for an SOB because my father was an SOB."

As the limo pulled away, Devon glanced again at the note Browne had given her. It was not the name and address of the nightclub. It read: COME BACK IF YOU WANT TO DISCUSS THE CYLINDER.

She went back upstairs and found Browne still behind his desk. "So soon?" he smiled. "Let's get right to it, then. I could see how intrigued you were by the Bolden cylinder."

"That's why I'm here."

"I have a proposition for you. I realize you have no idea of the cylinder's whereabouts. You had not even heard of it until today. Yet you may be able to help me find it."

"How is that possible? You've been searching for decades."

"Yes, retracing Owen's history was nearly impossible. He left a very broken trail. Look at how long it took me to locate your grandmother. But now you may be able to learn more about it than I ever could. Then you can share that information with me."

"Why would I want to do that?"

"Money? The more information you bring back, the more I will pay."

"Kind of like the deal you offered my grandfather."

"You mean, the deal he offered me. Are you interested?"

"I'd like to hear some details—with no strings attached."

"Fine. And if you're not interested, I'll bid you goodbye a second time. First, I have always believed that Joan Neptune knows more than she says. I only met her twice, and she made it clear she would never speak with me again."

"Why?"

"Because of my connection to Valentine Owen."

Devon was surprised. "What about my connection to him?"

"He died before you were born. Even your mother hardly knew him."

"Still, it's a nasty calling card."

"Why present it, then? You don't need to introduce yourself as Owen's granddaughter." He leaned forward. "I'll tell you what to say."

"You mean, you'll tell me how to lie."

"Oh, I don't think you need much coaching."

"What?"

"Not with your history—a criminal record, drug problems . . ."

"I don't believe this," Devon said, standing up and heading for the door.

"Suit yourself," Browne shrugged. "You're missing an opportunity."

"Go to hell."

Devon was furious with herself for going back. What did I expect? she thought, stepping into the cold.

She took out her phone and found an AA meeting in a Uni-
tarian church three blocks away. Before going in, Devon lit up
and huddled among the other smokers on the sidewalk. The
meeting was in the basement, a rec room with fluorescent lights
and linoleum tiles. Sunday school tables were pushed up
against the wall. Several dozen people were sitting on folding
chairs. The woman chairing the meeting was about Ruby's age,
wearing the kind of prim business suit Ruby used to favor.
After she had someone read the Twelve Steps and Twelve Tra-
ditions, the woman asked, "Is there anyone here for the first
time?"

Hands went up.

"Anyone under ninety days?"

Devon raised her hand slowly. "My name is Devon and I'm
a drug addict and an alcoholic. This is my seventy-third day."

Everyone clapped.

The speaker was a former cop. His qualification was no-
frills: before discussing the amends he had made, he described
the last time he had picked up, in a bar in Canarsie, only to
wake up the following morning in a men's room stall in Ban-
gor, Maine, with blood on his coat.

"And it wasn't my blood," he said.

Several people spoke from the floor in a similar vein. But it
was the slight, soft-spoken old man who concluded the meeting that caught Devon's attention. "Here's what I know after
forty years in the rooms: not drinking isn't the same as being
sober. Take an action."

Devon tried to stay with that as she walked outside. But
when she thought of Browne taunting her—*You're missing an
opportunity*—her anger rose up again. He was so devoured by
greed that perhaps he didn't realize he himself had given her an

opportunity she couldn't have imagined a few days before. She didn't grasp it herself until that moment.

Take an action, indeed, she told herself, stepping through a snowdrift and hailing a taxi.

Her driver skillfully worked the stagger on Park Avenue, and they didn't hit a single red light all the way to Harlem. He even knew where Algiers was, on the north side of 124th Street. It was a sleek, darkly curtained nightclub, no neon sign—no sign at all, in fact, just the name in discreet gold letters on a blue canopy.

Devon didn't want to sit at the bar. She took a table in the rear. A trio was setting up onstage. This was the kind of high-end club she had once dreamed of playing in. The room was beautiful to look at, humming with energy. Customers streaming in dressed to the nines. The waitress came over, and Devon ordered a plate of nachos.

"Anything to drink?" the waitress said.

Devon watched a tray of martinis and margaritas go by. A girl sitting alone at a nearby table was stirring a mojito. How easy it would be, she thought, to get drunk and tally for the thousandth time her thousand and one grievances against her parents, only to arrive at what? Her thousand and first drink? What did Giselle tell her when they were trash picking by the highway? *Instead of trying to control other people, control yourself.* Listening to Browne in his mausoleum, Devon had found herself drawn to that lost world where music was a religion and for a wild, fragile moment King Bolden was its high priest. His cylinder was the grail of that world. She had to hear it. If she never got near it, or if it no longer existed, then in order to write about it she would have to imagine and make palpable the music it preserved, which embodied nothing less than the genesis of jazz. If she could do that, if she could write about jazz, and interpret it, the way she had once hoped to perform it, it might light her way back to the parts of herself she had lost. The Bolden cylinder could help her begin a new chapter in her life. She was amazed at the power it had held over all these men for over a hundred years, driving some to revere it but keep it under wraps, and others to cheat, steal, and maybe die for it. Even the good men, who didn't see it as a dollar sign, became warped in the end, coveting it until it was not just a secret thing but a forbidden one. They locked it away so no one could hear it, just as Bolden himself had been locked away and never heard from again.

"Cranberry juice," Devon told the waitress. "Lots of ice and a twist of lime."

It arrived with the nachos.

Devon listened closely as the trio—piano, bass, drums—began playing an intense version of Art Tatum's "Deep Purple." The young pianist, leaning into the keyboard, working the pedals, was more Bud Powell than Tatum: playing soft block chords, elaborating right-hand melodies that broke off unexpectedly, allowing the bass and drums to converse—like the marathon duets of Mingus and Max Roach between Powell's solos.

Devon finished her juice and signaled the waitress. She had a plan, and it was time to put it in motion.

"Could you tell me if Joan Neptune is here tonight?" she asked.

The waitress looked at her more closely. "I wouldn't know, Miss."

"Is there someone here who would know?"

"You can ask the maître d'."

The greeter's smile on the smartly dressed young black woman at the door disappeared when Devon asked her the same question.

"She owns this club, doesn't she?" Devon said. "I wondered if you could give her this note."

Reluctantly the greeter took the note. "I'll give this to the manager. But I can't guarantee it will be passed along," she added politely.

"I don't need a guarantee. Please just say it's important."

"You're going to wait?"

"I'm at that table there."

Devon ordered another cranberry juice. She studied the crowd flowing in, classy, young, black and white. After a half hour, she began to think no reply was forthcoming. Then she saw a broad-shouldered black man in a brown suit make his way through the tables toward her, occasionally stopping to greet someone.

"Would you come with me, please?" he said pleasantly.

He led her through the maze of tables, around the stage, to a door marked PRIVATE. Around a corner there was a flight of stairs to a steel door, then a carpeted hallway at the end of which was another door marked PRIVATE. He opened it and disappeared.

The office she entered was spacious and well furnished and obviously soundproof: you would never know there was a nightclub below. The windows were curtained, the carpets thick. The track lights were dimmed over an L-shaped sofa to the right. In the middle of the room a tall, attractive black woman in her thirties was sitting behind a gleaming desk. She was wearing a green dress and gold earrings. A short, heavyset man, also well dressed, was sitting beside the desk. His eyeglasses were tinted yellow, magnifying his small eyes. The amber desk lamp was also low, so that the left side of the room was completely dark. Devon couldn't make out what was there, or how much distance there might be between the wall of darkness and the actual wall.

"Please, sit down," the woman said. She had striking bright eyes and beautiful hands. "Your name is Devon Sheresky?"

"Yes."

"I'm Adele. This is Leon."

Leon nodded.

"Thank you for speaking with me," Devon said.

Adele held up Devon's note. "So you want to write about Buddy Bolden."

"Yes."

"A big subject. What else have you written?"

"Reviews, criticism. For magazines. I want to do something more. An important story."

"Meaning?"

"A story that has yet to be told fully. Bolden's story." She hesitated. "And the story of the cylinder he recorded."

Adele looked at her more closely. "I'm not sure I know what you mean."

"I want to write about Bolden and Willie Cornish and Leonard Bechet. And Sammy LeMond. I'd like to know more about Mr. LeMond's relationship with Leonard Bechet."

For the first time, Leon's eyes strayed from Devon to Adele.

"How did you find your way here?" Adele asked.

Devon had been expecting this. "There is a letter of Leonard Bechet's in the musical archives at LSU in which he says he gave Sammy LeMond an Edison recording of Buddy Bolden. I'd like to meet Joan Neptune to ask her about this recording."

"What makes you think she knows anything about it?"

"How could she not?"

"Even if that's the case, why would she want to discuss it with you?"

"It's important musical history. I'm going to write about it. I hoped she would be interested in telling me what she knows."

Adele did not seem impressed by this answer.

Suddenly Devon had the feeling there was another person in the room, behind Adele, beyond that wall of darkness. She thought she'd heard a rustling of clothing, a breath. Leon was watching Devon again, but he never said a word.

"I will pass along your request to Mrs. LeMond," Adele said.

"Thank you. That's it?"

"Isn't that what you wanted?"

Devon hesitated. "Yes, that's what I wanted."

"Then good night, Miss Sheresky."

⁎

Back at the Pierre, Devon found Ruby working on her laptop at the desk in the sitting room. The screen cast a pale green light onto her face. She was wearing a lavender silk bathrobe—when had she bought that?—and her hair was still damp from the shower. Traces of her perfume were in the air. There was a bottle of champagne in an ice bucket. A room service dinner on the coffee table, the dish still covered, the silverware unused, a half-eaten roll on the bread plate. The television was turned on to the Weather Channel with the sound muted. Footage of a typhoon in Malaysia, followed by a mudslide in Peru.

Ruby heard Devon enter the room behind her, and without turning, said, "Give me a minute."

Devon put her hands on Ruby's shoulders. The muscles were tight. Her skin felt cold beneath the silk. Devon saw that she was writing in an emerald font.

"I'm changing my speech," Ruby said simply.

"All of it?"

"Just the middle. You'll see."

Devon massaged her lightly. "That was pretty rough this afternoon."

Ruby highlighted and deleted two pages of text, then looked up at Devon and assumed her clinical voice. "I never heard of anyone committing suicide like that. Medically speaking, it would be excruciating. As your temperature drops, your organs shut down, one by one, last of all your brain. You're aware of what's happening until you begin hallucinating, and by then you've lost all mobility. Amnesia sets in. You may not know who you are or where you are. Depending on his clothing, it may have taken him four or five hours to die. That's more than killing yourself: it's looking to suffer. It doesn't add up for me."

"I'm sorry you had to find out about it like that, Mom."

Ruby turned back to her laptop, and her tone again shifted. "I barely knew him, and he was a horrible man. For god's sake, this happened when I was your age. Younger." She started typing. "How was your walk?"

"Fine. I had some dinner, too. I see you haven't touched yours."

Ruby glanced over at the coffee table. "I'm working on it."

Devon drew herself a hot bath and soaked, sipping tea. She took two aspirins and stretched out on her bed. Her eyes were half closed when she heard a text message beep in on her cellphone. It was the first message she'd received in weeks. There weren't exactly a lot of people in her life just then besides her mother. It was an unfamiliar number with a New York area code.

CAN YOU VISIT JOAN NEPTUNE T'MW NIGHT AT HER APT @ 9:00? 2 EAST 111TH ST.—ADELE

Devon was surprised by the prompt response. She didn't think the meeting with Adele had gone well. Certainly not enough to elicit an invitation to Joan Neptune's home.

She texted back:

I'LL BE THERE. THANK YOU.

Lying awake for the next hour, she went over everything Browne had told them, but she kept coming back to Buddy Bolden alone on the asylum bandstand, blowing a battered horn. She drifted off to that image, lulled by what she thought was the whir of the ventilation ducts until, in her last waking moments, she realized it was Ruby, down the hall, humming to the music on her earphones.

NEW YORK CITY—DECEMBER 23, 10:00 A.M.

In the morning, Devon found her mother at the desk in front of her laptop, still wearing the lavender robe, as if time had stopped. Maybe for her it has, Devon thought. Ruby didn't look tired or anxious. Her expression was blank, remote, when she turned to Devon, as if she was laboring to register her presence. Devon was alarmed. The dinner tray had been replaced by a breakfast tray. Again the plate was covered, the silverware wrapped inside a clean napkin, the juice glass sealed. There was a half-eaten croissant in the bread basket.

"You didn't sleep at all, Mom?"

"Why do you say that?"

"Your speech—"

"Is finished. And we have two hours before I have to deliver it."

After showering, Ruby blow-dried her hair and applied her makeup. When she emerged from her bedroom, she was wearing the purple pantsuit, shoes, and every single purple accessory she had purchased the previous day, including her sunglasses and a pair of purple kid gloves Devon had not seen before.

My god, Devon thought.

"Well?" Ruby said.

"You'll knock them out, Mom."

"I plan to."

Devon had slipped on a black sweater and black slacks. She was curled up on the couch with the laptop. "Come and see this."

Online she had been reading whatever she could find about Buddy Bolden. She had just pulled up a *Times-Picayune* photograph taken on September 6, 1996. The caption read: A CROWD OF TWO THOUSAND WITNESSES THE UNVEILING OF THE BOLDEN MONUMENT AT HOLT CEMETERY.

"You're really taken with this guy," Ruby said.

"I want to write about him. Dig deeper. Start with a short piece and see what happens. I liked writing. It was something I could've done a lot better."

The article in the *Times-Picayune* described the ceremony on the 119th anniversary of Bolden's birth. The exact location of his grave was unknown, so they celebrated in a relatively open space that could accommodate the crowd. The Olympia Brass Band performed. The finest young trumpeters in the city alternated as soloists. The mayor gave a speech. At the banquet that evening, several old jazz musicians delivered testimonials. The last was the singer Blue Lu Barker, who made her debut the year Bolden died, when she was eighteen. She said King Bolden had finally received the funeral he deserved. "I only wish I could have sung by his grave in 1931."

"Then, in 2002," Devon said, "the City Council renamed the street next to the cemetery Buddy Bolden Place."

Ruby's mind was elsewhere now. "Honey, you'd better get dressed, too."

"I am dressed."

"I mean, for the luncheon. I bought you a dress. A surprise. It's hanging in my room."

"That is a surprise," Devon said warily.

"If you don't like it, you don't have to wear it. But I'd like you to wear it."

Devon expected something over the top, but the dress was sleek and stylish, a deep blue silk with puffed sleeves, from Armani.

"I didn't see you buy this yesterday."

"I did it on the sly. The color matches your eyes."

"Yours, too."

When Devon put it on, Ruby zipped up the back and clapped softly. "Fits perfectly, in all the right places."

"Thank you," Devon said, genuinely touched.

"Shoes to go with it are in the closet. Size eight and a half, Christian Louboutin." She looked at her watch. "Hurry."

During the twenty minutes it took Kenji to drive them to the W Hotel on Union Square, Ruby fell silent, just as she had en route to Emmett Browne's office. It had snowed through the night, and the snow was still coming down hard, swirling in the fierce gusts. Kenji negotiated the unplowed streets expertly. When they were a block from the hotel, Ruby roused herself and drank a glass of champagne.

At the W, as they approached Banquet Room B on the mezzanine, Devon was taken aback by the buzz of a large crowd. She had expected a gathering of anesthesiologists to be a quiet, staid affair. The reality was two hundred fifty doctors chatting loudly at twenty-five tables. There were centerpieces of red orchids and bowls of fruit. A lectern with a microphone stood behind the head table. Waiters were bringing in trays of iced tea and mineral water. Ruby had been vague about the scale of the luncheon, and she had neglected to mention—no small thing—that she was the only speaker. Other doctors would speak that evening before a holiday reception. But she wasn't planning to attend. "I make my speech and we're gone," she had told Devon, who didn't find this reassuring.

The doctors were about evenly divided between men and women. They had come in from around the country. All were conservatively dressed. The only flashes of real color were an occasional bright scarf or loud tie. Ruby drew a lot of stares and not a few whispers as she and Devon walked to their table, her purple positively luminous in a sea of grays and blues. She paused to shake some hands, but had trouble remembering people's names. One doctor, a much older woman, took Ruby's arm, as if wanting to detain her, but didn't seem to know what to say.

Waiting to greet her was the president of the American Anesthesiology Society, a tall, starchy, no-nonsense woman named Margaret Finley. She wore a black dress and modest gold stud earrings. Her musky perfume made Devon want to sneeze. Dr. Finley in turn introduced the nine other doctors at the table, including two acquaintances of Ruby's: Hiram Lake, a bearded doctor from Fort Lauderdale, and Karen Park, a Korean émigré who practiced in Seattle. Noting Dr. Lake's bemusement over Ruby's outfit, Devon could tell he hadn't seen her lately.

Devon had been worried from the first about Ruby's making a public appearance. But until they entered the banquet room, she hadn't really grasped—maybe hadn't wanted to—how much Ruby could damage her reputation there. She wondered if this was the true reason, unclear even to Ruby, that she had insisted Devon accompany her from Miami: to save her from herself before it was too late. A kind of human circuit breaker. If so, I've failed, Devon thought.

At twelve o'clock Dr. Finley went to the lectern and welcomed the group. Her remarks were cool and correct. No witticisms, no anecdotes. Not a wasted word. This was a woman who would anesthetize you with dispatch, Devon thought. Had these doctors elected her their president because they found her dryness appealing, or did no one else want the job? Ruby was unfazed by Finley's coldness. In fact, as Lake and the others noted, she literally paid no attention to Finley as she rummaged in her lizard handbag and casually gazed around the room.

Watercress salad and shrimp cocktail were served, then chicken cutlets, which Devon declined. Hardly anyone was drinking, but when Ruby suggested to Dr. Lake that they order wine, he agreed, no doubt figuring she was nervous.

"I'll keep you company, Ruby," he smiled.

Ruby told the waiter to bring them a bottle of 1988 Chateau Latour; when told they didn't have one, she asked for champagne.

Devon was seated between Dr. Park and Dr. Finley. Dr. Park talked about her own daughter, a Fulbright scholar in Prague—maybe the girl Ruby had wanted her to be, Devon thought ruefully. Dr. Finley didn't speak to Devon at all after watching Ruby put away two glasses of the champagne. Ruby ignored her food, eating only a single shrimp and two apricots—a fair-sized meal for her these days.

At 12:45 sharp, Dr. Finley introduced Ruby. It was more laundry list than introduction. Increasingly anxious, her eyes glued to Ruby, Devon heard it piecemeal: ". . . Phi Beta Kappa at Radcliffe . . . Tallman Scholarship from Penn . . . Heckman Award in Anesthetic Studies . . . winner of the Forrester Medal . . . UNICEF volunteer in Peru . . . currently senior anesthesiologist at Gehring Memorial Hospital in Miami . . ."

Ruby took a last sip of champagne.

"I know we are all eager to hear Dr. Cardillo's talk," Finley concluded. "The subject is postoperative cognitive disorder. Please join me in welcoming her."

To polite applause, Ruby walked to the lectern, carrying her laptop. She scanned the audience. Devon knew she had planned to read her speech from the laptop, so alarm bells went off when Ruby placed the laptop on a table behind her and clasped her hands on the lectern.

"Good afternoon. Thank you, Dr. Finley. And thank you all for inviting me to speak." She paused. "POCD. I call it amnesia by anesthesia. What are we, each of us, but our memories? Just as our bodies are ninety percent water, our lives are ninety percent memory. There are moments when we are fully alive in the present. But, as time passes, those moments become scarce. Perhaps because the weight of our memories, ever multiplying, pushes up against the present, diminishing it, eventually crowding it out."

So far, so good, Devon thought.

"Memory is our terra cognita," Ruby said emphatically. "No matter if the memories are good or bad, if we try to cling to them or escape them. Let's be honest: postoperative cognitive disorder is a euphemism for the fact that, if we've done our jobs as we were trained to, all of us here have erased patients' memories." She paused. "That may sound harsh. But maybe not harsh enough when you consider that, because of us, these patients are exiled to terra *in*cognita for the rest of their lives."

There was a murmur in the room, and Dr. Finley winced, exchanging glances with Dr. Lake.

"Brace yourself if you've never encountered the facts, which isn't likely, or if you've blocked them out, which is." Ruby paused again. "After surgery, forty percent of our patients experience long-term memory loss. Four in ten," she emphasized. Another pause, this one longer. "Let's assume one of those four suffers this loss solely due to surgical side effects: severe reduction of body temperature, neural trauma, postoperative inflammation. That still leaves three in ten patients whose memory loss can only be accounted for by the anesthesia administered." Longest pause of all. "I know most of you don't believe this. And I'm making it personal because for these patients it's as personal as it gets."

Though Devon recognized bits and pieces of the prepared speech she had heard before, she knew Ruby was winging it—and evidently *wanted* to wing it. At the same time, Devon thought, she still sounds lucid, and for all I know, what she's saying may be completely true.

"I believe we can solve this problem by eliminating certain substances from our procedures," Ruby went on. "Isofluran, for example, which we know erodes brain function. And desflurane combined with oxygen. And the low levels of CO_2 applied during extended procedures. What are the moral implications if we pretend there is no problem?" She paused several seconds, then said, "Permit me a digression."

Devon groaned inwardly. The pauses Ruby was inserting

for dramatic effect were increasingly out of sync with the ideas they punctuated.

"Psychogenic fugue," Ruby declared, lowering her voice as if she were sharing a confidence. "Psychogenic, as in 'to originate in mental or emotional conflict.' Fugue, as in 'fleeing one's own identity, seemingly self-aware, but later remembering nothing.' From the Latin *fuga,* flight. Fleeing reality. Wandering off after splitting off. Aka, an amnesiac gone AWOL after a shock to the system. In Dade County this year we had four reported cases of postsurgical psychogenic fugue, all of them missing persons." She paused one last time. "And then there is a case I learned of yesterday," she continued. "One winter night, years ago, a man fled New York for New Hampshire, drove into the woods, and died of hypothermia in his car. Was it a psychogenic fugue?" She looked around the room, as if expecting a show of hands, oblivious to the perplexed looks on some faces, the anger in others, and the astonishment of colleagues from Florida who had known her as a model of probity, a quiet, cautious physician. Some members of the audience were already heading for the door. "We'll never know. The police declared it a suicide. Did they look into the man's medical history? What had been the shock to *his* system?" Five, ten, fifteen seconds ticked by. Ruby couldn't speak. Ten more seconds passed. She stood frozen, staring out.

The audience no longer had to wait for an implosion—it had occurred—and more people were whispering among themselves or leaving their tables.

That's it, Devon thought, standing up.

"What have you been waiting for?" Dr. Finley muttered.

Devon walked over to the lectern, trying not to wobble on

the four-inch heels, and touched Ruby's arm. "Mom," she whispered, "it's time to go."

Ruby looked dazed.

"Please, come on."

She managed to get three words out. "I didn't finish."

"Yes, you did. You finished."

Ruby's face fell, but when Devon picked up the laptop and took her arm, she didn't resist. Leading her back to their table, Devon felt how unsteady she was. Dr. Finley remained seated, scowling at them. Dr. Lake was gone. Dr. Park and two other women came over to them.

"Can I help?" Dr. Park said to Devon.

"You could put the laptop in her bag and slip the bag over my arm."

"Okay. And I'll walk out with you."

For Devon, the walk to the door with Ruby on her arm felt interminable. Ruby was slumping against her, growing heavier by the minute. Dr. Park took Ruby's other arm. The doctors at the door parted to let them through.

The three of them rode the escalator down. They walked through the lobby and out the glass doors. Kenji pulled up in the limo.

Devon turned to Dr. Park. "Thank you."

She gave Devon her card. "If you need me, call my cell."

Within minutes, Ruby dozed off in the car.

Devon leaned forward and said, "The hotel. And after that, we won't be needing you anymore, Kenji."

✳

Ruby slept for six hours and twenty minutes, on her back, in her bathrobe, on top of the covers. When she woke, she found Devon sitting on the side of the bed, watching her nervously.

"I know what happened," Ruby said. "I'm sorry."

"You scared the hell out of me."

"I know."

"Do you really remember what happened?"

"I remember enough." She looked around. There was an ice pack and a bottle of water on the night table. "I'm so thirsty," she said.

Devon poured her a glass. "You want to talk about it?"

"Not now. Please." She spotted Dr. Park's card beside the lamp. "Karen?"

"She came by. You were lights-out so fast, I wanted her to check your blood pressure, your heart. I'm not a doctor."

"Oh god."

"It wasn't cool."

"I said I was sorry." She sat up. "I'm fine now."

"You're not fine."

"I am a doctor. You think I'm not aware of my condition?"

"What condition is that?"

"Please."

"You can't keep going like this."

"Devon, come here." Ruby embraced her. "Thank you for watching out for me. Why don't you send for some food? A sandwich would be nice. And coffee."

Ruby took a cold shower. Her head was aching. Her tongue felt numb. She had no idea how she had gotten a bruise on her hip the size of a plum. Accustomed to Florida humidity, her skin was dry from these overheated rooms. She rubbed cream onto her hands and face. She strained to focus her thoughts. Remembering her speech was like watching a film clip that skipped frames, with no continuity and huge gaps. Under other circumstances, it might have been funny that she couldn't remember what she had said about memory loss.

She put on a bathrobe and combed her hair. She didn't want to look in the mirror. It wasn't just that she appeared tired and ragged: there was a vacancy in her eyes that she couldn't ignore so easily now.

Twenty years of professional integrity out the window in twenty minutes, she thought, burying her face in her hands. Who among her colleagues would hear her name now without mentally penciling *crazy* beside it? In Miami, when she had felt herself losing control, unable to steer a straight line, she tried to convince herself she was in fact adopting a more demanding sort of control that required you to negotiate zigzags, loop-the-loops, and curlicues previously unimaginable. A psychiatrist friend at a dinner party had once told her that some patients simultaneously attempt to conceal and announce the onset of madness—itself an act of madness. He had likened it to a construction crew's unfurling one of those cosmetic trompe l'oeil banners down the side of a building: the pictorial representation made the building appear vividly intact even as it concealed demolitionists gutting the actual structure.

Devon ordered up a pot of coffee, three egg salad sandwiches, a plate of cookies, a glass of lemon juice, and some cayenne pepper, which she sprinkled into the juice.

When Ruby joined her on the sofa, Devon handed her the juice.

"What's this?"

"Just drink it."

"Whoa."

"All of it."

"Cayenne?"

"Uh-huh. I know something about hangovers."

The pepper went down Ruby's throat like fire. Then she surprised Devon, picking up a sandwich without a word and taking a healthy bite. When the sandwich was gone, she started in on another one.

"I was hungrier than I thought," she said.

Devon started pouring her coffee, but Ruby stopped her. "I need more sleep. I'm already tired again."

"Good."

"You know," Ruby said, "I always wanted to believe something my grandmother told me. She was a businesswoman, pragmatic, not formally educated, not given to big pronouncements. She waved a finger at me and said: 'If your life is a story that begins when you're born and ends when you die—and what else could it be?—you can write it yourself, or let other people write it. If you write it, you have to accept that sometimes something outside of you, that you can't explain, will push the pen this way or that, and suddenly your story becomes someone else's story—a person you love, or hate, or haven't even met—and all you can hope is that eventually you take it back and get to finish it the way you like.'"

"Do you believe that?"

"I do now," Ruby replied softly. "I just want it to be my story again. Not your father's, not my father's or mother's, not anybody else's." She stood up and headed for her bedroom. "Please don't wake me."

It was 8:00 P.M. on Thursday night. Ruby would sleep through to 1:00 P.M. on Friday afternoon, seventeen hours straight, twenty-three hours out of twenty-four. Longer than she had slept during the two previous weeks combined.

Even so, Devon couldn't let go of something Dr. Park had told her.

"Your mother ought to be put in the hospital, Devon."

Devon was taken aback by her bluntness, but not by the suggestion itself. "That could really push her over the top."

"She is over the top. This isn't something you just sleep off. At least let me give you the name of a friend in Miami, a doctor your mother would trust. She's going to need to see someone. If you want me to tell her this, I will."

"No, you can give me the name."

Devon didn't mention any of this to Ruby. She thought that what had happened at the conference was the end of something, not the beginning. If that wasn't the case, if Ruby doubled down on her denial and attempted to pick up where she'd left off, Devon would take Dr. Park's advice.

Devon traveled up the West Side Highway in an overheated taxi. It was slow going. The snow had finally tapered off, but twenty-six inches had fallen on the city. Some drifts were ten feet high. The plows and salters were out in force now, but even the parkway, one rutted lane in either direction, was thick with ice. The road divider was buried. The exit ramp at Seventy-ninth Street was blocked by abandoned cars. The high-rise windows overlooking the Hudson were intensely bright, as if, through the frigid air, those thousands of rooms blazed with fire, not lamplight. The temperature had dropped to 10 degrees. Chunks of ice were sailing down the river. Some were large, like mini-icebergs, shot through with sapphire light. Devon wondered how long they would remain intact when they were swept out to sea.

The taxi pulled up before a tall, well-kept building by the park. The bare trees in front were festooned with Christmas lights. The lobby was decorated with a fully trimmed ever-green, wreaths, and potted poinsettias. There was a basket of candy canes on the doorman's desk. Devon stepped into the elevator and was whisked to the twelfth floor. A maid in a pale blue dress ushered her into a spacious apartment. The ceilings were high and the darkness deep down the two hallways off the foyer. The scent of incense wafted from a distant room. Devon was careful not to step on the nightingales in the mosaic tiles. The maid took her coat and led her into the living room. The lighting was dim, but the fireplace was alive with flames.

"Mrs. LeMond will be with you in a moment."

Devon had been thinking so much about this apartment that she felt as if she had been there before. The oil portrait over the mantelpiece closely matched the image she had con-jured of Sammy LeMond: a handsome man in a white suit, with a trumpet under his arm, a white carnation in his lapel, and a wry smile beneath a carefully trimmed mustache. Many of his possessions remained in place after all those years: the white grand piano, a set of tropical landscapes with flame trees and toucans, the African masks on the opposite wall that stared back at her.

Barely audible above the crackling logs, a woman said "Hello" from a doorway across the room. Tall and erect, she walked out of the shadows toward Devon with a silent tread, her green dress barely rustling. When she stepped fully into the light, what struck Devon was the unlined face and sharp eyes of a woman who, even with her long white hair, could be mis-taken for fifty rather than seventy. More startling was how closely she resembled Adele, at Algiers, who could have been her daughter.

She extended her hand and looked Devon in the eye, not

unfriendly but wary. "Joan Neptune." Nodding toward the sofa, she sat down across from it.

"Thank you for inviting me," Devon said.

"May I offer you something?"

"No, thanks." Devon couldn't help staring at her eyes, a deep amber that caught flashes of orange from the fireplace.

"Then we'll get right to it," she said, crossing her legs, revealing a pair of gold slippers embroidered with stars. "You've been speaking with Emmett Browne."

"How—"

"Please. You mentioned something to the manager of my club that only Browne could have told you, about a letter in which Leonard Bechet says he gave my husband an Edison cylinder."

Devon panicked. "Is there no such letter?"

"There's a letter, all right, but Emmett Browne, the man who purchased it, has never made it public. And this isn't the first time he's tried something underhanded."

Devon knew she had to come clean. "Yes, he did tell me about it."

"Do you work for him?"

"No."

"Did he pay you?"

"No, it's nothing like that."

"What is it like, then? The truth, please."

"I have been a jazz pianist and a music critic. I am going to write about Buddy Bolden. Browne had sent my grandmother a letter saying there was a matter he wanted to discuss. She died this month and they never spoke. But I met him yesterday and heard about the Bolden cylinder for the first time."

"Why did he write to your grandmother?"

Devon hesitated. "I'm ashamed to tell you. My grandfather was Valentine Owen."

Joan Neptune sat back slowly and looked hard at Devon. After what seemed like an eternity, she stood up and said, "Come with me."

She led her, not to the front door, but farther into the recesses of the apartment, down a long hallway to a locked door. She opened a music box on a nearby shelf and took out a key. She unlocked the door and pushed it open. It was a double door, padded on the inside. The room within was pitch-dark and the air musty, as if it was rarely breathed. Joan Neptune threw a switch and three rows of track lights came on, blinding Devon before she realized she was standing in Sammy LeMond's recording studio. Nothing had been changed since his death. The large room was a time capsule of 1970s technology: the recording console, synthesizers, wall speakers, hanging microphones, reel-to-reel tape recorders, and bulky amplifiers. Even the coffeemaker and refrigerator in the kitchenette. There was a Ludwig drum kit with yellowed skins and a Hammond organ beside an electric piano. Only the various brass instruments, a clarinet in an open case, and a standup bass were timeless. A plaid sport jacket was draped over a chair by the bass. A Stetson rested on the floor tom-tom. There was a pack of L&Ms on a music stand and a pair of black wraparounds on the console. At the center of the recording area, partitioned by corkboard panels, a trumpet sat on a stool atop a sheaf of sheet music. This had obviously been a place of high energy, of ferment. It saddened Devon, for just then the room could not have been more silent or still. The fact it was filled with objects, musical and personal, only made it feel that much emptier. When she looked at the instruments and half-closed her eyes, she could imagine, could almost hear, the music they would have produced. But she also felt the bottomless silence of the decades in which the studio had lain dormant.

"I have something for you," Joan Neptune said.

Devon was surprised. The cylinder? she thought.

"I've waited years to give it to the right person, never knowing if he or she would come along. But now you're here."

She went over to a chair against the wall, beneath which was another trumpet. A Selmer trumpet, Devon noted with horror, as Joan Neptune picked it up and handed it to her.

"Recognize it?" she said coldly. "That's your grandfather's. He left it here when he stole the cylinder from my husband. It's yours now."

Devon recoiled, shaking her head. "I don't want it."

"No?"

Devon's anger was welling up in her. "My grandfather died before I was born. I'm ashamed of what he did. But I want no part of it. I made a mistake coming here."

Joan Neptune studied her closely. "I'll show you out."

Devon felt sick to her stomach as they walked to the foyer. The maid had left her coat on a chair. Joan Neptune opened the door, then paused. Her voice remained calm. "On which side was Valentine Owen your grandfather?"

"My mother's."

"Her maiden name was Owen?"

"Cardillo. She didn't want his name."

"Cardillo. So that was your grandmother's last name?"

"No, her last name was Broussard," Devon replied, stepping outside. She couldn't bear to be interrogated another moment. "I'm sorry for everything. I won't bother you again."

All the way down the corridor Devon felt Joan Neptune's

eyes on her. Only when she reached the elevator did she hear the door to the apartment close.

＊

Joan Neptune crossed her living room and looked out over the park. The clouds were low and flat, slate gray. The wind was so cold she could feel it through the double panes. She poured herself a white rum, neat, and sat down by the fire, beneath the portrait of her husband. As she'd grown older, she slept less—five hours at most, broken up. She knew that night she wouldn't sleep at all. The maid asked if she needed anything else, then left. As soon as she heard the front door close, Joan Neptune set down her drink and cried, harder than she had in years, since she had stopped crying for Sammy.

Devon put on her blue dress and walked into Ruby's bedroom. Still in her nightgown, Ruby was propped up in bed skimming a magazine.

"I just made a reservation for dinner at eight-thirty," Devon said. "A bistro on Fifty-seventh Street."

"I'm not really up for it, dear."

"It's Christmas Eve. You've been in here all day. It will be good for you to be around other people."

"I feel like I've been around hundreds of people lately."

"No, mostly you've been alone, or with me." Devon patted her arm gently. "Come on, Mom. Get dressed. It's our last night in New York."

"I thought you were staying on to research that article."

"No, I'm not sure where that's going right now," Devon said ruefully. "And I want to get back to Miami myself." She was still off balance from the night before. Once she got her mother home, she needed to clear out the debris she'd left behind in her own life and try to start working again, sober, focused.

"I hope you're not just leaving here because of me," Ruby said.

"No. Some things have come up. We can talk about it another time." She opened the closet door. "Now, how about this white woolen dress?"

"You win," Ruby said, getting out of bed. "Give me the dress. And I promise not to order steak."

Devon smiled. "You're getting your sense of humor back."

"Is that what you call it?"

Devon's phone beeped. "Text message," she murmured, flipping the phone open. "Jesus."

"What is it?"

Devon tried to gather her thoughts. "Joan Neptune's coming here."

"What—now?"

"Soon."

"How did that happen, Devon?"

"I was going to tell you—I visited her last night."

"I don't understand. You invited her here?"

"No."

"Then why is she coming?"

"Just get dressed, Mom, and I'll try to fill you in."

※

Devon answered the doorbell, and Joan Neptune, wearing a green suede coat and green dress, greeted her with an apology. "I'm sorry for last night. Please forgive me. I didn't know who you were."

"I told you who I was. Come in."

She was carrying a large leather handbag. She seemed giddy, which puzzled Devon even more. "Thank you for seeing me on such short notice."

"It's certainly a surprise. Let me take your coat."

"This is a beautiful place," she said, looking around the suite.

"My mother wanted to treat herself," Devon explained.

"Special occasion?"

"You could say that."

"Is your mother here now?"

"Yes."

"I'd like to meet her, if that's all right."

"May I ask why?" Devon said. "And why you're here?"

"Because I need to speak with both of you."

"What about?" Devon said warily.

"Trust me, please. I'll explain everything."

"All right. This way, then," Devon said, leading her down the hall.

When Joan Neptune entered the sitting room and saw Ruby, her smile widened.

Ruby rose from the sofa and shook her head in bewilderment.

"Hello, Ruby," Joan Neptune said, walking over and taking her hands. "I always knew this day would come."

It was Marielle.

✷

For a while, Ruby just stared at her. She couldn't help it. Hazy to begin with, she could barely absorb what was happening. Devon also had trouble grasping that this was her mother's aunt Marielle who had disappeared without a trace.

Sitting side by side with Marielle on the sofa, Ruby burst into tears. "I can't believe it's really you," she said.

Devon wondered whether Ruby could deal with another jolt, good or bad, just as she was regaining her equilibrium. She went over and put her arm around her mother.

Ruby called room service and ordered a pot of hibiscus tea, along with sugar and fresh limes. Devon had grown accustomed to her eccentricities. But Marielle looked pleased. "You remember," she said softly.

When the tea arrived, it was Marielle who served it, adding a teaspoon of sugar and a squeeze of lime to each cup, just as she had in New Orleans three decades earlier. When Ruby looked at Marielle's clear eyes and still flawless hands, her memories flooded back. Marielle's mud baths in the clawfoot tub, and the greenhouse herbs with which she washed her hair. Her freesia perfume. The panther brooch with the diamond eyes she was wearing now, that matched her earrings: black triangles speckled with diamond chips.

"Onyx," Ruby said.

"Yes."

Ruby shook her head. "But how?"

"You mean, how did I get here?" Marielle said. "I barely know where to start. I'm an old lady now, Ruby. And you must be . . ."

"Forty-eight."

"Forty-eight. With a beautiful daughter." Marielle turned to Devon. "Your mother is my second cousin once removed, which makes us second cousins twice removed."

"You realized it last night when I told you my grandmother's name."

"Yes. And I regret our misunderstanding. What matters is that we're all here now."

"Have you been in New York long?" Ruby said.

"Ever since you last saw me. A long time. I was married to a musician named Sammy LeMond. Our years together were the best of my life. Then he was taken from me."

Ruby covered her mouth. "Oh no." She hadn't gotten far enough past her initial shock at seeing Marielle to take in the fact that, if she was Joan Neptune, she was also the wife of the man her father had sent to his grave.

"Then you know," Marielle said.

"Just yesterday I learned what happened. It was bad enough then, but now it's a nightmare. I'm so sorry."

"It's not your fault. How could you have known?"

Ruby shook her head. "I couldn't. I never knew my father."

"But I know you. I never stopped thinking about you, Ruby."

"I wanted so badly to find you, Marielle, but I didn't know where to start."

"You never could have found me. I became Joan Neptune. No one knew. Not even my husband." She took Ruby's hand. "No one has called me Marielle since the day I left New Orleans. Until tonight. You see, Devon, I once knew a girl named Ruby Broussard, the daughter of Valentine Owen and my cousin, Camille Broussard. I searched for Ruby Broussard. And Ruby Owen. But until you said it, I had never heard the name Cardillo."

"It was my grandmother's name," Ruby said. "After New Orleans, I went to live with her in Miami. I took her name. Legally I could have been Ruby Owen. He was on my birth certificate. But that's the only place he was. Broussard? I hardly ever saw my mother again until this year."

"Devon told me she passed away. I'm sorry. I lost contact with her long ago."

Devon understood why Marielle had had such a powerful effect on her mother in her youth. Her strength was readily apparent, in her face, her voice, her gestures. She had a primal quality, a sense that youthful transitions were still occurring—or at least possible—long after she had passed middle age. She had a chameleon-like quality, in which disparate traces of the many lives she had once described to Ruby flickered in and out of sight. It was as if one of those African masks on her wall had come to life.

"Devon's a musician herself," Ruby said.

"I know she is. And all you know about the Bolden cylinder, Devon, is what Emmett Browne told you?"

"Yes."

"I'm sure Mr. Browne shared an interesting version of the story. Let me tell you another version, which happens to be the truth. It begins on my last night in New Orleans, the last time we saw each other, Ruby. You must have been told that I was called to the phone at Ciro's, went out to the parking lot, and disappeared. That phone call didn't just change my life: it made me invent a whole new one. A man on the phone told me I had five minutes to leave the restaurant and thirty minutes to get out of town. He ordered me to stay away from the airport and the train station—to just drive. *Don't go home,* he said. *Don't call home. Don't talk to anybody. And don't come back here, ever, if you know what's good for you.* Driving east, into Mississippi, across Alabama, I felt sick knowing how worried you and Theodora must have been. Honey, I never stopped thinking about you. But I knew that man was speaking the truth, and I did what he said."

"Who was he?" Ruby said.

"I don't know. I didn't recognize his voice. Maybe he was disguising it, maybe not. Didn't matter. He was threatening me, but there was fear in his voice, too. That's what really shook me up: I knew he wasn't lying. He might have been as scared as I was. We both knew what Chief Beaumont could do, to friends and enemies alike."

"But what had you done?" Ruby said.

"Done? It's what I knew, Ruby. It wouldn't mean much today, but back then it might have sent some important people to jail, including the chief. There was a contract put out. I never found out any more than that. I wasn't even sure what it was I knew that had suddenly turned toxic. I'd seen and heard plenty when I was with Beaumont's brother."

"And none of your connections could help you?"

"There was no one in that town who could check Beaumont. I had no choice but to run. I drove ten hours straight. Caught a few hours' sleep in a motel outside Atlanta. Then headed north. I checked in to a hotel in East New York where a black woman alone wouldn't catch notice. Had no luggage, so I bought a suitcase. Some clothes. It was when I signed the register that the name came to me. Joan Neptune."

"I hope you don't mind my asking," Devon said, "but weren't you afraid such an unusual name would arouse suspicion?"

"Names like Wilson or Jones—*they* sound suspicious. But who in her right mind picks an alias like Joan Neptune if she's laying low? It grew on me. Neptune was always my planet: the water planet. I waited a week, then rented an apartment. I needed work." She turned to Ruby. "I couldn't exactly do what I did in New Orleans. Not much market for that up here. But I knew I could draw on what gifts I possessed. So I set up as a psychic, taking on clients. I made a reputation for myself, and one day the police called on me to help them. I lived alone, kept to myself. Then one night I went to a club and met this man. And everything changed again. We traveled. He had tired of it when he was young, touring all the time, but I got him to go to Amsterdam with me, and Stockholm, and Venice. Cities with canals, cities built on water, like New Orleans. So that sometimes we both felt as if we'd gone home while being as far away from home as possible. He loved that. He loved the light that came off the water, and the smell of the canals, that mix of salt and fresh. He loved to wander, find a neighborhood we didn't know, a park, a restaurant. We would sit for hours listening to music. I almost had a child—can you believe it? I was forty-four, and he was fifty-six. But it didn't work. Nearly killed me. We decided then that we had each other and that's all we needed. His music, the club, our home. I had given up my practice. He had a sweetness about him. A soft spot for musicians who were down and out. He was a strong man, but he could be naïve, believing in people. I didn't believe in anyone except him, and I tried to watch out for him. And, for all my supposed know-how, I let him down when he most needed me. I warned him, but it wasn't enough. I never should have left his side. I remembered Valentine Owen. I knew how he had treated your mother and you. I knew he had done worse things, in New Orleans." She sat back. "You saw my home, Devon. Most of the furnishings were Sammy's originally. The paintings, the sculpture. There are a lot of things you could steal there. All kinds of people visited us: gangsters, grifters, tough guys. But only once did someone steal, and it was Valentine Owen. I'm sorry to be telling you this, Ruby."

"I want you to tell me."

"We all know people don't just steal money," Marielle said. "They can go after your confidence, your happiness, even your luck. Your father stole something valuable, all right, but much of the artwork was worth more than Bolden's cylinder. He stole the thing Sammy treasured most. A part of his musical soul. A link to all the trumpeters who preceded him, back to Bolden, and all the cylinder's caretakers. If Owen had stolen anything else, Sammy would have been angry, but it wouldn't have cut so deep. He was having trouble with his heart, and I know this was what did him in. As for Browne, his role isn't as innocent as he suggests. He conveniently changed one part of the story: Valentine Owen went to him *before* he stole the cylinder, not afterward. Instead of turning him away, or warning Sammy, Browne encouraged him to steal it. Later he told me he had no idea Owen had stolen the cylinder, but that's a lie. They plotted it together. He agreed to pay Owen a huge amount and then cover his tracks for him. He advanced him a chunk of cash. But once he had stolen the cylinder, Owen tried to shake Browne down, doubling his price. I was surprised a man like Browne didn't see that coming. Then Owen took off with Browne's money *and* the cylinder. Browne sent a man named Nate Kane after him."

"Was Kane the one who left him to die in the woods?"

"No one left him there. Owen drove there himself. Kane never caught up with him. He had nothing to do with his death." She paused. "I sent your father into those woods."

"You?"

"Ruby, I can't look you in the eye and tell you I regret what

I did, because I don't. But you deserve to know what happened. I was here in New York, in my apartment, the night he died," Marielle went on, weighing her words, "but I might as well have been in New Hampshire. I knew exactly what was going to happen. I could see it happening. The power of suggestion, properly directed, can override every instinct in a man, including his own preservation. In New Orleans we called it casting spells. Remember? Earlier that evening, I brewed Valentine Owen a cup of columbine broth with tamarind."

"How did you find him?" Devon said.

"My friends in the police department helped out. A detective named Gus, who had become an inspector by then. Owen was holed up at the Raleigh, a gloomy hotel on Fortieth Street. Two detectives staked out his room, and Gus called and told me to meet him there. I took my broth in a thermos. When Owen got off the elevator, the detectives grabbed him and took him to his room. I asked Gus and his men to wait in the hall while I went in to Owen. I made Owen drink the broth and told him exactly where he had to go and what he had to do. I repeated it to him several times, gave him more broth, and we sent him on his way. I was glad to take my revenge—I'm still glad. And you have to forgive me for that, Ruby."

"You don't have to be forgiven for anything."

"After that, I gave up all thought of finding you. I didn't want to be the one to tell you how your father died and what he'd done. And what I'd done. I wouldn't tell this story to anyone else, but you have a right to know. Before he died, Sammy suffered for days. Valentine Owen died in a single night. The New Hampshire state troopers found Browne's money sewn into his coat. That's how I confirmed that Browne knew about the theft."

"What about Browne?" Ruby said. "Why haven't you taken revenge on him?"

"Haven't I? He's been in that wheelchair for twenty-six years. He came down with MS after Sammy died. Of course, there was a history of it in his family," she added dryly.

Devon realized that was all Marielle was going to say. It was all she needed to say. Her eyes met Devon's.

"So you must still have the cylinder," Devon said.

Marielle finished her tea. "Of course I do. I got it back from Owen before he drove to New Hampshire. It never left my house . . . until today." She patted her handbag. "It's right here."

Devon was incredulous. "You're serious."

"I brought the Edison phonograph, too. I have a driver downstairs who'll bring it up. It's still hard for me to listen to the cylinder, but you can play it after I leave and then bring it to my house tomorrow."

"Tomorrow?" Ruby said.

"I was hoping you would come for dinner. Both of you." Marielle looked at Devon. "And maybe you'll show me what you can do on Sammy's piano. Duke, Errol Garner—illustrious hands have touched those keys. You know, I said I couldn't change what happened to Sammy, but there is something we can change after all these years. Sammy intended to release Bolden's recording on an album with other rare music by a few of his contemporaries—Manuel Perez, George Baquet, the Tio brothers. After he was gone, I planned to produce it eventually, as a tribute to Bolden—and to Sammy. But, like Sammy, I kept putting it off. I was going to find someone to help me. You're a musician, Devon, and you want to write about Bolden: I can't think of a better candidate. Would you be willing?"

"But you hardly know me."

"Oh, I think I do," she smiled.

"I'd love to do it."

"We'll discuss it at dinner. Do you mind if I talk to your mother alone for a minute?"

When they were alone, Ruby took Marielle's hand. "Thank you. She's given up on her music. She's had all kinds of trouble. And I haven't been much help."

"I believe you have, Ruby. You let her help you."

NEW YORK CITY—DECEMBER 25, 1:00 A.M.

Suite 16-02 at the Pierre Hotel. It was snowing again, fine flakes sifting through the vast darkness that enveloped the park, the myriad streets, the frozen rivers between which the island was set like a gem. The lights of nearby buildings barely penetrated the thick fog. Buses had stopped running. Traffic signals were clicking through their sequences at empty intersections.

In her bedroom, Ruby was on the window seat in a robe, her legs tucked beneath her, watching the wind rattle the trees, grateful, finally, to be in the moment. It felt like a luxury—as did her exhaustion. She was ready to fall into bed again.

Devon had switched off the lamps in the sitting room and placed candles all around. They cast yellow plumes up the walls and left a pool of darkness at the center of the room, where she set the Edison phonograph. She uncapped the gold cylindrical box Willie Cornish had brought home one hundred and three years before. And as Marielle had instructed her, she fastened the brass horn, screwed the cylinder to the mandrel, tightened the worm gear, turned the crank, and applied the needle. There was a low hum and a hiss of static. And from out of the darkness, King Bolden's cornet pierced the silence as he launched into the fiery opening bars of "Tiger Rag." Devon was electrified, like every listener before her—beginning with the band, the engineers, and a beautiful girl named Ella. Bolden was at once precise and unpredictable, improvising wildly, dangerously, transforming but never abandoning the melodic line, stretching the piece to its limits without allowing it to spin away from him.

Ruby watched a taxi crawl downtown and stop across the street. Two girls got out, then a young man in a black coat and yellow scarf. Wearing white coats and hats, the girls were nearly invisible against the snow. The three of them slipped and slid beneath the bare trees, laughing as they passed around a bottle of champagne, until one of the girls stopped short. She raised her arms like a diver and fell backward, landing gracefully, extending her limbs in the snow and flapping them slowly, five, six times, until she formed a snow angel. Then her companions helped her up and brushed her off while she took a swig of champagne. The young man threw his arms around the girls and they walked to the corner and disappeared.

Down the hall, "Tiger Rag" was winding down. As Bolden careened through his final solo and held that last high B-flat in his hotel suite on Oleander Street, it reverberated throughout the suite on Fifth Avenue. Devon clapped softly. Ruby stood up to draw the drapes. And down below, beneath the streetlamp's cone of light, the snow angel was filling up with falling snow.

ACKNOWLEDGMENTS

I would like to thank Noah Eaker for the generous, meticulous care he provided this novel from its origin to its completion. His devotion was unflagging and my gratitude is enormous. I owe very special thanks to Susan Kamil for all her support and encouragement over the years. And as with all my books, I could not have written this one—especially this one—without the insights, faith, and love of my wife, Constance Christopher.

The following offered invaluable information, for which I am grateful: *Hear Me Talkin' to Ya,* by Nat Shapiro and Nat Hentoff; *Treat It Gentle,* by Sidney Bechet; *Satchmo,* by Louis Armstrong; *Jazz,* by Gary Giddins and Scott DeVeaux; *Historic Photos of New Orleans Jazz,* text and captions by Thomas L. Morgan; *Early Jazz,* by Gunther Schuller; and, especially, *In Search of Buddy Bolden: First Man of Jazz,* by Donald M. Marquis.

About the Author

NICHOLAS CHRISTOPHER is the author of five previous novels, *The Soloist, Veronica, A Trip to the Stars, Franklin Flyer,* and *The Bestiary;* eight volumes of poetry, including *Crossing the Equator: New and Selected Poems 1972–2004;* and a nonfiction book, *Somewhere in the Night: Film Noir and the American City.* His novel for children, *The True Adventures of Nicolò Zen,* will be published in the coming year. Over the years, he has been a regular contributor to *The New Yorker, Granta, The Paris Review,* and other magazines. His work has been widely translated and published in other countries, and he has received numerous awards and fellowships, from the Guggenheim Foundation, the Academy of American Poets, the Poetry Society of America, and the National Endowment for the Arts, among other institutions. A professor in the School of the Arts at Columbia University, he lives in New York City.

About the Type

This book was set in Sabon, a typeface designed by the well-known German typographer Jan Tschichold (1902–74). Sabon's design is based upon the original letter forms of Claude Garamond and was created specifically to be used for three sources: foundry type for hand composition, Linotype, and Monotype. Tschichold named his typeface for the famous Frankfurt typefounder Jacques Sabon, who died in 1580.